MW00960856

Other publications by Tanya Fyfe:

Lost and Found in Missing Lake

The Dragons of Missing Lake

Website/blog: *www.tanyafyfe.com*

Secrets Abound in Missing Lake

Tanya Fyfe

Copyright ©2017 Tanya Fyfe

All rights reserved.

ISBN-10: 1545370303

ISBN-13: 978-1545370308

This book is dedicated to Loki Fyfe, our Boston Terrier grand-dog who moved in with us almost half a dozen years ago and subsequently stole my heart. Various health concerns crept up during her sixteen years including a heart murmur, her seizure disorder and eventually complete blindness but nothing could slow Loki down. She traveled back and forth between North Dakota and Montana like a pro, demanded chicken mozzarella from her Gampy, followed me from room to room and trotted around our farm during snow-less months with me by her side. As long as Loki had my legs to cuddle into at night under the covers and we didn't move the furniture around, she was ridiculously happy. As time went on, Loki became more attached and she was my constant companion, particularly during my writing or our evening Couch Time together. Almost every aspect of every day was based around our little black and white Boston and I miss hearing her cute little footsteps as she worked her way through the house to be with me. Loki sat on or next to my feet for the writing of all three Missing Lake books and she made it through chapter fifteen in this one. I told her how it would all end but it still isn't the same without her. I said goodbye to my forever little buddy on January 30th, 2017. I celebrate Loki's memory as I celebrate this book.

CHAPTER ONE

"Guys, I'd seriously rather drive to Iowa and enter a pig-calling contest than go to the dance."

I had been unsuccessfully trying to justify my position on the last dance of the school year to my friends, Ben and Derek. That statement earned me two sets of rolled eyes.

"Its not that I don't want to go. I just don't really know how to dance," I tried to explain but they weren't buying it. We had left the cafeteria and were headed down the hallway of our high school.

Our school's spring dance was coming up and I had been hoping to avoid it like I had the others all year. My excuses for the others came easily. For the Hallowe'en dance I told everyone I couldn't go because I lived too far out of town. For Christmas everyone knew I was putting in a lot of hours helping Dad train the sled dog team. February was a no-brainer. I still hadn't been cleared by the doctors for any kind of sports or activities after the concussion I got wrecking my snowmobile over the Christmas break. No Valentine's dance for me.

But the snow was all gone except for way up high in the surrounding mountains and we weren't running the dogs. The doctors had cleared me during a follow-up MRI in March so I couldn't use the injury excuse again. And living out of town didn't really matter because Dad and Jackie had said I could spend the night at Ben's after the dance.

The truth wasn't that I didn't know how to dance. I mean, I didn't, but that wasn't the reason I had been trying to avoid going.

I was preoccupied by dragons.

I had been hoping to see my silver friend, Zagros soon. He usually visited me on weekends but I never knew beforehand when he would be coming. I had to try to keep those days open and not be sleeping in at my friend's house in town. Zagros had a lot going on with Tabitha and him expecting baby dragons. He had concerns and questions and he always brought them to me, his Dragoneer. Zagros knew that I didn't know anything about babies or kids. I was just as worried as him about how we were all going to handle the twins hatching. I imagined trying to explain that to Ben and Derek. That my secret friend, who is a silver dragon, got his dragon girlfriend pregnant and now there were a couple of eggs being kept warm in a huge secret cave inside of a mountain north of Missing Lake.

The guys just stared at me with weird looks on their faces. I worried I might have mumbled something out loud.

"Nobody really knows how to dance, Luke," Ben told me. "You just kind of move to the music and try to stay in time with the beat. The girls get way more into it but the music is fun."

"I never know what to do with my hands," I tried. That much was true.

I had only been to a couple of high school dances as a freshman back in Bismarck, North Dakota, and the memories weren't exactly stirring. Sam and Alex and a bunch of us guys stood at one end of the gym and the girls all danced together in the middle. It hadn't helped that my Dad was one of the teacher chaperones for both dances I went to. Not that he said or did anything embarrassing. In fact, he had completely ignored me and my friends. Most of the student body really liked my dad as a teacher but it was still weird that he had been there. Maybe he had felt strange, too. Who wanted to watch their teen-aged son stand still at a dance?

At least one of the dances had been the Hallowe'en one where everybody dressed up in costumes. It was fun to see what everybody wore. One of the kids had a really cool Minions costume but his yellow face makeup didn't come off for a couple of weeks. He played hockey with us and his sweat came off of his face with a yellow tinge. I remembered that it stained his Home jersey and chuckled to myself at the memory.

"Yeah, same here but I make that work for me," Derek said, with his trademark grin spreading across his face. He started hunching his shoulders up and down, moving his arms like waves from side to side. His eyes were closed and he kept smirking as he did his version of dancing around us. Ben and I both cracked up.

"It's true. That's how Derek dances at these things. It's hilarious and he's out there for every song. Everyone loves dancing with him. Even the seniors get a kick out of him. You have to come just to see, right?" Ben explained after we caught our breath.

"Smooth moves, Slasinger. Can't wait to rip it up at the dance," a voice called out from down the hall. I looked up as two older guys came past us from the other direction. One of them, a junior named Callum, who was a really good basketball player, clapped his hand on Derek's shoulder as they passed. He caught my eye and asked, "Everything healed up, Luke? It was too bad about your wreck this winter."

I sometimes felt uncomfortable talking with the students who were older and obviously cooler than me. Callum was one of those guys who already looked like a man. He grew stubble by the end of basketball practice after school and he walked with a casual authority that made you pay attention. His face was ridiculously good-looking and everyone knew it, even us guys. He drove an older blue pickup truck that he worked on all of the time and everyone knew he called it Baby.

"Um, yeah, it's all good, Callum," I stammered as I looked at my shoes. "Thanks for asking."

He nodded and smiled before they walked off. I couldn't remember the other guy's name but I felt a bit less dorky after they talked with us. I turned back to Derek and Ben.

"So the guys actually dance here? With the girls?" I asked. I realized as soon as the words were out that it was a dumb question.

More weird looks on the faces in front of me.

"Uh, yeah, dude. We dance but no, not with the girls," Ben replied, rolling his eyes dramatically.

"We try to just dance with the teachers. Mrs.Dale never misses a song," added Derek.

"Right," Ben added, laughing again, "She especially likes the slow ones."

I joined in the laughter at the image that created. Mrs.Dale was our crusty librarian who never smiled. She was kind of mean and had always treated me like I was a bad kid after I got booted off the computers before Christmas. I often caught her staring over her glasses at me even if her head was down. She would slowly blink her eyes and glare at me. She did it more when I was using the computers versus sitting at a table.

I had wondered how strange it would be to have a dance with such a small student population. Missing Lake didn't even have two thousand people in it so our high school was pretty small. Some years they didn't have enough students for Junior Varsity and Varsity basketball teams and the freshmen and the sophomores all shared Home Room together. Everyone was pretty much friends with everyone else or at least we all knew each other so I couldn't see how a dance would be any different than getting together at Ben's house to listen to music.

The next closest high school was an hour and a half away up in Big Fork. I wondered if they had ever considered bussing kids from one school dance to another just to have more kids to dance with.

"Seriously, you should come. It's the last dance of the year and we're pretty sure Gwen would like it." I watched Derek wink at Ben when he said that.

My cheeks started to warm up and I figured I had started to turn red. It hurt a bit because I had just sprouted a new crop of pimples on my chin that week. I loved how my body liked to remind me that I was going through puberty but it wasn't willing to grow or put hair on my face. I had noticed a bit of a deeper sound to my voice, though. That had been a real sudden thing. My step-mom, Jackie had noticed it one morning when we were driving in to town but she didn't say anything.

I had asked her something and my voice cracked at first and after I cleared my throat it sounded pretty deep. Jackie had jumped a bit when it crackled. She didn't look over at me but it definitely looked like I had startled her. The sound of my voice startled me sometimes, too.

I was glad Jackie didn't talk to me about it. It would have been bad enough if Mom had been the one to jump. She definitely would have made a big deal about it and probably would have started crying. She was pretty emotional about things ever since my accident. I realized I hadn't called her on the phone in a couple of weeks. I wondered if she would say something about my voice. Maybe that was why I hadn't called, on a subconscious level, so I wouldn't have to have the 'you're growing up so fast' discussion again.

My mom lived in Vancouver, Canada, and hadn't been to Missing Lake yet. Dad, Jackie and I had only moved there the summer before and we weren't sure how long we would be staying. Jackie signed a two-year contract with the state to help run her veterinary clinic which was across the road from our high school. Before moving to the middle of nowhere in Montana we had been living in North Dakota. Mom had only visited there once but I used to go to Vancouver during the summers. I knew she was expecting a visit this coming summer but there was going to be a lot going on and I had just been there over spring break.

After the accident Mom was really pushing for me to get back to Vancouver for a few days. We always invited her to Montana but we all knew that wouldn't be a lot of fun for her. For starters, her husband Frank wouldn't come. He wouldn't like all of the dogs we had and neither of them would like the tiny community and being way off the main roads. Dad, Jackie and I all talked about it and we knew that summer was going to be pretty crazy with me hopefully getting my learner's driving permit and keeping the dogs in shape. The main focus for the summer, though, was going to be the dragons.

There was absolutely no way we could explain the dragon situation to my mom so we all agreed to compromise and fly me to Vancouver for spring break. Mom had been ecstatic.

Our spring break had been the first week in April and I flew from Missoula to Seattle and then up to Vancouver. I didn't need to wear a big sign around my neck saying I was a minor without a parent anymore. I had done that years before when I flew to Bismarck but apparently, at fifteen years of age you are supposed to have your stuff together. Our only concerns had been with flying internationally and passing through Canadian customs once I landed in Vancouver.

Dad, Jackie and Mom had all coached me on what to say and what not to say. I had crossed the border enough times that I got annoyed with what had felt like badgering but I tried to listen politely.

"Only answer their questions with a yes or a no."

"Try to have eye contact and keep your head up. Mumbling teenagers look suspicious."

"Have your passport ready to hand to them as soon as they call you."

"Don't shove your hands in your pockets."

"Don't carry any packages or luggage for anybody else across the border."

Everyone had treated the trip like I was going off to some mysterious far-off country where nobody spoke English and kids my age were already in the military. The kids at school made Canada sound so foreign as well. I kept trying to explain that it was just like the States. Both countries have the same fast food chains with the same types of hamburgers, the same television shows and movies and the same music.

It had been a neat opportunity to tell my friends about Tim Horton's and poutine, though. In general they all thought Timmy's sounded terrific but the fries and gravy thing grossed most of them out. Poutine, and seeing Mom of course, was one of the things I had looked forward to the most.

My flights went fine and the lady at the Canadian Customs had been very friendly. She almost looked like she felt sorry for me when I said I was visiting my Mom. She told me to have a nice visit and I passed through giant glass doors that led to the rest of the terminal. I scanned the people who were waiting everywhere but it was Mom who saw me first. I heard my name and before I knew it I was swept up in her thin arms in a bear hug I hadn't known she was capable of.

It was fun going back to see her and even Frank was pretty cool with me. It rained the whole week I was there, which is typical for Vancouver in the springtime. We went to some fun restaurants like the one way up high in a building right downtown. It rotates and you get to see a full circle's worth of the city in an hour. The food is really expensive and it's not as good as some other places but the view is incredible, especially at night, when the city starts lighting up and everything sparkles.

Even though I had lived there for a few years I caught myself staring at so many beautiful things. The ocean, the harbor, the floating gas stations, Grouse Mountain, Stanley Park, the skyscrapers, the bridges... all of it was so familiar and brand new at the same time.

I hadn't fully appreciated the multi-culturalism that exists in Vancouver and probably a lot of the West Coast until I went back there after living in Missing Lake. The different kinds of restaurants were incredible and Mom enjoyed taking me to them. When I had lived there as a younger kid I didn't really like eating out at what I used to call 'Sit Down Restaurants' but I absolutely loved it being older. There was a Greek restaurant in North Vancouver I could have eaten at every single night. The memory was magical because the reds and yellows of the street lights and neon signs were shining in the slick wet pavement in the rain and it was almost like there were Christmas lights everywhere. The sky was dark because both times we ate there it was getting late and we had the prettiest waitress helping us both nights. Her name was Jaclyn and she remembered us the second time. She winked at me as we left on my last night there and Frank saw it, too. He smacked me on the upper arm like Ben and the guys always did.

The calamari there was incredible but the best part was an entire half of a chicken roasted in a lemon sauce. I wasn't sure what spices they used but the memory of its taste made my mouth water whenever I let my mind drift back to the two meals we ate there.

After a couple of days, though, I was ready to go back to Montana even though I loved the restaurant scene. I hadn't kept in touch with many kids from Vancouver when I moved to North Dakota and the years that had passed were significant ones. We were all doing the adolescent thing and we were all very different from when we were just little kids playing street hockey.

I found myself thinking about the dogs and little Baxter who usually slept with me. It was so quiet and lonely lying in bed without a snoring Boston Terrier snuggled into my legs. I missed the incredibly fresh air that we breathed living at the base of the Rocky Mountains. While the smog around Vancouver isn't as bad as a lot of other big cities, particularly when it rains, it's bad enough that when you blow your nose it sometimes comes out black. I wondered what that looked like in my lungs.

I missed my friends and I sort of missed school but I really missed the anticipation of seeing Zagros or Tabitha again. We never knew when we would see them or if they would come to us or we would go to them. I remembered how the entire dog kennel became still, frozen almost as we watched the giant silver dragon with jet black eyes land in front of us. I even missed being able to freely talk about that strange part of my life with Dad and Jackie.

Mom made sure I had a great time in Vancouver but it never felt like home. It always felt like a holiday. She did ask once if I wanted to move back but I knew I didn't. I wasn't sure what home was supposed to feel like and why I thought of Missing Lake as home when we hadn't even lived there a full year but that was how my mind saw it. Besides, I had really big things to look forward to and be a part of when I got back home.

Zagros and Tabitha had two eggs to hatch.

Dragon babies. Baby dragons.

I must have smiled as I was lost in thought because the guys took that as a positive sign.

"See, telling him about Gwen did the trick," Derek announced as he reached up to slap Ben's shoulder.

I didn't bother correcting him as we walked down the school hallway towards our lockers. I could never share the secret of the dragons with my friends. It would put them all at risk. I had already become accustomed to being mistaken whenever I drifted off and thought about the dragons and the huge significance of the two eggs. I had Dad and Jackie and our friend, Oscar to talk to and I also told our Boston Terrier, Baxter things. I told the sled dogs about the dragons whenever I was out poop-scooping their kennel area or just playing with them. Even if the dogs didn't answer they were really good listeners. And the sled dogs had all seen Zagros a few times so maybe they understood what I was saying or who I was talking about when I would ramble on about the eggs and our responsibilities.

I followed the guys and we joined up with Gwen and Bethany and headed off to World History class. Gwen was wearing a green shirt that looked nice with her hair coloring but I didn't want to say anything. I hadn't seen her wear that shirt before.

It had made me feel a little funny inside when Derek hinted that Gwen would like me to be at the dance. A slight twinge of guilt passed through which made me shiver as I remembered I hadn't told anybody about Liz, the girl I met in Vancouver.

I made a mental note to make time to call Mom soon.

"Oh, honey, it's so good to hear your voice," my mother's voice squealed over the phone line.

I was at Jackie's veterinary clinic on her land line. We still didn't have cellular service up at our farm out of town and it was expensive to use the satellite phone so we tried doing our calls from the clinic whenever we could. Jackie was in the exam room with her final appointment of the day so I couldn't help her clean the clinic up completely. It seemed like a good time to call. I knew Mom would have her cel phone with her.

"And just listen to you," she began. I rolled my eyes for my own benefit. "Your voice sounds so grown up. Luke, I swear it sounds different from the last time we talked. When was that again? Has it been that long? It definitely didn't sound like that when you were here last month."

We small talked about school and English and the weather and the fact I needed to call a little more frequently.

I finally decided to give her something she was desperate for.

"I'm thinking of going to the spring dance."

She actually gasped. I thought she was going to drop the phone.

"Oh, Luke, that's wonderful. Who are you going with? Your friends? Of course you are but I mean any special girlfriend? What's that one's name, Gwen? Or Bethany? Or someone else, maybe? Did someone new move to town? What are you going to wear? Will your dad get you to Missoula to get a new outfit? Is it formal wear?"

Holy smokes. I had known Mom was dying to get me to show an interest in girls but she sounded insane rambling off questions. I couldn't get a word in until she ran out of breath, which was after an impressive amount of time.

I never knew why it was so important for her that I live what she thought was a more regular teenaged life. She had grown up in Vancouver all her life and was very popular when she was in school. I had seen pictures and she was very pretty and there were always guys hanging around. Sometimes I wondered if those were the best years of her life and that's why she thought I should try to do things along the same timeline. She must have been happy when she and Dad first got married and they always told me I was the best thing that ever happened to them but maybe high school and dating were it for her. I hoped the best times were ahead of me.

"Are you there?" she asked over the phone line.

"Oh, sorry. I was kind of overwhelmed there, Mom."

“Give me a break, Luke. I’m just so excited about this upcoming dance. Tell me all about it.”

I sighed.

“If I go,” I began. I made sure to emphasize the ‘if’, “I will probably just hang out with the guys. I might stay overnight at Ben’s afterwards so that Dad doesn’t have to come back into town late at night. I’m sure he wouldn’t mind, though. He might even be chaperoning so maybe I would just come home with him.”

“What are you wearing? Dressing up?”

“Nobody really dresses up in Missing Lake, Mom,” I explained. “There aren’t any clothing stores other than for touristy things. I guess maybe the girls will because they like to but I don’t even know that. A lot of families here don’t have much money from what I know. They aren’t even doing a Prom this year because of the cost of things. All of the parents voted on that a few months ago.”

That had been a huge deal for the community and school. The student body had been given a vote about whether to have Prom or not and we voted to let the Parent-Teacher committee decide. There weren’t many strong opinions on either side other than Anne-Marie, who desperately wanted a new sparkly dress. Because our school was so small they had opened up Prom for all of the grades years before we came to town. Several families didn’t have extra money to spend on fancy outfits, though. One of the kids suggested we have a casual Prom but the parents didn’t like that. What would be the point?

I had to agree with that. If you are having an event where everyone buys or rents something they would never wear again just so you can march through the gym arm in arm for your parents to take pictures, what was the point? There weren't any fancy restaurants to go to unless you drove at least an hour, if not two and nobody wanted their kids on the mountain roads late at night. The senior class was pretty small so they agreed on a big year-end barbeque either at the school or the picnic and park-like area by the lake.

We didn't have high school Proms up in Canada so Mom wasn't too clear on the significance of cancelling it.

"You are going to wear something nice, though, right?"

I resisted the smarty pants comment about sweatpants that went through my head and assured her I would clean up nicely for the dance. If I went.

"Are there any special girls you have your eyes on?" It had been risky bringing up the dance, knowing the girlfriend topic would come up again.

"It's not like that, Mom. Gwen and Bethany are just good friends. There aren't enough guys to have a group so guys and girls all hang out together here. I am pretty sure the whole thing will be just like Ben's party only it won't be as relaxed and fun because a bunch of teachers will be standing around watching us."

I had explained all of that to her every time she brought up the subject of girlfriends and falling in love. She may have been trying to distract me from the dogs. I knew, deep down, that she hoped my love of running sled dogs with Dad was a phase I was going through and a girlfriend would eventually steer me into another phase.

I could never explain to her how it felt on the back of the sled. How the cool air moved past my face as the sled runners swooshed across the snow and how there was a real peacefulness to being behind panting, running dogs. Or how it felt to love and care for our huskies and to learn to work as a team together because I couldn't really explain it to myself. It was just something we really enjoyed doing and we wanted to get better at it. Dad and I wanted to hit the Oregon race and Race to the Sky and other qualifying ones and someday hopefully compete in the famed Iditarod. I liked having goals and something to work towards. I liked learning what worked for our team and how I could almost feel in control if we had trained and motivated them correctly. I also liked how Dad and I were part of a unique community of individuals all trying to promote the sport in a positive light. I thought all of that was more important than your kid finding a girlfriend.

She had even introduced me to Liz, probably hoping we would fall madly in love during our one-hour coffee shop visit downtown and I would want to move back to the city again. Liz's mom and my mom did yoga together and her family had just moved to Vancouver over Christmas. Her mom didn't think Liz had a lot of friends and my mom was desperate for me to have a date with a girl so we met at a funky coffee place and talked for an hour.

Liz was one of the prettiest girls I had ever met. I could picture her crazy curly blond hair flying in all directions when she laughed. She talked with her hands more than anyone I had ever met before and she made me laugh within the first few minutes of meeting. She was already sixteen and was a competitive snowboarder. She drank something called a caramel macchiato which was sweet and a bit foamy when she gave me a sip from her mug.

"Do you know how to slow dance? Has anyone shown you?" asked the voice on the telephone.

I paused. That had come out of nowhere. Particularly since I had been remembering my one-time coffee date with Liz.

Mom took my silence as a no.

"Make sure you hold the girl around the waist and do it right away in case she isn't sure. The girl always puts her hands around your neck, okay?"

"Mom," I tried to cut her off. I felt horrified that she chose to have this discussion with me and my face started feeling warm again which made my pimples itch.

"I'm just telling you so that you don't feel embarrassed. The last thing you want is your arms on her shoulders, Luke. Some parents never tell their kids about this and then they get embarrassed and I don't want that for you," she told me.

"Yeah, I would have been fine if you never told me. I doubt I'll be slow dancing much anyhow, Mom. If I go to the dance at all."

"Well, I won't tell Liz's mom about the dance. Liz really liked you, Luke."

I felt the heat creep up my neck and onto my cheeks. Mom and Frank hadn't asked much about the coffee date afterwards and she hadn't mentioned Liz's name since then.

"Although I'm sure there are lots of pretty girls, maybe even some in the grade below yours who would love a chance to dance with you," she added, filling in the silence when I hadn't responded. I didn't bother to hold back a heavy sigh. "And you know, if you see a younger girl who maybe looks a little awkward or is standing by herself there is absolutely nothing wrong with asking her to dance. That could be the highlight of her year, Luke."

She eventually dropped it and we got the basics of everyday life out of the way. My grades. The dogs. Her job. Frank. The weather in Vancouver. We talked a little bit about me going back there to visit again during the summer which made me nervous but she didn't press the subject. She probably sensed that I was losing interest in the discussion and I tried to keep my answers short so we wouldn't go off on any deep, meaningful tangents.

After we had hung up I cruised around on the clinic's Internet for a while until Jackie's final appointment left the exam room. A lady was carrying a cute black and white puppy that had really floppy ears. It looked like it was going to be a big dog by the size of its paws. They looked like frying pans dangling from his arms and legs. With all of the time I spent helping Jackie in her clinic I never learned all of the dog breeds and puppies could look like just about any breed so I was surprised when the lady said, "It's a Great Dane."

“No kidding,” I said, getting up from behind the main desk to pet it.

“He’s cute but I’ll bet he’s going to be huge,” I said. The lady laughed and the puppy made squealing sounds and wriggled in her arms. I reached out to hold the puppy so the lady could pay for her visit. It was all I could do to hold onto the little guy and he was very generous with his puppy kisses. I knew Baxter would sniff me all over when I got home. He would know I had been unfaithful by cuddling up with another dog.

After the client and her puppy left, Jackie locked the door and turned the blinds.

“Have you noticed an awful lot of Great Danes for such a small community? Or are they more popular than I realized?” I asked, plugging the vacuum cleaner into the wall socket.

“I have, actually. They’ve always been an attractive, fun breed but for such a small population there are a lot. This last lady told me there is a young family who has bred their Danes a couple of times so maybe most of the pups end up staying local,” Jackie replied. “They can be a lot of fun if they are handled well early on but they can be full of health problems at young ages, kind of like other giant breeds.”

I didn’t press for details because she turned and went to clean up the exam room. I remembered her telling me something about that before with Saint Bernards. Or maybe Mastiffs.

Jackie and I got her clinic cleaned up and her computer shut down for the day without many more words. I respected her silence because some days in her clinic all she did was talk and sometimes it wasn’t always happy things she was saying. Other times I wondered if she thought I preferred the silence. Especially after I had been on the phone with Mom.

I saw the ABBA CD cover on the front seat in the truck and knew I needed to get a conversation going before disco sounds of the seventies were coming through the speakers.

“So I think I probably will go to the spring dance next week if you and Dad are still cool with me staying at Ben’s.”

“That’s super, Luke. Did you tell your mom?” she asked as she started the truck.

“Yeah, and she went a bit crazy with her questions and ideas of what I should wear,” I answered, laughing a little as I relaxed into the passenger seat. I felt pretty safe bringing it up with Jackie because she usually didn’t ask embarrassing questions or probe into my personal life.

“Do you know how to slow dance, Luke?”

TWO

"Which game did you see when you were back in Vancouver?"

Dad was sitting at the kitchen table sipping his coffee. He had made his classic Saturday morning omelets and I was stuffed. Jackie had already cleared the table and we had loaded the dishwasher when Dad brought up the National Hockey League game I got to watch over spring break. I had told them about when we drove home from the airport but I knew Dad liked talking hockey with me.

"The Sharks," I quickly answered, excited to talk about hockey again myself.

Since coming to Montana we didn't have a lot of exposure to hockey but Dad and I had always loved the sport. We didn't get any major newspapers and there was no Internet at the house for us to follow the league online. Mom had outdone herself with those tickets. Even Frank seemed to have a good time but most Canadians did at those games. Unless your team was losing and the Vancouver Canucks did not disappoint us.

"They beat the Sharks two-to-nothing, remember? It was an awesome shut-out. You would have loved it, Dad."

He smiled at me and sipped some more coffee. I had poured myself a half of a cup as well. As long as I wasn't doing anything potentially frightening I could stomach more and more coffee in the mornings. With a good amount of milk and sugar, of course.

"The reffing was pretty good, too," I added, knowing that Dad liked every aspect of the game from the warm-up to the little local kids skating between periods to hearing who the three stars were following the game. He didn't like the fighting but most people in Canada sort of respect that it was a big part of the game. Tensions can build up and players sometimes did things that the refs didn't catch or maybe a certain player got picked on when he was on the ice. If you let a couple of shoves or punches get thrown then a message is sent and frustrations are released without someone getting all angry and doing something really stupid, like checking a guy from behind. It wasn't cool to let a fight go beyond a couple of hits, especially if helmets come off and it definitely was bad if one guy was covering up like a turtle on the ice to avoid the hits.

"Do you miss playing the game much?" Dad asked as he got up to refill his coffee. His mug had a musher and a dog team pictured on it.

"Yeah, you know, I do sometimes," I answered. It was true. Our sports programs in Missing Lake were very limited and I missed the variety of opportunities we had back in Bismarck, like hockey.

Like most Canadians I started playing hockey when I was a little kid. I wasn't the fastest skater or strongest shot on the team but I loved playing the game.

"I miss watching you play, too, son," he said. "You played fair and kept your head up."

"From Sam's emails it sounds like I would probably be the smallest guy on the team right now, though and definitely not playing Varsity," I told him. “It would kind of suck to not be able to play with my friends and I wouldn’t want to get checked by a guy twice my size any more than the one time it happened, to be honest.”

Dad laughed and nodded, saying, “I probably wouldn’t want to watch that happen anymore, either, Luke.”

Sam was my best friend back in Bismarck. We emailed back and forth weekly since the high school got Internet and computers so I was in touch with what was going on back there even if I couldn’t relate to most of it.

He was moved up to Varsity hockey full time after Christmas and the team placed third at the State Championships. He was still going out with Kristi Rushman and had been driving for months. His parents got him a used pickup truck and he was already writing about colleges and universities he was thinking about.

A lot of what Sam told me felt far away and not just because he was in Bismarck and not because college and university were still two years away. It was more of an emotional distance, something I couldn’t grasp in my heart and mind because it didn’t mean anything to me yet. I wondered if it ever would. Would I want to have a girlfriend who did everything with me and knew my secrets? Would I ever be excited to pick a college and career enough to spend my spare time focusing on it?

Dad had already left the table when he asked if I wanted to practice driving again.

“We could go into town this afternoon and work on things if you’d like,” he offered.

“As in Missoula or just Missing Lake?” I asked.

“Just Missing Lake for now,” he answered, “Technically you don’t have your Montana learner’s so we should stay off the main roads and highways. Not that we have any highways right here but we can use the school parking lot. I don’t think anybody would care on a weekend. With you turning sixteen next month you can apply for your learner’s permit then.”

“It’s too bad the school here didn’t have Driver’s Ed,” I said, getting up from the table with my coffee mug. “Not that I would have had a lot of time to practice this winter especially after the accident. Plus, all of the snow we got here might have made practicing difficult.”

“I think once you get your learner’s permit you still have to drive with one of us for six months but by the middle of the school year you should be on your own as long as you don’t have any violations. And you won’t, right?” Dad had a smile on his face when he asked me that. I chuckled and we made plans for more driving that afternoon.

Baxter laid on my bed when I showered. He had the funniest expressions of any dog I had ever known. Our sled dogs had their own expressions and personalities, too, but Baxter’s pushed-in face somehow made him that much more hilarious. His big eyes stuck out almost on the sides of his head and he would quickly tilt his head sometimes when I was talking to him. It cracked me up every time.

I had my Montana Driver's License Manual on the bed and after I got dressed and gelled my hair a little I came out to find a black and white lump of snoring dog laying with his head on the stack of papers. We had downloaded the manual online at Jackie's clinic but I hadn't been expecting more than eighty pages to start coming out. I had been thinking maybe twenty, tops.

Jackie's clinic printer had run out of paper mid-way through the printing and I got embarrassed asking her where more was while she was vaccinating a cat. The owner seemed nice, at least, and said they didn't mind me interrupting them. I wouldn't have knocked on the exam room door if I hadn't known what kind of appointment it was. At a veterinary clinic some appointments were very private. You didn't even want to be in the same building for those ones let alone the same room.

Most of the kids at school had been practicing their driving or even getting their learner's permits. Nick Carter finally got his and Bethany was missing a day of school the next week to hopefully get hers. My birthday was June ninth, the last day of school so we were all planning to spend a day in Missoula the following week when I could hopefully pass the exam.

My driver's license had been a long-standing joke in our little family. I had a permit in North Dakota when I was fourteen and had eventually passed my road test before we moved to Montana. It seemed like most of the states had their own rules for kids learning to drive and what ages they could do it. Fourteen seemed pretty young. Most of us could barely see over the dash board back then. Dad even called us Driving Caps because if you were behind a short kid all you could see through their rear window was their baseball caps.

I had practiced a lot with Dad when I had my North Dakota permit, even though I failed my road test once in Bismarck. I was pretty sure I could handle it again. Besides, one of the reasons I probably failed was Jackie's Michael Jackson CD blasting through the speakers when I started the truck with the little old lady examiner next to me. I'll never forget how white she turned, with her hand reaching up to her neck as she gasped. Great way to start your road test.

When you became a new driver in the states they didn't make you stand out like they did in British Columbia. There they stuck an enormous green sticker with the letter 'N' for New Driver on the back of your vehicle. I saw a ton of them when I had visited over spring break and immediately felt sorry for whoever was driving. If you screwed up somehow everyone would think it was because you were new to driving but I knew lots of adults who screwed up with their driving all of the time. Like my friend, Alex's mom in Bismarck. She was always putting her makeup on in her rear-view mirror or swerving as she talked because she would be looking at us in the back seat. A person like that should have a big letter 'B' plastered on their car for Bad Driver.

One of the main differences in Missoula was the speed limit on the Interstate. Montana drivers liked to drive fast. I was sure the local examiner would make us go on the Interstate for the road test a little ways like they did in Bismarck.

Anne-Marie, a snobby rich girl at school already had her permit and a little car, too. You had to have someone older than eighteen in the vehicle with you for the first six months after you got the permit so she couldn't even drive the thing to school unless her parents took it right back home again.

I knew that I didn't need a whole lot of road work at that point but I figured Dad just wanted to get out of the house and hang out together. It wasn't like there were any sporting events that fathers and sons bonded over within a convenient driving distance. Missoula was a good two hours away.

As I reached over to try to extract the manual from underneath snoring Baxter he reminded me of another particular quirk of the breed. They are known for their horrendous gas.

"Who do you think gets to name the baby dragons when they hatch?"

My hands were at ten and two, my seatbelt was fastened and there was no music playing from the CD player. The road was bare and the sky was blue but I still swerved in the high school parking lot when Dad asked me that, seemingly out of nowhere.

And yet it was a question that had rumbled around in my own mind since we first saw the two eggs created by Tabitha and Zagros, our dragon friends.

We also weren't sure who was supposed to be the baby's Dragoneers. Oscar had never been a part of this type of situation because Tabitha had never been pregnant before. Even the dragons weren't completely sure, or, if they were, they weren't telling us. Dragons liked having a bit of mystery surrounding them, it seemed. Not that I had a world of experience with the species. The fact that we were some of the only people in the world who actually knew they existed probably made me somewhat of an expert.

"I think the dragons get to name them, don't you?" I asked without turning my head. Even though we were in a large rectangular parking lot without any obstacles around us I still wanted to practice staying focused on the road in front of me.

"I've thought about that, too, Luke. But I wonder if we all have a say in it or what. Oscar wasn't in charge when Tabitha was born and Zagros' most recent Dragoneer died. Wasn't his name Lawrence? And even Lawrence's father and grandfather had taken care of our silver boy before that so who knows who got to name him?"

I remained quiet as I negotiated in and out of parking stalls, making sure to come to a complete stop before putting the gear into Park, shoulder checking before backing up and using all of my mirrors.

I hoped Zagros would visit again soon so we could talk about all of those things. Zagros was helping Tabitha and Oscar prepare for the hatching as much as he could. Tabitha's lair in the heart of Mount Thuban was larger than the one Zagros created for himself by our house when I became his Dragoneer. It would be more appropriate for the eggs to hatch there. They had already organized a sort-of holding area to contain the baby dragons if they couldn't watch them for a small amount of time but none of us knew if it would hold them. Zagros had flown through the night to South America where two of his own dragon friends had raised young ones and got some ideas and advice.

I had so many questions for Zagros. Like, when is a dragon considered an adolescent, or when are they officially an adult? When do they learn to fly or breathe fire? Oscar had explained to us that it was a rare occurrence to have eggs because of the small number of remaining dragons around the world and the necessity of keeping their existence a secret. With a small population of the creatures remaining it was apparently a pretty big deal that Tabitha had not just one, but two eggs to hatch.

Oscar's Dragoneer friend from Hawaii, Nahele had already flown out to meet Zagros and see the eggs. Jackie, Dad and I had made a trip up to the lair when he was in town. His easy-going personality and big smile lit up the dark tunnels as he told stories of his dragon, Kanoa. Kanoa had apparently been talking about a girl dragon who also lived on the islands. Oscar and Nahele had always thought their dragons would someday meet and have babies but Oscar assured him that Zagros was an excellent suitor for Tabitha.

"Yes, but Kanoa is a golden dragon and we had hoped his stronger, sturdy scales would lead to stronger young dragons," Nahele had argued. "We need to keep the species as strong as we can as long as we are alive, right?" He had laughed and winked at me.

"Just like with our children, Nahele, we can not make decisions for our dragons. We must trust them and let them find their own partners,"

Oscar had responded, clasping his hand on Nahele's enormous shoulder. He wore a large button-up floral shirt that screamed, "I'm not from here" but it wasn't like he would ever fit in with his dark, bronze skin, Hawaiian accent and affinity for giving the Shaka sign with his hand.

Nahele had told us all that his youngest son was very excited about the eggs and still wanted to pursue a career path as a Dragoneer. It was funny to think of being a Dragoneer as a career. In my case it had been more of a request. Or a statement. "You, Luke, are going to be a Dragoneer," was pretty much how I remembered it. Tabitha hadn't given me much of a choice. Nahele's oldest son had recently won a big surfing event and was definitely heading away from the world of dragons.

Surfing sounded like fun but it also was probably really dangerous. It was never something I had wanted to do even though I spent a lot of years living right by the ocean in Vancouver. I figured maybe if we went to Hawaii sometime I could try surfing. I would probably need lessons beforehand.

I had asked the Dragoneers if there was significance to dragon coloration. Jackie and I had talked about that when we first met Oscar and Tabitha.

"The colors can be significant as far as the dragons' earthly and spiritual connections," Oscar explained as we all walked through the tunnel towards the eggs. "Our large silver friend, Zagros, for example, likely has a strong connection to the lunar cycles."

"Or they can be significant physically," added Nahele. "With bronze or gold dragons, their scales tend to be stronger. I am not sure why this occurs but it has been consistent with what Dragoneers around the world have noticed. It makes them less able to be readily injured in fights or accidents and the scales themselves do not loosen or fall off easily."

Tabitha had been missing a few scales around the wound by her wings the very first time we had walked the very same path we traveled that day with Nahele. The wound that wouldn't heal and eventually sent Oscar to Jackie's veterinary clinic where he risked sharing the one secret he shouldn't have to help save his beautiful dragon friend.

"Do the dragons without the heavy scales have more problems with wounds and injuries?" I asked.

Nahele shrugged his large shoulders and looked at Oscar.

"I don't think we have any actual data on things like that, Luke," Oscar answered. "The things we wrote down when Mr.Takahashi was here and the good doctor did her official exam and measurements on Tabitha may be the first modern things written about dragons."

"Are there old documents somewhere?" I asked. I heard some excitement in my own voice as well as a bit of a gurgle that reminded me I was strolling through puberty while strolling through a mountain tunnel.

"Yes, the dragons all speak of them but as far as I know, unless Nahele knows differently, nobody is certain where they are or what language they are written in."

Nahele nodded his head and said, "That is as much as I know, too. Kanoa says there are ancient scrolls and carvings that indicate dragons had human Dragoneers as far back as the beginning of time but they are somewhere in Europe, we believe. Nobody knows for sure how many dragons really exist and where they all are, exactly. Our younger dragons may not know of the older ones and the more they have to stay hidden the less contact they have with each other. The European continent is a large place." He looked over at me and asked if I had ever been to Europe.

"No. Just Canada and the States. I haven't even been very far in either of those countries," I said.

"You should come to Hawaii some time. My son would like to meet you and everyone needs a bit of Aloha in their lives." Nahele clapped his large, meaty hand on my shoulder and gripped down, shaking me a little. His strength surprised me and I almost lost my balance.

We all chuckled as we continued along our path. The orange glow from the actual lair ahead of us was becoming brighter and the sound that reminded me of rushing water started to get louder.

The thought of going to Hawaii made me smile. Several of my friends and their families took holidays there during the cold, blizzardy winters of North Dakota. Or the Caribbean. Bismarck was basically right in the middle of the country so it took the same amount of time to go east as it did to go west. They usually all came back with burned red skin, though. And they were colder than ever when they got back out on the ice for hockey.

"Can you predict the coloring of the offspring by knowing the colors of the parents?" Jackie had asked. I could hear her mind buzzing. She used to have horse clients back in North Dakota who bred Paint and Pinto horses and they actually have figured out how to predict a foal's coloring and sometimes even the type of colored pattern just by knowing the genetic makeup of the parents. Dad and I would sit at the supper table listening to her explain things like how a particular stallion would always create painted foals but others might have solid ones, regardless of what the mare looked like. Homozygous genes, like we learned about in science had something to do with that.

I wondered if she was going to start trying to figure out dragon genetics. I wasn't sure how she could send blood off to a laboratory without it being flagged or labelled nonexistent.

"Son." Dad's voice woke me from my memory. "Are we still driving?"

I was just sitting there, the truck in Park, with my hands still at ten and two. I wondered how long I had sat like that.

"Maybe let me take over and we'll grab a soda at the Merc before heading home. That's probably enough driving and dragon talk for the day."

"I just find the dragons so distracting, you know? I start thinking about them and then I remember things that lead to more memories and usually more questions. I have so many questions and concerns about the babies from what color they are going to be and does it matter, to how are we all going to protect them. I didn't even realize we were just sitting here." I undid my seat belt to get out and trade seats. Dad chuckled.

"New driver rules. Don't drink and drive, don't text and drive and don't dragon and drive."

THREE

I dreamt about dragons that night. With Baxter curled into my legs under the covers I dreamt that I was able to ride on a dragon as we flew through the sky. The details weren't clear or I didn't remember them when I woke up but the dragon had been black. The dragon and I didn't communicate like Zagros or Tabitha did but I knew I wasn't scared. I was just flying around feeling the wind in my face like on the back of the dog sled but riding a black dragon instead.

I was pretty sure I would never have dreamed that if we hadn't met Oscar and Tabitha.

Dad and Jackie had gone into Missing Lake together for a sort of lunch date. A new café had opened up and Dad hadn't tried it yet. It was mostly a breakfast and lunch place called The Silver Bullet but I had heard they were going to start doing suppers as well. Most of us kids had tried their soups and sandwiches at least once. Jackie had eaten there on her lunch breaks already but Dad hadn't joined her. They invited me but I wanted to clean up the dog kennels. Poop scooping was a major pastime of mine.

I had been in the kennel with the newer dogs, Martin, Burnett, Candy and Lucy, telling them about my upcoming plans to maybe go to the dance and then hopefully get my learner's permit for Montana. Martin's personality had become more playful since most of the snow had melted and we weren't running them. His one blue eye and one brown eye always looked so cool and they were such a striking foursome, each of them with different coat patterns in black and white.

I explained to the dogs that I wasn't super keen on going to the dance but I probably should make an effort to fit in more with my friends. Martin got up and moved around the kennel with me as I went from poop pile to poop pile. He sat down when I stopped to scoop and cocked his head almost like Baxter as I spoke. Then he would lift his paw at me as if to get me to pet or rub him, not clueing in that my hands were both busy.

I eventually stopped and gave him what he wanted. His sisters were on top of their dog boxes. I wasn't sure if they were listening to me or not. Burnett was looking off towards the other dogs, barking occasionally as I talked, seemingly at random but perhaps not.

"It isn't that I don't like girls or don't like music. I actually really like the music," I told them. "I just think there are so few kids in the school and we're all like a family, almost. I wouldn't want to dance with my sister so why would I want to dance here with my friends?" I turned and looked at Martin.

"Would you want to dance or cozy up with Lucy, for example?" He kept staring at me and I had to laugh. Dogs were dogs and for the most part there was no concern about siblings. Besides, Jackie made sure our farm was never in the puppy-making business. Every dog in sight was fixed.

I put the scoop down and leaned on it as I thought about that. Why did they call it getting fixed? That implied that the animals were somehow broken beforehand. They weren't broken, they just had all of their puppy-making parts and the desires that went along with them.

I looked back down at Martin who still sat there, watching me.

"Am I broken?"

"Woof," Martin replied, which made me laugh. Jackie took care of Martin and his brother within days of them moving onto our property. Everybody fixed.

I let my mind drift some more as I continued to scoop. I left the foursome and moved to another dog pen. Maybe I was broken, or not working correctly. I didn't want to go to the dance and I never really saw myself getting married down the road. I liked spending time with the dogs more than anyone other than Tabitha and Zagros but they weren't humans, either. Why did I like the company of animals so much when I had perfectly good friends both in Montana and North Dakota? Why was Sam already into having a full-time girlfriend when the thought of it kind of freaked me out?

I knew kids were supposed to talk with their parents about stuff like that but I didn't want to. Dad was very cool when it came to that type of thing but I didn't want it hanging there between us. Things between him and I were sometimes best just being done, not talked about. Like the deodorant that appeared out of nowhere on my bathroom counter one morning. Okay. Message received.

I knew I wasn't completely broken because I had felt a funny feeling when I met Liz back in Vancouver. A weird thing in my stomach that hadn't been nauseating or uncomfortable. Just weird. And I sometimes found myself looking more and more at Gwen during classes we shared.

A breeze came rushing off the mountains towards our house. I could hear it when it began and as it swept into our little meadow towards the house. I loved how you could hear the weather changing in Montana, especially with the wind. It was windy almost all of the time in North Dakota so getting to hear a solitary breeze coming towards you seemed really cool. The wind was loud enough to almost drown out the barking dogs and just about knocked me off balance. I turned towards the mountains where it came from with my eyes closed and let it seemingly blow right through me. I didn't know why but it made me smile.

By the time the wind had moved on I realized that the dogs weren't barking or making any noises. They were all crouched down facing the house with focused looks on their faces. That sort of thing didn't happen in a husky kennel when the handlers were out in the pens with them. Unless there was a dragon landing in your front yard.

I turned to face the house and was once again blown away by the sheer magnificence of a tremendous silver dragon with his shimmering wings outstretched and glistening in the sun. He reached towards the same ground that I stood on with almost pointed toes and slowly lowered himself. My mouth was open even though I had witnessed both Tabitha and Zagros land before but the sight was something I didn't think I would ever get used to. I hadn't heard the swooping sounds of him flying because of the giant breeze that had blown through and I didn't know how long the dogs had been lying still since my eyes had been closed. I wondered if he had been using the breeze to fly with and thought about how risky it was to come over in broad daylight but knew his lair wasn't very far from our farm and it wasn't like many people lived where we did, basically in the middle of nowhere.

"I used the wind as you suspected, my friend. And it is good to see you," his powerful voice came through inside my head. He had landed completely and lowered his front arms to the ground. "Most people do not look up during strong winds such as this or they must close their eyes to avoid debris getting into them. These winds travel the world and the dragons know when they are there and we can use them for daytime travel."

I had started to move towards him as he spoke to me without moving his mouth. The dragons could communicate with their Dragoneers in whatever language we spoke. I had made sense of if by comparing it to thought transfer. I had watched an old episode of Star Trek where they talked about thought transfer and that made sense as to how these giants from another era could speak with us. But they had to choose who could hear them or communicate back. Zagros told me that he could read my thoughts as well, that I didn't need to speak out loud to him but I still usually did.

"I'm so happy to see you," I said as I approached him. While he was a huge force in my life we hadn't actually been face to face more than ten times. Zagros and Tabitha seemed more in tune to our activities and actions. It was Zagros who had saved my life when I had my snowmobile wreck.

He lowered his head towards me and I reached my arms around his neck. It had become a thing between us where it was okay for me to hug my dragon friend.

"I am pleased, as well, Luke," came the voice inside. "I have missed sharing thoughts about our world and upcoming hatchings with you. Tabitha and I are both very excited."

Zagros followed me as I walked back towards the dog kennel. I remembered that I hadn't latched the door shut behind me when he appeared and then landed. Not that the dogs were going anywhere. They had their eyes glued to the dragon.

As we got closer to the kennel I heard one of the dogs growl. That was the first time I had heard that, having been out with the dogs when Zagros had appeared another time. Even Dad had been with the dogs the first time he accidentally met Zagros and nobody had growled, from what he remembered. I wasn't sure which dog it was and I wasn't sure how Zagros would feel but he seemed to know exactly who it was as he turned his head slightly to the side. He stared at Harry, our oldest husky, and the growling stopped. I wondered if he communicated something in dog language inside of Harry's head.

"I did," answered the voice. "And that will be the last growl from him."

I suspected Harry's instinct was to be protective of me and his dog pack buddies. He had been around our family the longest and most of the team always seemed to respect him. He had led the team that pulled me out of the forest when I couldn't walk after my accident.

"He was protecting you all, you are right. I respect that but he understands I am not a threat," the voice told me. After I latched the kennel door Zagros and I walked back up towards the house. The dogs remained quiet and fixated on us.

"What kind of things are you thinking about with the eggs? Are you nervous?" I asked, sitting down on a large boulder in our front yard. Zagros sat on his haunches on the grass and I felt the ground shudder. He wrapped his thick tail around his legs.

"I mean, I wouldn't know the first thing about having kids. I don't even know if I want to have kids," I added. "It would definitely be a long time from now if I did."

"Births are rare in our world and not many of the dragons we have met have had hatchlings. We are nervous that we will not be good parents or that we will not know what to do. Or that we could make mistakes. And we have to do everything twice because there will be two of them. Truthfully, it is more me who is worried. Tabitha seems to think we both will do just fine."

I laughed and said, "Well, don't look at me!" I watched the corners of his mouth pull upwards as he snorted a heavy puff from his nostrils.

"We are all in this together and I am thankful for that. Tabitha is, as well. My friend I visited is certain we will be alright and that the knowledge will come to us as things change or something is needed. He claimed that his young one began wanting to fly within months but that it can take up to one year for them to gain the coordination and strength. I worry about this time in their lives, Luke."

I asked why it worried him so much.

"Because they might try to fly and injure themselves. They might not have the full strength to hold their bodies in the air or to land carefully and they could fall. They might catch their wings on tree branches and tear them. What if they go out and get tired and can not get back home? Or they might fly off and not be able to complete a turn to return back, risking being seen by humans at any time. The world is so different now from when dragons could freely move about. There are things that track the sky from all countries and we have to be so specific about our height and air space. It is one more reason many of us do not meet one another and why our species is so threatened."

I didn't know what to say so we sat in silence for a few moments. I couldn't imagine what those limitations and boundaries were like.

"Well, you somehow figured it out, right?" I asked. His dark eyes were riveted on my face as I spoke. "And Tabitha did, too, so maybe you will just have the knowledge to be able to teach them these things before they do something like fly off when they aren't ready."

"I do not remember life when I was that young so I do not know. Do you remember when you learned to walk?"

I shook my head and laughed again. "Dude, I barely remember what happened last week so I'm in the same boat as you on that one. At least both you and Tabitha are around to help take care of them and you have Oscar and all of us to help, too. Even if all I can do is listen to you when you have questions. I doubt I can do much for teaching a baby dragon how to fly."

"What if I do something wrong, or teach them incorrectly? Or what if I lose my temper?" My dragon friend had a concerned look to his face. It appeared as though his forehead was wrinkled and the corners of his mouth looked downturned.

"I just feel this responsibility I have never felt before, Luke. It is a strong urge to protect and care for young dragons I have not even met. To make sure they survive into adulthood so that they can continue our species on their own many years from now is overwhelming at times," he told me.

"Many male dragons do not participate in raising their young ones because they live elsewhere around the world and do not get to see the female regularly. Tabitha and I are very lucky to have this remote area that is large enough to sustain both of us so I plan to assist in the development of the hatchlings."

I nodded but I couldn't relate. I remembered a senior in Bismarck who got pregnant and the whole school knew about it but nobody really talked about it. It was close to the end of the school year and as dorky freshmen, Sam and I never hung out with the older kids. I wondered if she'd had anyone to talk to about responsibilities and things or if she was worried about her baby like Zagros was worried about his. I never thought about who the father was in the case of the Bismarck girl. Things like that didn't occur to me back then. I wondered if the guy was involved in the baby's life.

"I don't know," came the voice in my head. I assumed it was in reference to the girl I had been thinking about.

"But it isn't just the flying or staying safe that worries me," he added. "Tabitha and I can do everything we possibly can to protect these young wyrns and keep them safe but the world around us that your people control is changing in ways that may be harmful. Do you worry about this yourself? About your own future?"

I didn't answer at first. That was a heavy question.

Everyone talked about climate change and how the planet was heating up. We all knew California needed more rain and even North Dakota didn't get much snow that winter. More and more people were being born around the world and I had started hearing about there not being enough food to feed the future population. Most kids my age didn't talk about things like that but I had heard Dad and Jackie and other grown-ups have those conversations. On the Internet home pages at school sometimes I would see an article about the future but I rarely clicked on it unless it was NHL Stanley Cup predictions.

I saw Zagros nodding his head. He must have heard everything I had been thinking.

"I guess I haven't given that kind of thing much thought, other than how it affects our sled dog teams," I told him. "If there isn't any snow then we can't train. Dad told me that Missing Lake is a pretty reliable place for snow but other mushers in different places have had recent years where there isn't enough. I can see how you'd be concerned, though, with two babies due to hatch soon. Especially since you guys live so long."

"Do you think there is anything we can do?" asked the voice in my head.

"Maybe just hang in there and trust that we humans aren't going to screw it all up. Some countries are really making changes." My mind flashed to the city of Vancouver with all of the recycling they did and how much time it took the week I went back there. At first I had been annoyed by having to separate everything and clean out the containers but after a couple of days I actually felt pretty happy doing it. As if I was doing something to help the planet on my own. I had even wondered about getting a recycling program going at the school when we went back after summer break but I was worried that would make me the king of the nerds.

"And maybe you and Tabitha can teach the kids, or dragon babies to always listen to you and to not ever fly off on their own without supervision. I know my folks taught me things like that when I was young. I was never to talk with strangers or go off with anybody and I just always trusted that my parents were right because I knew they loved me and wanted to protect me," I added. I watched Zagros nod his head up and down when I spoke.

"I understand that and appreciate your thoughts and suggestions. I also remember some of your thoughts when you were away," Zagros said. I hadn't given much thought to Zagros being in my head when I was up in Canada. I smirked and just as a memory flashed through my mind I saw the sides of his mouth curl upwards.

"And I like your new friend, Liz."

That evening, after we had cleaned up the supper dishes, Dad went to let Harry and Ella out of their crates. The two of them were pretty much retired and because of their age they got to eat and sleep indoors at night. Harry loved going out in the morning with us and he spent all day with the younger dogs and most days Ella joined him but sometimes it seemed she preferred being more of a house pet. Harry was twelve years old and during the winter months Jackie had started him on daily anti-inflammatory medication for what she figured was arthritis. If Ella looked a bit stiff she would give her some, too.

Baxter got along with Harry and Ella. They didn't all cuddle together but they didn't fight, either. We just always made sure Baxter had eaten all of his food by the time the big dogs joined us.

"Hon," Dad said as he followed the dogs into the living room, "Do you notice anything different about Harry?"

Jackie and I both turned to look at our big grey and tan boy. He had looked normal to me. Dark brown eyes stared back at me, all four long, lean limbs stood tall and his ears were up and alert on top of his head.

"Why?" Jackie asked, kneeling down next to him and rubbing her hands along his body. I knew she was feeling around for lumps that could be lymph nodes or growths that weren't supposed to be there. I felt a sudden pang of fear as I flashed back to when our husky, Robson had enlarged lymph nodes and what that all had meant.

Dad moved in closer to where Jackie and Harry stood. I felt frozen to the ground.

"Well, he just didn't come out his kennel right away and you know that's not normal for him. Then when he did get up it was really slow and he looked almost wobbly."

Jackie's hands were moving around his face and neck, feeling, palpating, questioning.

"His lymph nodes are down," she said and I let out a big sigh. I hadn't realized I had been holding my breath as I watched. Jackie and Dad looked over at me and Jackie smiled.

"No obvious lymphoma from what I can tell, Luke," she said while her hands moved all around. Harry just stood there but I could see his eyes moving from Jackie to Dad to me and then over to Ella, who had made herself comfortable on our couch. I watched Jackie's smile quickly disappear when she lifted Harry's upper lip and slid her fingers along his gum line. Harry didn't cry out or move at all and when Jackie gave him a rub on his forehead and stood up he went and laid down in front of the couch like he often did in the evenings.

"What? What? What did you see in his mouth?" I stammered.

"I just didn't like the color of his gums, Luke," she replied, turning to face my dad. "At his age there are a couple of things I worry about, especially if he had just been acting weak."

Dad nodded and said, "There is no question in my mind he wasn't right but he looks good now."

"And he's eating normally as far as we all can tell, right?" she asked both of us. Dad and I both nodded. I definitely hadn't noticed any change in his appetite, although Dad was the one who did most of the feeding.

"Yes, no change at all. I'm sure he'd eat Ella's food if I didn't separate them," he said.

Jackie looked like she was lost in thought. I felt beads of sweat build up on the back of my neck. I wasn't ready to lose another of our dogs.

"Luke, if I bring Harry in with me to work tomorrow do you think you can come by at lunch and help me take a couple of x-rays of him?" she asked me.

I nodded and said, "Sure. In fact, we are getting our last Sharing session assignment for the year tomorrow so probably all of us will come over. Do you think Harry will be okay all day at the clinic?"

"Absolutely. I don't have a packed morning so I can keep him by my desk with me. Sherise isn't coming in this week because she is visiting some long lost distant cousin in Wyoming so I would need the help getting Harry up on the x-ray table. I doubt he'd lie still, either, so I'll probably need you and one of your friends to help hold him, too, if that's alright."

"Do you think he has something going on inside that you'll see on an x-ray?" I asked. I heard that high-pitched sound squeak out. Sometimes I hated being fifteen. We were having a serious, grown-up conversation about an animal companion I loved and was concerned about and my body chose that moment to betray me.

"Not necessarily," she said, allowing the words to trail off as though she was, necessarily, looking for something specific. I didn't push the subject.

We all agreed how to handle the next day and I didn't ask any more questions about her medical thoughts on Harry. I didn't want to know anything bad and I figured more questions would lead to her telling Dad and I something sad. I knew she would probably tell him more when they were alone together but I was fine left in the dark.

I sat on the couch next to Ella and reached down to rub Harry. He looked up at me with such affection it melted my heart. He had to be fine. He just had to be.

FOUR

"Did you guys hear about Prince?" Bethany asked as we put our notebooks away in English class.

"Who?" asked Ben who had been making every effort to casually slide his long body into the desk that was definitely too small for him. By the time he had finished his legs were stretched out in front of him.

"Prince! The singer, or artist, sometimes an actor. Prince?" Bethany's expression was of complete exasperation. She looked at Gwen and me for some form of assistance but I wasn't sure what she wanted.

"Um," I began, "he's a singer from Minnesota. Jackie probably has some of his stuff. Purple Rain and all that."

"Right. I think I've heard that one on some eighties channel," Gwen said, nodding her head. "What's the big deal?"

"He died last week!" Bethany exclaimed with her eyes wide open. "They found him dead at his house and nobody knows what the deal is." She looked at each of us individually with her mouth open. I still wasn't clear what her expectations were.

"Oh my God, people," she said, lifting her hands dramatically in the air as she rolled her eyes.

"I heard about it and my folks are kind of bummed," came a voice from behind us. It belonged to Harrison. It had sounded like his voice had changed over the weekend. I brought my hands up towards my pimply face.

"My mom is crazy in love with Prince, you guys," Bethany told us in a louder voice for the entire class to hear. Everyone had been seated and it looked like even Ms.Tanner was listening.

"She saw him in concert when she was our age and even as a grown-up. He is her all-time absolute favorite singer and performer. She still has all of her old Prince cassette tapes and every single CD that was ever released. You should see her playlist. She knows every song by heart and is a bit of a mess over the fact he's dead," she explained. I saw some heads nodding up and down.

"I'm sorry to hear that but, honestly, I didn't know anything had happened. I hope your mom is okay," I offered.

"That's because you live out in the hinterlands, Luke," Ben said, clapping his hand on my shoulder. "We're surprised you know what day of the week it is." I heard a few chuckles.

"I don't know. I rely on Jackie for that," I said, which led to more laughter.

"Was he sick? I'm sure I never heard anything," asked Gwen.

"No, and they don't think it was suicide although he was seen at a hospital just the other day. My mom said the autopsy results weren't in yet," Bethany answered. "I don't think he was into drugs or alcohol but I honestly don't know. My mom is keeping the whole family updated on it all. My dad is really patient with her and her love of Prince even though it isn't his favorite singer."

Ms. Tanner made her way to the front of the class and held her hands up as if to signal it was time to stop talking. She always made a big deal on the days she announced our newest Sharing assignments so she probably wanted to get right down to it.

Instead, she turned to Bethany and it almost looked like her eyes were moist.

"Bethany, you are correct, the world lost a musical genius when Prince passed away. He didn't live out loud like many artists of these times and perhaps that is why some of you haven't heard much about him. He was a little before your generation but most of your parents probably remember him. His film, Purple Rain was a large hit in nineteen eighty-four and he was very talented. His music will live on. Your mother has her memories, which I am sure are cherished, of seeing her favorite performer live," she said as she slowly brought her hands together in front of her and closed her eyes.

She stood like that for several seconds. Ben and I looked at each other and I saw a couple of kids squirm in their seats. It was awkward. I wasn't sure if we were all taking one of those moments of silence to remember the guy or she was just spaced out.

After a loud sigh Ms. Tanner opened her eyes and said we would move on to our final Sharing assignment of the year. The assignments were songs we got to analyze and discuss in group formats and talk about what we thought the singers were trying to tell us. My step-mom, Jackie was helpful with our little group. We always went over to her veterinary clinic across the street at lunch after we got our assignments and talked with her about whatever song we were doing. I wondered if she had heard about Prince's death. I was sure she wasn't a huge fan like Bethany's mom sounded but I knew she had some of his CDs.

Ms.Tanner had been setting up her CD player so we could listen to the song she had chosen.

"We are stepping into contemporary times for our last song of the year, Class," she began as she fiddled with the dials on the little machine. "This is a singer you and your parents may not have heard of but he uses powerful words with sometimes delicate sounds and this song, in particular, evokes several feelings in me as I listen and I think you will see what I mean.

His name is Matisyahu and this song, *Hard Way*, was on his two-thousand and fourteen album, Akeda. Part of what makes him unique is the fact he used to practice Hasidic Judaism but had recently broken from the main sect. This played a large part into who he was and what he said in songs and in interviews. He tried to have a message and I'm sure he still does but perhaps that message is slightly different now. I have only just recently heard his music and this is the first time I have used this song so I am interested as to what you all will think. While I want you to discuss the lyrics and what they might mean I also want to challenge you all to share with us how the song makes you feel. Or if you have any specific images or thoughts that come to mind as you listen to and learn about the song. I want to encourage you to try to avoid the Internet for this particular song and just share at the end of the week the images and discoveries you may each have experienced."

We looked around at one another with questioning looks on our faces. I hadn't heard about the guy before and from the looks my classmates had on their faces, they hadn't either. I hadn't even really made out what his name was when Ms.Tanner had said it.

"I am going to have you all listen to the song without seeing the words the first time and then I'll hand them out and we'll play it again before you go into your groups for discussion."

I watched her hit the Play button on the CD player and a guy's voice and what sounded like a piano simultaneously filled the room. The song didn't have any other music until about half-way through, when it started to have a neat vibe to it and more instruments. I definitely couldn't follow what he was saying until we got the lyrics sheets and we heard it again.

Within minutes Bethany, Gwen, Ben and I were pushing our desks together so we could talk in our own little group. It was a little strange to hear Bethany talk about Prince instead of her Springer Spaniel, Mollie. We had become accustomed to learning all about the liver and white pup whenever we had Sharing sessions.

"Seriously, you guys, I have never seen my mom so down about something. She had his music on all weekend. Some of it is actually pretty good but it's obviously, like, old funk versus newer funk."

I hadn't realized funk had a timeline.

"And he has this one song about when it was nineteen ninety-nine and everyone thought the world was going to explode or all the computers were going to crash when it turned midnight and the year two thousand happened. He sings about everyone partying like it's the end of the world. That one really got my mom down."

"Whoa, whoa, Bethany, slow down," Ben said as he waved his hands in front of her. "We have one song to analyze already and I'm thinking it's going to be a tough one looking at your faces as we were listening. We don't need Prince's songs to complicate things right now."

"Besides, how is Mollie?" I asked. I had hoped to lighten the mood.

Bethany looked straight at me with a confused look on her face.

"Mollie? I don't think she knows who Prince is."

The way she had replied so seriously got all of us laughing loud enough to attract Ms. Tanner's attention with a look that read, 'Be quiet, you troublemakers.'

I watched Gwen pull a few blank papers out of her binder. She seemed to like to organize our group whenever we did activities together. It was a grown-up quality she had and I respected it. I noticed she had sparkly green and blue earrings in that looked pretty with her almost-red hair that Jackie called strawberry blonde. She took a finger and pushed some of the hair off her cheek and behind her ear. She looked directly at me and I felt the heat creep up my neck and onto my face. She smiled and we both looked away.

"Right. So. What's the singer's name again?" Gwen pointed all over her lyrics sheet and came to rest up top. "Ma-tis-ya-hu," she said, pronouncing each syllable slowly. I looked down at my own sheet and the letters of the guy's name definitely looked jumbled. I mouthed the name to myself and heard other groups in the class working on the pronunciation as well.

"Do you think that's his real name?" I asked. I had been paying more and more attention to names of people and things the closer we got to the dragon eggs hatching.

"Who knows? Maybe that's something we could look up but I don't know if it matters," answered Bethany.

All names mattered, I thought silently to myself. Bethany obviously had never met a dragon.

"The song sounds sad," Ben said.

"Yeah, I totally agree. The guy might be depressed. Like, clinically depressed," I added.

"Probably bummed out because nobody can say his name," said Ben, which got him and me laughing loudly again. Neither of the girls laughed.

"Guys. Seriously not funny. Time to grow up a little bit, maybe?" That was Gwen again. Trying to keep us in check. I saw Bethany glance over at Ms. Tanner who had been watching us.

"I think he's depressed, too. I mean, he's saying he knows nothing and has to learn things the hard way. What do you think he's talking about?" Gwen asked.

"The whole song is called *Hard Way* so it must be the main theme of things," added Ben.

"I have no idea. I didn't get the kingdom and palace bit from listening but now the words are here I guess that might be something important," I offered. I had hoped I could get through a suggestion or two without laughing, especially if Ben kept up with the jokes.

"At least we know we aren't going to be wrong about anything we say. I like that Tanner lets us just put stuff out there," Ben said.

Gwen chimed in, "And she's never done this song before so she might be interested in what we have to say."

"Hey, he actually says something like that in the song," Bethany said, turning the lyrics over and pointing at some near the top of the page. "'*Everyone's right or wrong. Everyone's got an opinion*' he sings. That's kind of cool. Do you think that's important?"

I shrugged my shoulders and said, "It might be. I still need to wrap my mind around the song because it doesn't really have a normal beat that you can lock into your head and it's not a song I know."

Gwen nodded.

"Do you think Jackie knows about Ma-tis-ya-hu?" she asked as she looked down to read his name off the lyrics sheet. I had noticed she used her pointer finger to glide along his name as she read it out loud and wondered if she always read like that. I hadn't noticed that before but I hadn't been paying as much attention to her habits and behaviors.

"I don't think so. I know she has a boat load of CDs but I couldn't tell you if this guy is in her collection. I definitely haven't heard him when she has music on in the house or the truck. She has a lot of music that isn't from the seventies and I know she likes some modern music like Coldplay so maybe."

"Does she like Taylor Swift? I love her music," said Bethany, emphasizing the word, love, by closing her eyes and leaning into her hands that were clasped in front of her. I looked over at Ben who rolled his own eyes.

I chuckled softly so I wouldn't get any looks from Ms.Tanner. It was funny how my friends thought I knew more about Jackie than I did. Sure, we rode in and out to school almost every day together but a lot of that time we didn't talk. Sometimes I had my headphones on or if the roads were bad Jackie liked to be focused. And some days after work she just wouldn't say much. Those times I figured she'd had some difficult appointment to do and being quiet was her way of dealing with it. I wasn't really sure how veterinarians coped with the sad appointments without losing their minds. It was one more reason I never saw myself being a vet.

Then, other times on our trips her disco-ball tunes were playing in the background. Or we were talking about Tabitha and Zagros. The Matis-whatever guy was definitely different from the Bee Gees or Boney M. I figured I would prefer listening to his music as long as he had some more upbeat songs, too.

I guessed that I knew Jackie pretty well but I never really sat down with her and asked her about her life or her family. Dad probably knew all of the background things about her and if he liked her enough to fall in love and get married then that had been fine by me. I wondered if a step-kid was supposed to ask questions about their step-mom's past or even what music, other than disco, she liked.

I knew she had always wanted to be a veterinarian since she was a kid and that she had grown up with lots of animals. I also knew that she never wanted to have kids of her own and that she had always been pretty cool with me. Right from the beginning she never wanted me to call her 'mom' because, as she said, I already had a Mom. She liked cooking but she didn't care for baking and she had a pretty funny sense of humor. She was also pretty good around dragons.

"I don't know," I finally answered when I realized all three of my friends were staring at me. "Should I know these things about my step-mom?" I looked over at Gwen, whose parents were also divorced. She lived with her mom and step-dad and her real dad had started dating a new lady before Christmas.

"I don't know. My step-dad and I aren't close like you guys are," she said, looking down at her hands on the lyrics sheet. "We get along and everything but he isn't really interested in me so I haven't been that interested in him. That sounds kind of bad but it isn't. He's a good guy. He isn't interested in anyone, really, other than my mom. He likes being alone and writing. And Dad's new girlfriend, Bitsy is too new to really know anything about her."

Ben turned to me and said, in a very serious voice, "Luke, leave it to me. I'll get to know your step-mom for you and tell you what you need to know." The girls looked at each other and giggled.

He sat back in his desk with a big smirk on his face and added, "It's just going to take me several years and lots of one-on-one time with her so be patient. Your old man might even get a little jealous, if you know what I mean." He winked his eye dramatically at me as he said that.

Thankfully the class had ended because all of us started laughing out of control again.

"Hi, Gang," Jackie said to us as we entered her veterinary clinic with our lunches. Derek Slasinger had joined us even though his English class hadn't been assigned the song yet. His English class was after lunch.

Jackie was wearing one of her lead aprons she used when she had to take x-rays. She smiled directly at me.

"Want to get Harry and help me take a quick picture while your friends work on their lunches?"

I hadn't forgotten about Harry's x-rays but I also hadn't mentioned it to my friends.

"One of your sled dogs is here?" Bethany asked. She almost ran to the kennel room.

“Hey, can I help with that?” Derek asked, putting his wrapped sandwich on a counter top next to a small round container with liquid that had a cover slip on it in the exam room.

Jackie and I exchanged a glance and she smirked at me and cleared her throat. I suggested to Derek that he not put his lunch immediately next to the container.

“Why? What’s going on in the container?” he asked, bending down close to look at it.

“Fecal sample. Stool sample,” Jackie replied with another smirk. “You know, dog poo. Looking for worm eggs and that sort of thing.”

Everyone’s mouths dropped open and a few groans went through the clinic as Derek quickly took his sandwich to the kennel room where Ben was microwaving his lunch.

“Don’t worry,” Jackie said, chuckling, “you can’t catch anything from it. It’s just not somewhere you should put your food.” She joined the others in the kennel room where her small x-ray table and machine were set up.

“I could certainly use one more of you to help. Harry is a big dog and he might not like laying still but I only have two other lead aprons.” I was putting one on as she talked, wrapping the ties around my waist and tying them together in front of me. I reached for the last lead apron and held it out to Derek who almost shoved Ben out of the way to take it. I helped him tie it together and started to get a leash for Harry, who had been watching us quietly from a crate on the bottom row of kennels.

"Does this apron make me look fat?" Derek asked Ben, Bethany and Gwen who were all watching from the doorway. We all laughed, even Jackie. Derek was twirling around with a fake worried expression on his face.

"The risk of any exposure is very minimal with the proper protective equipment, Derek, but do you think you should call your parents to see if they are alright with you helping?" Jackie asked as the laughter died down.

He shook his head. "No, they'll be cool about it. My mom thinks your job rocks and she knows we come over here when we're doing Sharing things. They probably already think I've scrubbed in on surgeries or whatever."

"Why would they think that, Derek?" she asked.

I watched a bit of red creep up onto his face as he looked around at us and stammered, "Um, well, it might be maybe because I sort of told them that you kind of let me help one time."

That got more giggling going from the others and Jackie rolled her eyes and shook her head.

Jackie ushered the others out and had Derek shut the kennel room door behind them. He helped me lift our big husky with his long, dangly legs onto the table while Jackie helped us gently lay him on his side. I wondered what Harry was thinking while we handled him and remembered how Dad and I had helped Jackie take x-rays of our other sled dog, Robson months before. Like Robson, Harry never complained or whimpered once.

We wore lead gloves as we helped lay him on his side which made it even more challenging to handle him. My hands felt twice as big as normal, like they used to feel inside my big hockey gloves when I had first started playing hockey. I also couldn't bend the fingers at the joints as much as I usually could so I had to almost lean into Harry and use my body to hold him still. I noticed Derek was watching and copying me as I went.

Jackie pushed some buttons on the bright yellow box suspended above Harry and a light shone onto his abdomen. He was laid on his side and the key was for Derek and me to not let him move. She manipulated something on the yellow machine and cross hairs showed up in the light. The cross hairs moved until Jackie seemed satisfied with where they were.

"I'm just trying to zero in where I want the focus of the beam, boys," she said, not looking at either of us. "Make sure to keep your heads and bodies back as much as possible and definitely stay out of the light. Harry let out a long breath and Jackie put a gloved hand on Harry's neck to help hold him still. I was holding Harry's front legs right up by his head and looked into his dark brown eyes. I tried to communicate in my mind with him, the same way the dragons did with us. I silently told him everything was going to be just fine and that this would be over in a few moments as long as he laid still. He held my gaze and I almost convinced myself he understood.

There was a loud beep and the light on Harry's abdomen flickered off for a split second before Jackie said that was great.

We turned him onto his back for what Jackie said could be a bit of a challenging position. Derek had to gently pull Harry's back legs towards him as I held his front legs out of the picture. The light beam was mostly focused on his abdomen but Jackie still wanted the arms out of the way of the lower part of the chest.

Another loud beep and light flicker and we were finished. Derek had a huge grin on his face.

She helped us lift him off the table and said she would process the film later that afternoon. We took our aprons off and I took Harry for a quick bathroom break outside. Jackie said he would be fine hanging out with us in the exam room as long as we didn't feed him. When I brought him back inside he walked over to each of my friends and sniffed them before he laid down at Jackie's feet. She sat on the floor with her back to the cabinets and Harry rested his head on her legs.

"What are you looking for with your sled dog, Dr.Yale-Houser?" Gwen asked. "Is he sick?"

"He didn't seem sick when I was with him but then, I had the business end of our little transaction there," Derek said. I shook my head and laughed to myself. I wondered if Derek had the ability to ever be serious but at the same time I enjoyed that about him.

"He seems pretty happy right now," Bethany added, nodding her head towards our resting husky.

Jackie explained that there were some odd symptoms that may or may not have meant something that she and my dad had noticed and that he was a senior citizen in dog years so she didn't want to miss anything. That must have been an adequate explanation because nobody asked anymore questions about the x-ray other than Ben asking how much the machine cost.

"Well, these ones are a few thousand dollars but most clinics are trying to move towards digital systems, which get into tens of thousands depending on what brand and how much technology you want as well as what size clinic you are operating. This was a second-hand unit the state bought from a veterinarian in Missoula who was going digital and he gave us a really good deal on it along with the processor to develop the films," Jackie answered. Ben nodded his head and went back to his heated-up lunch that smelled really good.

"Dr.Yale-Houser, did you hear about Prince?" Bethany asked. I had wondered to myself how long it would take her.

"Oh, wow, yes, I saw that on the Internet this morning but I hadn't heard until then. Holy smokes, I didn't see that one coming," Jackie replied.

Bethany told Jackie all about her mom so the rest of us, other than Derek, got to hear it all again. I had to resist the urge to roll my eyes several times to Ben but I didn't think it would be polite and it would probably hurt Bethany's feelings if she saw. We learned that Jackie was a fan but not a diehard and that she was fairly certain my dad wouldn't know who Prince was. The Prince discussion gave the rest of us a few minutes to eat our lunches before Jackie turned us back to the main reason we were there.

"So, what are you guys assigned for the last Sharing event of the year?" she asked with a tone of excitement in her voice.

Gwen put her sandwich down and pulled some papers out of her knapsack.

"We don't know the singer and his name is hard to say so hang on," she began, flipping through until she pulled out the top page of the lyrics.

"Ma-tis-ya-hu," she said, again saying each syllable slowly while following along on the page with her finger. She looked at Jackie with questioning eyes. We all did.

Jackie closed her eyes and then opened them as she looked off towards the blinds that were drawn on her windows. She made a funny shape with her mouth that I took to mean she was thinking or trying hard to remember.

"Yessssssssss," she said, still looking off at the window, slowly nodding her head. "Yes, in fact, I think he sang a song they played over and over before the Vancouver Olympics several years ago. It was a great song but it wasn't written for the Olympics. Just a funky song about everyone from all over getting along. I liked it but that's the only thing I have ever heard from him."

I wondered what time line of funk she was referring to and was pretty surprised she had heard of him before. Or that he had been around a long time, even.

“Seriously? You know him?” Bethany asked.

“No, not really. I just remembered his name because the song back then was really good and they used it in a lot of television ads. I had to look him up and for whatever reason his name stuck, I guess. I don’t have any of his music and couldn’t tell you anything more about him although he had long braids in his video for the song.”

“Is that because he is, or was a certain type of Jewish person?” Ben asked. Derek immediately turned his head towards Ben.

“How on Earth do you know that?” he asked.

“Ms.Tanner told us today in English,” Ben started to say as he was chewing the last of his lunch. He held a finger up and finished chewing. I saw Jackie smile when he did that.

“Even she doesn’t know much about him or the song. Or, at least that’s what she told us. This is the first time she is using the song for one of these sessions and something about the fact he used to be Jewish and now he isn’t.”

“Right,” I added as I remembered the discussion. “Ms.Tanner thinks maybe the whole religion thing has something to do with the song.”

“It’s a slow song, sort of,” Gwen said as she looked back down at her lyrics. “And maybe kind of depressing or sad. Luke will have his copy of the lyrics to look at when he goes home with you.”

“Yeah, but at the same time it has a really nice sound to it musically so maybe we need to look at it from a bunch of different angles,” I said.

"Right, and if you have the internet here maybe you can listen to the song yourself if you have a slow moment. As long as your assistant doesn't mind," said Ben, nodding his head in the direction of the waiting room. He had been referring to Jackie's assistant, Sherise, a short, stout, quirky lady who had a bunch of cats and a pot-bellied pig.

"Sherise isn't here right now, which is why I needed your guys' help with Harry today but yes, that's a good idea, Ben. I'm sure there will be slow moments throughout the afternoon. Missing Lake doesn't have a whole lot of activity these days," Jackie told us.

"It will soon enough, though," Bethany told us. "Once Memorial Day hits all of the tourists and summer people come back and this place gets rocking through until Labor Day. It's probably why they opened up that new café when they did. Good timing."

Gwen was nodding and said, "Hey, I'm going to be working part time there once school is out."

"Are we old enough to have real jobs?" Derek asked. When nobody replied he added, "No, seriously, aren't there, like, child labor laws or something?"

"Derek, my mom's friend owns the place and I'm sure she has checked into all of these things. Besides, it will only be two or three shifts a week."

"Their clubhouse sandwiches are so good," Bethany said as she tossed her lunch wrapper into the garbage. That led to a brief discussion about what items from the menu we had all tried and what we recommended and why.

Jackie brought us all back around to the point of our visit as we all stood up to go back to school.

“I’m sorry I couldn’t give you guys anything on this song yet. Maybe give me a couple of days and feel free to come back over for lunch if that works for you all and we can have a real discussion about it then. That gives you guys some more time, too, right? And Derek will have had a chance to have heard the song as well.”

“Good thinking, Doc,” Derek said as he clapped his hand on her shoulder. “That’s why you are the brains of this operation.” We all laughed.

“And thanks for the heads-up on the, uh, poop situation back there,” he said quietly, yet loud enough we all could hear. He turned and shot each of us one of his classic grins.

“If we plan ahead I can bring lunch in from the café,” Jackie said as she held the door open for us. “Sort of like a celebration of our own Sharing sessions. I’ve enjoyed all of these talks we’ve had.” I looked back and saw her smiling as we all nodded in agreement.

We crossed the street back to our high school and Ben leaned down towards me. He said, “I have absolutely no problem going back this week. Maybe we should go every day? Just to keep on top of things in case the song is really complicated.”

I looked up at his toothy smirk and smacked him on the arm. Gwen and Bethany both groaned and rolled their eyes which only made Ben smirk some more. I liked that my friends were predictable. Goofy, but predictable.

At least, I thought they all were.

FIVE

Harry's x-rays had turned out to be normal. Jackie showed them to me when I had gone back to the clinic after school. The images were a bunch of grey, black and white but, like she had done with Robson's x-ray, she slowly pointed things out so I could try to make some sense of the images. Harry had been right there so when she pointed to the last ribs on his rib cage she also showed me where they were on his body. He stood perfectly still for Jackie as she drew lines with her fingers along the side of his body, tracing where what she said was the liver was supposed to be.

I looked back and forth between the real life dog and the two dimensional strange image on the lighted view box on the wall. It seemed weird that you could zap some rays through a body and come up with an image like that.

It was confusing to try to figure out the two kidneys because they were sort of on top of one another. The ribs were the same on the side view but once she put the second film up, the one where Harry had been on his back, the ribs were easily identifiable. The kidneys were, too, although I didn't realize that until Jackie pointed them out to me.

The spine was obvious, as well, with gaps between the vertebrae and triangular bits on top that looked like shark fins. His spine curved just like his real-life back did and the vertebrae got smaller and smaller towards Harry's tail. I hadn't ever imagined that their tails had vertebrae just like the rest of their backs.

I mentioned that to Jackie and she nodded. She asked if I saw anything unusual about Harry's spine but I reminded her that I could barely figure out which body part was which let alone know if something was odd.

"Here and here," she said, pointing to two spaces between the vertebrae. The spaces were black because x-rays don't show muscle and tendons. Or, mostly black. I focused more closely exactly where she was pointing and then looked at the black spaces between other bones along the spine and realized there were some fuzzy grey bits on the edges of the bones. Between the vertebrae.

"What is it? I think I see the fuzzy bits on the bones. Is that what you're showing me?" I asked.

"Yes, exactly. It's some arthritis that our old boy has and is totally normal. It has nothing to do with his pale gums the other night and everything to do with being an older, athletic dog. Humans get arthritis, too and it looks similar in any joint. I see this a lot in older dogs when I take radiographs for other reasons," Jackie explained.

"Should we not pet him along his back, then? Is it painful?" I looked down at Harry who looked right back up at me as if he understood the question.

Jackie shook her head and answered, "No, not at all. These bony fragments and rough bits have taken a long time to develop. You can tell that by how their surfaces are mostly smooth, not jagged. I have seen a lot more and lot worse arthritis in some dogs. I would imagine all of our team will have some of this even at younger ages just because they are very active, working dogs. But it doesn't look too bad to me and I keep Harry on anti-inflammatories all of the time now so hopefully that keeps any discomfort to a minimum. It's good for us to know he has it but it isn't surprising."

Jackie was good at explaining things in normal words. I had often heard her in the clinic telling clients about medical conditions or diseases that were confusing at first but then she would put it all in words that made sense. I wondered if they had classes on how to do that in veterinary school.

"Were you looking for something specific as far as how he was the other night, though?" I asked as I reached down to give Harry a few rubs. I made sure to stay closer to his head and neck, avoiding the areas in the lower spine where Jackie had shown me the arthritis.

Jackie paused before answering and she spoke slowly at first.

"Kind of," she said before pausing again. She tipped her head to the side as she stared at the black, grey and white film that was like visual mumbo-jumbo to me.

I figured doctors who looked at x-rays had to have good imaginations. Especially the radiologists who looked at them all of the time. I met one when I had my snowmobile accident. They showed me my own x-rays at the time and the broken collar bone and ribs were pretty obvious but when they talked about fluid around my chest I never really saw what they were talking about.

With Robson's x-rays, Jackie had to point everything out to Dad and me. She found a light grey growth by his heart and she had explained it as being some metastatic cancer. I remembered that his heart hadn't been very heart-shaped at all. I couldn't remember what shape mine had been when I saw my own x-rays. A lot of memories around the time of the accident were still pretty fuzzy in my head. The most important thing was that I always remembered the New Normal, as Dad, Jackie and I called it. That was the version of the accident that didn't involve being saved by a silver dragon.

"I was looking for abnormalities around his liver or spleen, to be honest. Things that would indicate another type of cancer that's pretty common in older, large breed dogs."

Jackie's words startled me. I had been picturing Ben, Derek and our friend, Josh visiting me back in the hospital. That had been a pretty special day. I shook my head to clear the memory although I hadn't really wanted to.

"And you're sure you don't see anything?" I asked, not trying to hide the hope in my voice. Harry's dark, moist eyes were riveted on me. I kept petting him.

"Well, the thing is, radiographs don't tell the whole story. They only show me when things are big. Just because we don't see anything obvious right now doesn't mean something isn't lurking in the background," she answered. That got me even more confused, which she must have seen on my face.

"An ultrasound or MRI is a wonderful way to actually peek inside the tissues to see if something is growing within," she explained, adding, "Which we don't have access to at my clinic."

"Are there any vets in Missoula that have those?" I asked.

Jackie nodded her head. She took the x-rays down and put them into a big golden envelope with a label that read, "Harry Houser". I saw a little heart Jackie must have drawn next to his name.

"There is an internal medicine veterinary specialist in Missoula, actually. I called him up today and he'd be happy to do an ultrasound if and when we get time to go down there. I'm thinking we can wait and if Harry has another episode of weakness or pale gums then we'll get that done."

"Why would we wait? Shouldn't we just go and do it?" I asked. It seemed ridiculous not to get all of the answers as soon as we could, especially if someone in Missoula had the equipment. Missoula wasn't that far away and Dad or Jackie went there at least once a month.

"Let's just get through this week, Luke. Harry clearly isn't suffering and if what I'm suspecting is there it isn't very big, at least from what I can tell on the x-rays. Okay?"

I nodded and hooked Harry up to his leash. The clinic was already cleaned up and the computers were shut down for the day. As we headed out to the truck I asked, "What type of cancer is this one called, the one you're suspicious of?"

Jackie had her hand on the driver side door and she paused and looked down at her feet. I saw her shoulders slowly rise and fall with what sounded like a weary sigh. She looked at me across the hood of the rig and said, "Hemangiosarcoma."

...

"So you think you'll go to the spring dance then, Son?"

Dad and I had been poop scooping out in the dog yard while Jackie was inside making supper.

"Aw, geez, Dad, not you, too?" I heard the exasperation in my own voice and immediately regretted it. Dad never was big on whining or complaining from me. He stopped shoveling and turned towards me. I felt the need to explain myself.

"I'm sorry, Dad. It's just that Mom and all of the kids at school have been asking and the conversation is getting old," I said, looking at my feet.

"I didn't realize everyone was making such a big deal about it, Luke. It's just a dance," he said.

"I know. That's what I say but Mom wants me to fall in love at the dance and have a girlfriend and I just like listening to the music," I told him. That was the truth. The idea of hanging out with my friends with cool music playing louder than we could play it at our homes sounded pretty good but once you added dancing into it the image became less appealing to me.

Dad chuckled and started shoveling dog poop onto his scoop again.

"Luke, I'm sure your mother has her reasons. She only wants what is best for you, even if she sounds like she is ready to look into arranged marriages on your behalf."

I laughed and nodded. I wondered silently if that was the whole set up with her friend's daughter, Liz.

"I will go to the dance, Dad, but not for the reasons Mom wants me to go."

I looked up and saw him smiling in my direction. I had to know, though, if he was going to be chaperoning. I doubted it would change my mind if he was going to be there but I still had to prepare myself.

"No, sadly, I won't be part of the youth movement this time, Luke," he replied after I had asked. "Yes, as unfortunate as it is, Jackie and I will have to stay home together that night all by ourselves and I will miss out on you possibly finding the young woman of your dreams while you guys listen to Coldplay or whoever is popular right now blasted through the gymnasium speakers." Dad looked off in the distance with what I thought was supposed to be a sad expression. It made me laugh.

"I can still stay overnight with Ben, right?" I asked as we transferred poop to buckets and buckets to wheelbarrows. The forest surrounding our property not only offered great training for the sled dog team, it also provided ample dumping grounds for the poop. The wheelbarrows were the only way when you had that many dogs. Dad and I scooped the kennels usually twice a day. Dad got full honors for the morning session during the school week but we shared the job in the evenings and on weekends.

"Absolutely," he answered as he hoisted up the wheelbarrow. Thankfully we had kept up on things so there was just the one to hike out back. I offered to do it but he said he was fine. It wasn't like I minded cleaning up the kennels. That was just part of the responsibility of having the team. When Dad first got into mushing and increasing the number of dogs we all sat down and talked about the commitments we would have to make and how much time it would all take. Mixing their feed during training season and then getting out to feed and water them all. Communicating and playing with or handling the dogs daily. Poop scooping and then poop removal. These were all very important aspects of having an active dog kennel. It was also why I knew I probably wouldn't get to go to Hawaii anytime in the near future.

I hadn't shared it with Jackie or Dad but I had been thinking a lot about traveling to meet other Dragoneers and their dragons. I thought about Hawaii and Nahele and how cool it would be to meet his son who was following in the family business. As I walked back to the house I let my mind drift to the image of palm trees swaying in the breeze. I had never seen palm trees other than on TV and in movies. Dad liked watching old *Magnum, P.I.* shows which were all filmed in Hawaii. It looked really sunny and beautiful there.

I turned to look once more at the scenery around me before I went inside. Rural Montana was pretty spectacular, too. The high mountain peaks looked almost purple as the sun disappeared behind them. We had trees that were all green again and creeks that were full from the winter run-off that still continued from the bits of snow high in the mountains.

Montana had four distinct seasons, which I had never really appreciated in North Dakota. In Bismarck we had a short spring and a short fall. Summers could get really hot and winters could be dangerously cold, with wind blowing constantly in each season. The trees would change color in the fall but you wouldn't get to see the pretty colors for long because the wind would blow the leaves all onto the ground.

Vancouver had four seasons but I had been pretty young when I lived there so I hadn't really cared. Plus it rained most of the time, regardless of which season it was, so even if it was spring you weren't outside enjoying it.

Montana got rain but just enough to make it beautiful. Spring really looked like the world around us was waking up and I was looking forward to a full summer. We had moved to Missing Lake late the summer before and most of our time was spent getting organized into our new life with the house, dogs and Jackie's clinic. Then it was school, training and my accident. When I really thought about it, I was looking forward to the whole next year.

I closed the door behind me and the unrecognizable but intriguing smell of whatever Jackie was making made my stomach rumble.

I figured I was pretty lucky to be in Montana in the middle of nowhere. I knew I would have plenty of time as a grown up to experience big city life if I wanted, if I ever decided to go to college or a trade school somewhere. But right then I was content with the forest, the mountains, the creeks, the dogs and the wildlife around us.

And the dragons.

"Luke, is that you?" Jackie called down from the kitchen. "I need you to bring up a container of chicken broth from the garage pantry area."

“Okay,” I called back up the stairs as I went back to the garage. Dad and Jackie had been stocking up on big items whenever they went to Missoula to do shopping. The store in Missing Lake was pretty small and didn’t carry everything a person needed despite having a pretty good variety of supplies. They had food, clothing, fishing supplies, books, movie rentals, and hardware supplies, some small appliances like toasters and coffee makers and also souvenirs.

I had actually taken Mom a couple of things back with Missing Lake written on them. They had these really nice candles that I thought she would like. She told me in an email since then that she burned them a lot of the time and thought of me.

I found the carton of chicken broth and, hoping that was what Jackie wanted, went upstairs. At the top of the stairs I had to navigate around Cooper, our new black cat who had moved in with us after Josh’s family left town. Or fled town.

Cooper didn’t even bother to move. She had become quite comfortable in our home although her sister, Olive was still a little bit wary. I liked having the cats around. They generally seemed to like Baxter and their presence made me feel a bit closer to Josh, even though I knew I probably would never see him again. I was sure his mom would have told him the cats came to live with us. That had all been arranged through Jackie’s clinic. I liked the idea that he knew I was helping take care of them and that maybe, if he thought about the cats, he also thought about me.

"Hey, thanks, Luke," Jackie said. She was standing in front of the oven and reached her hand out towards me.

"Nice of Cooper to make the stairs a potential death trap, hey?" she said to me.

I chuckled and replied, "Yeah, if the lights were out and it was dark you could be in for a big surprise at the top of the stairs." Jackie nodded and poured the chicken broth into a pan on the stove.

"What are you making? It smells really good," I asked.

"A new curry recipe I found online today. I was searching for Matisyahu and got pulled into Pinterest for a while when it was slow this afternoon."

Pinterest. I didn't think a lot of kids my age were into that but all of our moms were. They did crafts and recipes and then shared them to boards or something. I stuck with Facebook for the most part. It was a wonder I could even do that without Internet access at our house.

It occurred to me that Jackie was bringing up the Sharing singer.

"Oh, right, did you come up with anything?" I asked, sitting down at the kitchen table.

"He's an interesting guy, no question. His Jewish religion really was a big part of his life and music early on. He is the guy who sang that song they played before the Vancouver Olympics in a few commercials. He has a really unique sound, I think," she told me as she stirred the sauce she had been making.

"Did you listen to the song we're doing? I think Ms.Tanner doesn't want us to totally get the facts right about what, exactly, the song is about. I got the feeling she wants to know how we feel and stuff. It's her first time using this song," I explained.

Jackie turned and smiled at me. "So you guys are guinea pigs then?"

I had no clue what she meant by that so I shrugged my shoulders.

"Guinea pigs? It's an expression about being test subjects. Remember that report you did on laboratory animals and how their medical care is much more regulated now?"

I did remember and nodded my head slowly up and down.

"Of course. Right. So, yes, I guess our sophomore class is Ms.Tanner's science lab," I offered.

I watched Jackie as she looked back and forth between a piece of paper on the counter and her sauce. She reached for a dish that had something powdery-looking in it and dumped it into the sauce on the stove.

"All right," she said. "I have never made this before but it looks like its working. Can you get the milk out of the fridge and the lemon juice, please?"

After handing both of them to her separately I watched her add them to the concoction on the stove. Jackie's own little science laboratory. The sauce bubbled gently while she kept stirring it, adding the milk in small amounts while glancing back to her recipe she must have copied down at work.

It smelled good but it definitely didn't smell like curry. I had a few East Indian friends in Vancouver and generally I knew what curry smelled like. I didn't question Jackie, though. Usually she was an awesome cook.

Dad came in from the poop dump and joined us upstairs.

"Smells good, Hon, what is it?" Dad said as he came up behind Jackie and planted a kiss on her cheek.

I took that as a good time to get cleaned up for supper and visit Olive in my bedroom.

By the time Jackie said supper was ready I was covered in orange and black cat hairs from lying with the little cat.

I joined Jackie and Dad at the table and scooped up some rice from the bowl in the center. Dad had done the same. I loaded up a ladle full of the fragrant, golden sauce and topped my mound of rice with it. It looked like it had peas, celery, onions, and chicken in it.

"Dig in, guys. Let me know if I have a Pinterest win here!" Jackie said with a smile on her face. She looked like she was excited for us to try the curry.

Dad and I blew on our forkfuls and at the same time put them into our mouths.

And at the same time we both started making retching, gagging sounds. The most intense, bitter flavor mixed with onion coated my tongue and I couldn't get it out of there fast enough.

I managed to spit some of mine out onto the plate but poor Dad looked like he swallowed all of his. I noticed the horrified look on Jackie's face as I pushed away from the table and ran for a glass of water. I drank it all within seconds and refilled it for Dad, who was just barely catching his breath.

"What the Hell, you guys?" Jackie asked. "Are you okay? What's going on?"

I looked over at the bowls, containers and the recipe on the counter and went towards them.

"Jackie, this isn't curry you used," I said as I read the label on a small spice container filled with yellow powder. I watched as she and Dad both looked up at me, his water glass completely empty.

"It's turmeric."

"Oh my God, I can't believe it," she responded as she got up and took the pan of sauce to the sink. "It must have been awful," she said, looking down at the pan. "I guess that's why I didn't think it smelled very much like the curry I remember having before."

I didn't know what to say. I knew she had worked hard at it and looked so pleased when we were going to try it. The awful bitter taste was still in my mouth. I didn't know how to really describe it and hoped I would never have to.

Dad, though, always knew what to say. He was the king of seeing something humorous in any situation.

“Pinterest fail, Hon. Epic Pinterest fail.”

SIX

Yo, hey, Sam. How's it going? How's Big Joe? Did you guys get that wound on his tail fixed up? Jackie said some labs are just extra exuberant (that's her word) about their tail-wagging and it isn't uncommon for them to open a sore like you described. She said to definitely finish the antibiotics your vet sent home. When was prom for you guys? I told you they cancelled ours, right? We have a dance coming up and I'll probably go. Dad isn't chaperoning this one. I'll stay overnight with my friend, Ben, who I've told you about. The really tall guy. Hopefully it'll be better than the dances we went to before. Do you and Kristi even go to dances? Are you allowed to dance with anyone else? Lol. Okay, well, write when you can.

Luke

I was at Jackie's clinic computer killing time the day after the brush with death we had after ingesting Jackie's attempt at curry. I had been so surprised, not just by the awful taste but because Jackie was usually so good at cooking. Plus she was a stickler for getting things right and following the rules. It was one reason she drove with her hands at 'ten and two' most of the time. If anything, I had always thought of her as a bit of a geek but then I wasn't sure if adults could be geeks.

I paused before I hit Send and thought about that. How kids had names or classes for certain types of people and how that probably changed when we got older. That was one neat thing about going to such a small school. We all had to get along because we pretty much saw each other every day, no matter if we were a jock or a science geek. It didn't matter what grade you were in, either.

Missing Lake's high school also had freshmen through seniors, which some larger schools didn't have. That meant we had kids during all levels of development, both physically and socially. Maybe kids from smaller schools became more tolerant adults. I wondered if anybody had ever studied something like that.

It wasn't like we didn't have our groups or types of people. That Junior, Callum was obviously one of the cool guys. He just moved like he knew he was cool but he wasn't rude or anything. I never saw him bully anyone and he was a great team player in basketball. He always encouraged the other players and complimented them on solid passes or smart plays. Even his truck was cool, from what I had heard. As if being cool made everything you touched cool, too.

I knew I wasn't cool but I was okay with that. I didn't think I was necessarily a geek. I actually didn't think any of the kids I knew in my grade were geeky. I thought of myself as more of a dork but mostly because of all of the time I chose to spend at home with the dogs. I was okay with being a dork.

I didn't think Ben was necessarily a dork but he wasn't really cool, either. His little athletic brother was going to be very cool when he grew up. Cade was enrolled in a summer camp for talented basketball players somewhere in Florida that was actually called an Academy. Ben said his younger brother was begging his parents to let him go there for the full school year but his parents said it was too far away. That seemed pretty cool to me that he even wanted to move away from his family just to pursue his athletic dreams. Maybe it was cool that I moved away from a vibrant big city to live in the prairies with Dad and Jackie. I hadn't chosen that just because of the dogs but the longer I lived with them the more I knew I would never go back to living in Vancouver. I also had dragon friends to think about and I was pretty sure they couldn't live in a big city.

"Luke, are you alright?" Jackie startled me. She had come out of the exam room with an older couple who had one of those puffy, friendly dogs like a Shih Tsu but it didn't look quite like what I remembered. I quickly sent my email off to Sam and turned to face them from behind the main desk in the waiting room.

"Yeah, totally. I was just lost in thought, I guess," I said.

"Luke, this is Mr. and Mrs. Compton and their dog, Bentley," Jackie said. I stood up and shook their hands. Mr.Compton had a firm grip for an older guy. Dad would have been pleased. Mrs.Compton had Bentley in her right arm so she just squeezed my hand with her left hand and said, "So pleased to meet you, young man. We had heard about your horrible accident this past winter and were so happy everything turned out well."

I smiled and nodded as I looked at my feet. I remembered Dad suggesting that I not look down when adults talked with me.

He had just told me again the last time we were getting a few supplies at the Mercantile and the owner, Jeanette had asked me if I was looking forward to summer vacation. I had immediately lowered my head and realized that Dad was standing next to me so I lifted it up and answered her.

Driving home that day he told me that kids could look and feel more confident if they tried to maintain eye contact with adults and that it was something I should practice and be more aware of.

"I like your dog," I said, as I came out from around the desk. Mrs.Compton handed him to me. "What is he?"

Mr.Compton smiled and rubbed the little grey and white dog's head. The dog wasn't very heavy at all and seemed content to be handed off to a complete stranger.

"He's a Malti-Poo and a spoiled little smart ass but we love him to bits," Mrs.Compton told us. I couldn't hold back my laughter and Mr.Compton and Jackie joined in.

"I have two spit fires to take care of in my golden years," the older man said to me as he nodded over to his wife. I watched as she winked back at him which made him smile again.

I held the cute little dog while they paid their bill. Bentley had been in for annual vaccinations and a basic exam. Jackie had been trying to promote routine exams for pets since we moved to Missing Lake. There hadn't ever been a full time veterinarian before she opened her clinic so a lot of the local animals hadn't had regular check-ups most of their lives. She told me that she always liked those visits as they were great times to educate pet owners about all sorts of different things. Plus she got to meet some terrific animals like little Bentley.

I helped her clean up the clinic after the Comptons left. I didn't mind doing it and it meant we got to get home sooner than if I just sat at the computer. If I had research or homework to do, though, Jackie never minded if I didn't help.

"The Comptons seem like a neat older couple," I said to Jackie.

"They're hilarious, really. You wouldn't believe some of the things that come out of that sweet little old lady's mouth in the exam room," Jackie said. She told me that Bentley was a huge part of their lives and that he was really important to them.

"Their oldest son was killed in a car accident in Bozeman a couple of years ago and I guess it just about destroyed them both. Mr.Compton told me he didn't leave the house for weeks and Mrs.Compton said she cried almost all of the time. Their youngest son was quite concerned so he brought Bentley to them as a puppy and even though they didn't want him at first I guess he's become their therapy in a way," she explained.

"Because he makes them happy?" I asked. I understood that. Baxter always could cheer me up or at least be a companion for me if I was feeling down about something.

"Yes, that is a big part of it but also because he made them start living again. They had to get out of bed in the mornings because the puppy needed to be fed or let out. They had to start going outside again because Bentley needed walks. Mr.Compton told me it just suddenly started to happen and develop into a routine and before long they both realized they were able to laugh and enjoy life again, even if they had an enormous sadness in their hearts." Jackie looked up and smiled at me and I thought I saw a glimmer of tears in her eyes.

I nodded my head and thought how powerful one little grey and white dog could be. I knew what all of our pets meant to our family. Plus I knew a lot of people whose pets meant the world to them. Like Bethany and her Springer Spaniel, Mollie. I didn't know what Bethany would do when it came time to go to college. I was pretty sure that dorm rooms didn't allow rambunctious spaniels for roommates.

Thinking about Bethany reminded me about our assignment in English class.

"Any more thoughts on our Sharing song?" I asked as I swept the tiled floors.

"Yes. I actually listened to it today at lunch a few times. I like it," she began. "It has a light sound to it and even when it picks up a bit I still like how it sounds. I think there is some real innocence to the beginning."

I had no clue what that meant which Jackie must have anticipated because she kept on going.

"I think he is singing about losing this innocence somehow and that he got hurt in the process. He says he's not okay and then he has all of these sad sounding images he sings about."

"I'll have to look at the lyrics again," I told her. "I haven't memorized the song at all. I find it's hard to keep this song in my head the way the music changes and it isn't a song I've heard before."

"I printed off the lyrics, myself. They are by my computer there," Jackie said, pointing towards her computer.

"Why do you think he says he knows nothing?" I asked as I glanced through the written words again.

"I'm not sure but he is pretty hard on himself with that. Or maybe it's a lyrical attempt at being self-deprecating. Where you put yourself down in front of others even if you don't necessarily believe it. He has definitely learned something in life even if it was done, as he says, the hard way."

"Do you think this has to do with his religion? One of the kids at school suggested that."

Jackie paused before answering, leaning forward on the mop she had brought into the room.

"I think so. I dug around a little bit into his actual meanings and what inspired him to write this song. It was a period in his life where he was questioning the word of God and he was listening for some inner intuitive voice to help guide him. But I thought your teacher didn't want to know the actual meaning of the song."

I nodded and said she was right but that I was curious on my own.

"Oh, well, definitely then. At the time he felt like he was bound to a lot of big things, most likely his deeply held religious beliefs and that he felt like he was losing control. Something along those lines. I also read how the whole album that this song is from dealt with the madness in his life at the time."

"From leaving a religion?" I asked. In my mind I flashed back to that song we did by the band, REM, *Losing My Religion*. It seemed as if they were somehow connected.

"Absolutely, Luke. Religion can be a main driving force for many people. And it can be any religion, too. Some people yearn to feel close to a spiritual understanding of the world and all that is around us and a church can be a great place for them to share this with others who feel the same way. I think most religions are about finding peace and contentment in your life along with perhaps the purpose of it all. But you're talking with someone who isn't overly religious, remember. Maybe one of your classmates will have a unique perspective on that."

I thought about that as Jackie wielded her mop around the clinic. I wasn't sure about most of my friends in Missing Lake because we never talked about things like church. It didn't come up in our conversations and I never thought to ask anyone. I had a feeling it was going to come up in English class with the song we were assigned.

"Aren't most religions about being kind to others and stuff like that?" I asked.

Jackie continued mopping as she talked.

"I believe so. It's similar to what your father always tells you. Be a good person and do good things. Now, religions are going to be much more complex than that but one of the messages most religions probably want to share is similar to that."

I nodded and let that sink in.

I watched Jackie close her computer for the end of the day when she finished mopping. She had shown me the closing procedures before but that felt like something too important for me to do. I didn't like the idea of losing files or screwing up her records somehow.

At that point, the telephone rang which caused both of us to jump. When the clinic was closed for the day Jackie always let the answering machine answer so we both ignored it until the caller started to leave his message.

"Hello, Dr.Yale-Houser. It's Oscar."

We both reached for the phone but Jackie got it first. She gave me a thumbs up and a big grin.

They didn't talk for very long but it made for a fun conversation on the ride home. That was a bonus because on the drive into school that morning we had listened to the Bee Gees' Greatest Hits. She had been going through a classic rock phase before that, which I had been enjoying. We had the Rolling Stones one day and Bruce Springsteen another but the Bee Gees were alive and well that morning in her pickup truck. I hadn't been looking forward to more *Night Fever* on the ride home.

"I guess Tabitha and Oscar have been talking about names for the babies. Apparently the Dragoneers for the parent dragons get to suggest names but, ultimately, it's the dragons who decide," Jackie excitedly told me as we drove the windy highway home.

"Where do we look for names, though? Did he tell you?" I asked. I wondered how I would look things like Naming Your Dragon up online at school.

"Sort of. I guess Tabitha was a bit vague about that. The names have to have meaning to both the dragon parents as well as the Dragoneer. And of course it all depends on whether they are boy or girl dragons," she answered, hands at ten and two on the steering wheel.

"The names have to have a meaning? What does the name, Tabitha, mean?" I asked.

"I guess Tabitha is the 'keeper of the eggs', Oscar told me," she answered, looking at me with a wide grin on her face. "How fitting is that?"

"But she didn't have eggs when she was born. She was just young. Who would have named her that?" It didn't make sense in my head. I felt a need to know what the meaning of Zagros' name was.

"Yet it must have meant something to her Dragoneer and her own dragon parents when she was born, or hatched, right? The meanings can be literal or theoretical, apparently, or they can be a place or monument or even something spiritual. Oscar sounded just as excited as we are to be a part of something so important. A dragon's identity begins to take shape when they hatch and are then named." Jackie had so much excitement in her voice that it was infectious.

"Shouldn't we get to know the babies a bit and see how their personalities develop before we saddle them with something so important? How do parents do it when they have a baby? What if your parents call you Bob and you're really more of a Zachary kind of guy?"

Jackie laughed and nodded her head, saying, "You're talking to the wrong person there, Luke. I have no clue about that. Although I think your parents got it right with your name. You seem like a Luke."

I asked her what she thought a Luke should be.

"I don't know. Down to earth. Rugged. Honest. Tough. Not the kind of guy to mess around or play games with And before you ask I have no idea why I think that." We both laughed.

"Do you think your name has something to do with how you turn out in life? Like, if you are named something unusual and different, will you grow up to be unusual and different? Do people expect that of you if you aren't named Bob?" I had been mostly wondering out loud when I asked that, not really expecting an answer.

"You know, that's a super question, Luke. And it's probably different in every culture and for different species. Names that seem unique in North America might be completely normal in another country like Mexico or Russia or Japan. Or even within a country, like our friend,

Nahele. He's an American from Hawaii but his name is unique here in Montana."

I laughed again and said, "You just answered my question. Nahele is a pretty unique character, no matter where he is from."

"One thing I don't want to do is come up with a list of one hundred names each day. I think the three of us can toss ideas around but you are officially Zagros' Dragoneer, so you are the one to give the suggestions when the time comes," Jackie told me with more seriousness in her voice. "You definitely can't let this affect your schoolwork, either. You can research names and meanings and things after your homework is done each day. And I don't want you lying awake at night fretting over this or getting distracted during the day. You know you have a slight tendency to do that when you are solely focused on one thing."

She was right. Even my friends noticed it about me. They would snap their fingers in front of my face or wave their hands to get my attention if they thought I was drifting. It had been bad when we had first met Tabitha and also after my snowmobile wreck.

I figured I was pretty justified, though. When we met Tabitha it was as if everything I had learned in fifteen years of life was wrong. That there was a different world I was living in, I just hadn't known it. Jackie and I both kept her existence a secret from Dad for the longest time, too, and that had been so difficult. I would have to think two and three times about a word or statement before I said it and then I would forget what I was supposed to be saying. I was always on guard with my conversations with Dad and my friends and the guilt of our secrecy ate me up inside, too.

Then Dad accidentally met Zagros and thought he was having a nervous breakdown. He flipped out when we told him the truth and didn't talk to Jackie or me for a couple of weeks. I had been terribly distracted back then. I didn't know if he and Jackie were going to break up or if he would send me back to Vancouver to live with my mom or what. I thought being distracted was acceptable given what we were all facing, not to mention a second dragon.

And after my accident we were creating the New Normal which was another lie but one done to protect the dragons here and all around the world. I had to cope with my injuries as well as my guilt about how my own foolishness could have cost me my life and how upset Jackie and Dad would have been. It could have exposed the dragons when everyone was out looking for me and then when Zagros saved my life. Distraction was alright then, too.

"Don't get me wrong, it's a wonderful thing to be thoughtful," Jackie said. "You just need to learn to not let it take over your day to day life. Everyone drifts off now and then."

"What?" I said, in a far-off voice, jokingly pretending I hadn't been listening.

"No, I get it," I told her after she stopped laughing. "This is a big responsibility but it's probably one of a billion responsibilities we're going to be facing and I can't wrap my brain and my life around it. I still need to try to be normal, right?"

"Exactly. The eggs aren't hatching today. Oscar said Tabitha suspects they might hatch in early summer. Of course, these are her first eggs so she isn't totally certain either. It's not like there is a pregnancy center for dragons. At least not one in Missing Lake," she said.

"Right. She can't just get online in a chat group and be all, 'Hi, I'm an enormous crimson dragon living in a mountain with twin eggs to hatch. When does that happen, again? Hashtag, dragons-be-born.'" We both laughed. I didn't know if Jackie even knew what hashtags were but I put it out there. I was fairly certain Dad didn't use them. He could barely use a cellular phone.

"I'll try not to get too distracted, I promise," I said after we had driven a bit in silence, just about at our own driveway.

"I'll say again, it's a good thing to be thoughtful," Jackie told me before she added, "It's very Luke of you."

SEVEN

"So what are you guys wearing to the dance?" I tried my best to sound casual and cool. I knew guys didn't normally talk about what they were wearing but I had no clue and I didn't want to ask Dad or Jackie.

"I was hoping to get to Missoula for a tuxedo fitting beforehand," Derek said, with his trademark grin on his face, "but it just didn't pan out."

After Ben stopped laughing he smacked me on my arm.

"Jeans, Luke. Just jeans. Not much different than what we're wearing now."

I looked down at my clothing choice for that day. T-shirt from a store in the mall. Jeans. Check.

"Let's not be like the girls and call each other to see what we're wearing, okay?" Derek asked. I felt a bit of a flush as I remembered doing that to Sam for our first dance back in Bismarck.

"We're just glad you're coming. It's fun to hang out and listen to the music and watch everyone, too," Ben added. We had been waiting for the girls to join us before going to the veterinary clinic to have one more session hashing out the latest Sharing assignment for English class. It had been amazing weather that week, with the trees all becoming bright green and the sun putting out a bit more heat each day. Some of the kids had even worn shorts to school, which I hadn't been ready for just yet.

It had started to become difficult to sit in class while spring was taking over the view through the windows. As much as I loved winter and the incredible journey Dad and I were on with our sled dogs there was nothing like watching the world wake up to warmth again.

"What are you guys talking about?" Bethany asked as she and Gwen joined us on the front steps of our high school.

"Nothing much," I answered. We picked up our knapsacks and headed to the street where a blue pickup truck was passing by. It slowed to a stop and the driver's side window came down. Callum. The really cool basketball player. We watched as he rested his muscular arm on the ledge. It looked like he already had a sun tan. Bethany and Gwen were a few steps ahead of us but it didn't appear that Callum had stopped to talk to us.

"Great, I'll see you guys Friday," was all I heard and then Callum lifted his arm to wave at Ben, Derek and me.

"Keep the faith, bros," he called out and drove off.

I saw Bethany and Gwen look at each other and heard them giggle. It occurred to me that only someone as cool as Callum could stop their truck on the main road through town just to talk with friends.

I felt a jab in my side and looked down as Ben pulled his elbow away.

"What do you think that was all about?" he asked quietly as he jutted his chin toward the girls and slowed his pace. I figured he wanted the girls to get ahead of us but we didn't have far to go. We were already at the clinic's front lawn.

“What? Callum? How should I know,” I answered. Before I could ask why I realized Ben was frowning.

“You don’t think… wait… what do you think?” I stammered. I watched my tall friend shake his head as if to shake some unpleasant thought from his mind. It happened to wipe the frown off of his face, too.

“Never mind,” he mumbled as we joined the others in the clinic.

Jackie’s assistant, Sherise Laird was still on vacation and there were no other clients around. We generally all funneled into the kennel room because that was where the microwave was to heat our lunches and we usually wanted to see if there were any animals in there. I hadn’t been expecting to see any because Jackie couldn’t do surgery with anesthesia without another person to help but the girls were knelt down in front of what looked like a spaniel of some sort. The dog looked happy and started thumping its tail against the metal cage.

“That’s Seemore,” Jackie said before the girls asked anything.

“He looks a lot like Mollie but different,” Bethany said, turning to Jackie.

“He’s a Britany spaniel. They’re red and white and they have slightly more refined features. They’re very nice and smart, like Springers,” she answered.

“How come he’s here?” I asked. I laid my jacket on the x-ray table where I saw Ben and Derek had laid theirs.

Jackie looked at me and smiled. “No surgery, just a toe nail trim and his owners were here but they asked me to keep Seemore while they ran some errands and tried out the new café for lunch. I knew you guys were coming over so I would be here over the lunch hour."

After we all visited the happy dog we moved to the exam room where Jackie had a surprise for us. She had me tell everyone not to bring a lunch but we didn't know what she had been planning. On her examination table that had a towel laid across it she had sandwiches brought in from The Silver Bullet. There were clubhouse and turkey and roast beef to choose from. I was as surprised as everyone else even though she had mentioned bringing us sandwiches when we first talked about the song together.

"Help yourselves, guys," Jackie said, handing out napkins and paper plates. "There is pop and water in the fridge. I thought I would celebrate your last Sharing session of the school year with you. I have enjoyed thinking about various songs in different ways, especially songs I hadn't given much thought to in a while. It's been a neat experience for me."

We thanked Jackie and small-talked about the food and how happy we all were that the owners had opened the café. Gwen sounded excited to help out there once school was over and we all agreed to try to come in and get together when it was her shift to work.

We didn't end up having much time to discuss our discoveries with the song, *Hard Way* because of the fun lunch but we did make a bit of progress. Bethany had thought about the connection to the REM song we had done in class, too.

"Do you think Ms.Tanner is religious?" Gwen asked after Bethany made the suggestion. Gwen had her notebook out, as always. Over the school year the rest of us gradually had stopped taking our own notes. We referred to Gwen if there was something one of us had missed when Sharing came around and she never complained about her role as group secretary.

“I don’t know if she even thought about the two songs,” Ben said. “I think the stuff that goes on in her head is pretty random.”

I chuckled and added, “Right, as if there are a few too many cobwebs up there.” Everyone laughed.

“Can she legally get us to talk about religion?” Derek asked. “No, I’m serious,” he added probably because our faces were all blank. I had no idea what he was talking about.

“She isn’t forcing us to talk about anything, Derek. Just our own thoughts and feelings about a song we’ve never heard before. If our thoughts go that way then that’s our fault. She isn’t forcing that out of us,” Gwen said. She had a perplexed look on her face and her freckles were all scrunched together towards her pointy little nose. I quickly looked away.

“Right, so maybe she’s using subliminal suggestions like they do in commercials where you see or hear something that makes you say or do another thing but it actually has nothing to do with what you saw or heard,” he explained. I looked around at the rest of us and even Jackie looked confused.

“But why would Tanner do that?” Bethany finally asked.

"Because she's crazy," Derek replied without any hesitation. "She was a hippie, you know. She could be anti-government or something and she's lulling us into her trap of trust until she springs something like this on us as our last assignment."

I saw Jackie's shoulders shake as she must have stifled a laugh.

"Derek, I think you watch too many shows on conspiracy theories," she said. "I think she just likes the song and wants your guys' opinion on it all. If you happen to make the connection that this song highlights exactly what Michael Stipe and REM meant in *Losing My Religion* then that's just a neat thought. Remember, though, Michael Stipe was most likely referring to losing his mind or being at his wit's end and I think there is a similarity although not necessarily about religion. Maybe Matisyahu was partly inspired by REM's song."

Bethany and Gwen looked at each other.

"Oh, good one, Dr. Yale-Houser, good one." Gwen said the words slowly while she nodded her head up and down. We all watched her scribble a few words in the notebook.

"I definitely think the singer is sharing that he has a void in his life after departing from his deeply-held, former religious views and that's a big part of the song, regardless of whether or not you want to talk about religion," Jackie said, looking directly at Derek with a smile on her face.

"Oh, I don't mind talking about it. I'm just questioning the legality of it all," he answered.

"He does say something right at the beginning about quenching his thirst," Bethany said, "a thirst that he can't escape, right?"

Ben nodded his head.

"So the singer, himself, maybe doesn't have any answers for quenching his thirst. It's just there and he knows nothing but he is learning, even if it's the hard way?" It was more of a question than a statement. I wasn't sure what to say.

"I think that's a great thought to end on, gang," Jackie said, standing up. "It is just something more to consider when you listen to the song and then talk about it tomorrow in class."

We all cleaned up our plates and got ready to head back to school. We made sure to say goodbye to Seemore, who started thumping his tail loudly again and said our thanks to Jackie for lunch and the discussion.

"Hey, thanks so much for letting us hang out with you at lunch and talking about the music and stuff," Derek said as he shook Jackie's hand.

"Again, it has been as much fun for me and a great break from science and medicine," she replied.

Out of nowhere, at least to me, Ben wrapped Jackie in a hug as he towered above her. Jackie was not a big person. Even I was taller than her but seeing Ben like that made him look like a giant. He caught me rolling my eyes at him and smirked at me. Jackie seemed startled by the hug and didn't really hug back. She more or less patted him on the back, having to reach up a bit to do it.

"Good grief, Ben," Bethany said as she, too, rolled her eyes once we were outside.

"Way to go, Rothman," Derek said to Ben when we made our way back across the highway to the high school. Ben looked like he was strutting.

Various kids were sitting out on the front lawn under the few trees that were greening up. Most of them had no jackets on. The two seniors who had become engaged that year were holding hands and kissing under one of the trees. That seemed out of place and maybe even inappropriate. I didn't remember anyone doing that back in Bismarck but that might have been because I never would have noticed. I immediately pictured Sam and Kristi Rushman making out in front of people at our high school in North Dakota and I felt my stomach plunge.

"Oh my God, it's Emily Young and Kyle O'Regan," whispered Gwen. "Wow, they aren't afraid of much, are they?"

"That's what I was thinking," I whispered back. All of us slowed our walking and our heads were turned towards the trees.

"Guys, we are all totally staring," Bethany announced in her own hushed voice and she was right. I lowered my own head and picked up the pace a bit.

"I don't see the big deal," Derek said. "Everyone knows they're engaged. They've obviously kissed before and hey, it's spring. Love is in the air," he added as he made a swooping gesture with his arm that knocked into Ben's nose on the way up.

"Geez, Derek, I can pick my own nose, thank-you very much," Ben said. He felt around his nose with one hand and shoved Derek away from him with the other. The girls laughed and waved as they headed off down the hallway in a different direction from our lockers.

"So what was up with Callum and those two?" Ben asked once we had reached the lockers.

"For real? How would I know? I almost forgot about it," I lied.

"I think that's just how he is. You know, friends with the entire school, most popular man in the world. He'll probably be the President when we all get older but that will be after his long, successful career as a star NBA player and then a brain surgeon," Derek said. He sounded like he was thinking out loud, not actually involved in a conversation.

I removed a couple of notebooks and then hung my knapsack back up. I had started doing that a few weeks prior to have less things to carry but sometimes my arms felt empty and I didn't know what to do with them. The empty hand usually ended up in a pants pocket.

"I agree with that," I told my friends. "I'm sure he was just making sure everyone knows about the dance and he was just being friendly."

The look on Ben's face told me he suspected something else. He shook his head slowly from side to side and frowned.

"I don't know. I'm thinking maybe he likes one of them."

"Does that bother you?" I asked. I felt confused. Ben never talked about the girls in any sort of girlfriend way. Had I been a bad buddy because I never asked him? I realized I didn't really ask Sam about Kristi when we emailed. Instead I mostly made jokes and that probably wasn't very nice of me. It might even be immature. Just because I wasn't ready to think about asking someone out didn't mean my friends weren't. I knew that Ben felt if it was a choice between him and the athletic, older, confidant, charming Callum that it was a clear decision who would get the girl.

"No, Idiot. I'm thinking about you and Gwen," Ben said in a lowered voice. He looked all around him as if making sure nobody could listen. I heard Derek chuckle even though his head was inside his locker.

I felt the heat rise in my neck again but I wasn't sure what to say. I wanted to be angry that they kept bringing it up and I felt embarrassed that I had just been concerned about Ben's feelings and my own lack of interest but I couldn't make sense out of any feelings at all. I just shook my head. I was pretty sure my face was red, which made me feel even more embarrassed.

"Ben, Gwen is a friend, just like Bethany is our friend. Gwen pays the same amount of attention to you guys and everyone else she's around so stop bugging me. I'm going to the dance to hang out with all of you, not to hook up with Gwen." I hoped I hadn't sounded bossy or rude. I closed my locker door a bit harder than I had intended to.

The rest of the afternoon passed without any more discussion about Gwen or Callum. I had one class without Ben and Derek which had been just fine. Nick Cutler asked if I was going to the dance and we talked about it a bit. He had been grounded for something he did to make his dad mad but his mom persuaded him to let Nick go. It was the last dance of the school year after all.

Whenever I talked with Nick I felt sad for him that he didn't have the kind of relationship with his dad that I had. His dad worked in Missoula and stayed there during the week so it wasn't even like they were in each other's faces. It was totally the opposite with Dad and I. We did spend time together with the dogs and even sometimes when he subbed at school I would see him. I had a lot of respect for my dad but I never sensed that from Nick with his. There had always been rumors that his dad knocked him around at times and that he had quite a temper. He wasn't a man I ever wanted to meet but I was curious about him. I would never ask Nick but I did wonder if the rumors were true.

Or if it was almost like Josh and his family, who had to hide from his dad. Josh could never talk about it because it would put his family at risk if his dad ever found out where they were. I realized as time passed that he had sort of told me about his past. He hinted about having secrets and he was very private if anyone asked about his mom or sisters. And he was obsessed with having a bad person's blood inside when I was in the hospital and had needed a transfusion.

Maybe Josh sensed that I had a big secret and maybe he knew more than he let on. He would have known it had nothing to do with my family because I didn't hide my relationship with my dad. All of my friends had met him through his substitute teaching at least once and they all saw him and I joke around together.

But I had secrets. I had two very big secrets with Tabitha and Zagros and my role in their lives. And their roles in my life. My secret, like Josh's was so important because the lives of those I cared about would be at risk if I said anything.

Josh and I bonded in a way that didn't require a name. We weren't Best Friends or Brothers From Another Mother. We never hung out together after school but I knew I was one of the only people he liked to be with, even if we didn't have much to say. At first I figured it was because we both were pretty new and hadn't grown up with everyone else in Missing Lake. With time, though, after he left, I started thinking that there was more to our friendship. Maybe Josh knew a lot more about me than I realized.

"Luke, are you in there?" a voice snapped me back to the real world.

"Yeah. Yeah, Nick. Sorry, I drifted a bit there," I stammered. "Hey," I added, "what does everyone wear to the dances here?"

Nick threw his head back and laughed.

"Jeans, buddy. Or shorts if its warm tomorrow night but I'd stick with jeans. A nice shirt." He laughed again. "What are we? Girls?" Nick shook his head and clapped his hand on my shoulder before turning away.

EIGHT

"Do you want to go right on time or is it better to be more fashionably late?" Dad asked at supper before the dance. Jackie had made her green bean and cashew chicken pasta, which was one of my favorites. She had said something about carbo-loading before the dance.

I finished my mouthful and shrugged my shoulders.

"I don't know, to be honest. I told Ben that I would meet them there but I didn't ask if they were going to be right on time or not. It starts at seven."

Dad would have known what time the dance started but I still felt the need to say it. As the day had gone on I became less convinced that going to the dance was a great idea but it was too late to change my mind. Everyone was expecting me and they would bug the heck out of me forever if I didn't go. Things with Ben and I had been fine during our Sharing session earlier that day and I was looking forward to sleeping over at his house after the dance.

It was as if Jackie had been reading my mind because she reminded me to call them for a ride home if I changed my mind on staying overnight or if I wasn't having fun at the dance.

"I can't see that happening, though," she added as she scooped a second helping of pasta onto her plate. "Dances are fun and your friends are all pretty neat kids. At least the ones I've met."

“Yeah, most of them are a lot of fun. Derek makes everyone laugh a lot and Harrison seems like a smart guy. He had a lot to say today in our Sharing class,” I told her. I watched Dad sneak a piece of chicken down to a very quiet Boston Terrier who was sitting as if at attention next to his chair.

“Rob, he’s going to get fat if you keep doing that.” Apparently Jackie saw it, too.

Baxter made a whimpering sound as if he had understood what she said. Maybe he had. Jackie told Dad and me off whenever she busted us giving him our food. She was a bit of a warrior on pet obesity and, having canine athletes as our team mates, we certainly understood the need for our dogs to be healthy. Still, it was impossible to resist those big round eyes that stuck out almost on the sides of Baxter’s head when he sat next to you silently willing us to give him our food.

He never sat next to Jackie when we ate. Dogs are smart.

“Oh, come on, Hon, it’s one piece of chicken,” Dad protested.

“That was the fourth or fifth piece, nice try,” Jackie responded. I hadn’t noticed the other ones. Jackie was getting good at watching us, apparently.

“There are a couple of people I don’t really know that well, like Anne-Marie. I don’t know if she goes to the dances or not,” I said. “She doesn’t seem to have many friends and she talks about getting out of Missing Lake as fast as she can after high school.”

"I wouldn't be surprised if most kids want to move on after high school here," Jackie said. "There aren't a whole lot of options for work and there aren't any industries for kids to learn trades. I suppose if you had a family business like the Mercantile then you might stick around but even then, a degree in business or marketing first might be wise."

Dad and I nodded our heads. We were both pretty busy with our meals to comment much. I appreciated how the conversation had moved away from the dance at that point, though, so I needed to keep it going.

"Would you consider mushing to be a family business?" I asked. Dad winked at me from across the table.

"Noooooooo," Jackie answered, really drawing out the response. "Although I guess it could be." She appeared to be thinking about it while she ate another forkful.

"There are some families in the mushing world who basically have it in their blood. Like the Mackeys in Alaska." She was referring to a famous family of mushers who have taken turns winning the Iditarod race. The dad and his sons and their kids all mushed competitively and ran terrific Alaskan Husky breeding kennels.

"Those families pretty much know nothing else," Dad finally offered. "I would want for you to learn other skills, get a different career path and then, if it is still a passion of yours, come back to the mushing. Of course, that doesn't mean you have to go to college right away if you wanted to stick around and mush another year. It's completely up to you, Luke."

"That's still a couple of years away, Dad. Let me get through my sophomore year first, alright?"

We laughed and ate in silence for a couple of minutes before Dad asked about the Sharing session from that day.

I shoveled more pasta into my mouth and thought back to earlier that day at school. Ms.Tanner had outdone herself with a flowery scarf around her neck and some sort of head piece that had flowers on it, too. It wasn't a hat or a headband or anything I had seen before but it seemed to suit her. She had huge hoop earrings in that went down past her chin and sparkly bracelets that made noises when they bumped up against each other. Her long skirt touched the floor and even went past her feet. Ben had leaned over and whispered that she probably didn't have shoes on but at one point early on she spun in a circle and I could see sandals. I thought they were called Birkenstocks, which I wrote on a piece of paper and handed to Ben. I still wasn't sure if that was correct or not but he burst out laughing, which caused Ms.Tanner to stare at both of us. Thankfully she hadn't seen the note.

The Sharing session was a different one because we weren't necessarily analyzing the song. Ms.Tanner mostly wanted us to comment on it and give our thoughts. Which was funny because, as Harrison pointed out, the song says, *'Everyone's right or wrong, everyone's got an opinion.'* She wanted us to talk about how the song made each of us feel and if we liked it or not.

Bethany got the discussion going after we had all moved our desks into our Sharing circle. It still made me a bit sad to not see Josh's desk.

"I wasn't sure when we first heard the song but I can honestly say I like it," she began. "It doesn't have a catchy beat or anything and we won't be playing it at the dance tonight because I'm not sure if it's a slow dance or a fast one but I like it."

Ms.Tanner had asked, "What, specifically do you like about it?"

That made Bethany pause. She looked up at the ceiling before answering.

"I like how the music is wispy and light and how he sings for awhile before the music picks up."

Karol-with-a-K almost jumped out of her desk, adding, "Yes, I know what you mean. And when the music picks up the feel of the song changes until the end when it slows down again. I like that about the song and he has a really nice voice, too. Did anyone else look up other songs of his?"

"Of course," answered Anne-Marie. She had a way of putting people down just by answering a question. As if Karol's question had been stupid.

"I think his older song, *One Day* is an even better song and it has a great video with it, too," she told us all. Anne-Marie didn't seem to ever talk with us. She talked at us.

"I like that song, too. They used it when they advertised for the Olympics in Vancouver," I offered.

"Houser, can you get through one Sharing session without mentioning Vancouver?" asked Jason. I knew he was joking. It got everyone laughing a little which always helped open up the Sharing sessions.

Everyone agreed that they liked how the song sounded and the way the music changed. It was Harrison who pointed something out that none of us, including Jackie had mentioned.

"So, I was listening to the song on my computer over and over with the words in front of me and I noticed something about when the music changes. When it's mostly just piano, at the beginning and end of the song, he is singing about you. As in, *'your thirst'* and *'something you can't* escape' at the beginning and *'you say it's your cage'* and *'you're your own worst enemy'* at the end." I leaned forward and noticed that some of the other kids did as well.

"In the middle part of the song, though, when the music picks up, he is singing about himself. With words like *'who am I to say'* or..." Harrison paused and fingered through some notes on a piece of paper in front of him. "Okay, or *'I'm descending down'* and *'I opened up a door'*. There are a lot of examples if you look. He's changing the perspective of who or what the song is about."

I had my lyrics sheet in front of me and Ben leaned over to look at it with me. The entire class became silent as we read through the words. I tried to play the song back in my head and it looked like Harrison was right.

"Wait a sec, though," Trista said, turning to her right where Harrison sat. "The second verse he is singing about himself using *'I'* but the music is slow and light there." I began to get confused about where the music changed and where it didn't.

"Right," Harrison turned directly to Trista when he spoke, "but the music did pick up after the first verse and then slowed when he started singing again."

"So?" she asked him. I watched him fold his arms across his chest as he leaned back into his chair and looked at all of us.

"I don't know. I have no clue what it means. It was just something I noticed," he said before he chuckled.

Ms.Tanner had looked pleased as she walked around behind our circle of desks. Her skirt grazed the ground behind her as she slowly took each step and the bracelets she wore on both arms made jingling sounds.

"That is a terrific observation, Harrison, thank-you for sharing it with us. What do the rest of you think? Are the wording and musical changes significant?" she asked us.

I had a thought that was incomplete but I figured a class like that was all about thinking freely and sharing what was on my mind.

"Maybe he's totally admitting to himself this problem he has when the music is light at the beginning and the end, and that it's more like a confession. He's asking himself who will quench his own thirst and who will make him happy even though he says, *'you'*. It's almost like he's writing in a journal or talking to himself and then the middle bit of the song he's trying to answer his own questions. He isn't making excuses, he's just answering the questions, like here." I pointed down at the lyrics sheet on my desk, "he comes right out and says '*I opened up a door*' so he admits that he created the situation he's in."

I was almost breathing hard after I had dumped all of that out there. I hadn't meant to ramble but it had seemed like a good idea when it first hit me.

"I like that," Harrison responded, leaning forward in his desk. We were almost opposite each other in our circle. "And maybe when he says '*you*' at the beginning and end it is him talking to himself. Like when you look in the mirror and say, 'Harrison, you are looking fine today.'" We all cracked up again.

"What's the deal with the '*palace made of glass*'?" Karol had asked. "Because it crashed all around him and the kingdom was broken and he's all kind of messed up in the middle."

"I think that was his career and his life, right?" Bethany took a stab at an answer. "Because he says he opened up the door and that might be when he quit the serious version of his religion which probably made him question everything at that point."

"Whoa, Bethany. Deep," Jason said, which made most of us chuckle. Particularly when she stuck her tongue out at him.

"I still don't know about that second verse, where the music picks up but slows again and he switched to saying '*I*' instead of '*you*'," Gwen said as she stared at her lyrics sheet. "He sounds like he's feeling some anguish here and things are bad, like the sky is gray, the dog has strayed and there's no barricades for a hurricane. All things he can't control."

She looked up from her paper, turned to me and asked, "Do you think that's significant?"

Our eyes locked, which surprised me, which was probably why I didn't look away immediately. Gwen held my gaze with a questioning look on her face. I wanted to answer her question to make her smile so I could see her dimples but I didn't know the answer. I didn't want to let Gwen down, though. I felt like she specifically chose me to answer her question. She looked like she was really interested in what I had to say.

It was Anne-Marie who broke our moment with a long-winded description of how the singer was clearly depressed and he did mention that he was off his medications and in fact, she, the expert on life thought he was using a self-deprecating tone in much of the song which was a ploy to make people feel sorry for him which she, clearly, did not.

Gwen and I had returned to looking at our own lyrics sheets by the time Anne-Marie finished sharing her understanding of the song. I hadn't really been listening. I had been thinking about Gwen and I and our direct eye contact. I realized I hadn't felt any heat or redness in my neck which I figured was probably because I wasn't over analyzing her question to me. I had just wanted to answer it.

I was remembering that shared look when Dad brought me back to the supper table.

"Luke. Are you in there?" he asked.

I was sitting there with my empty fork in the air and he and Jackie were staring at me.

"Oh, right. Sorry. I was just remembering things we talked about in the Sharing session," I told him.

"Did anyone have any revelations we hadn't talked about? It is an interesting song and since we didn't know much about the singer it's not like we could easily tell what he was thinking when he wrote it," Jackie said.

I told them about what Harrison noticed and how the discussion ensued. I told them how Jason didn't have much to say but that he wasn't a huge talker. I explained my rambling as thinking out loud but that was okay in Sharing sessions because Ms.Tanner kind of encouraged it.

Dad seemed interested in the fact the whole class liked the song. Not just how it sounded but the words, too. Even Anne-Marie who had informed us all before the session ended that she thought the singer was being a bit passive-aggressive. I told him that Ms.Tanner had chuckled at that.

"He does call himself his *'own worst enemy'*, though, so maybe he knows that," Jackie said. She stacked Dad's and my empty dishes onto hers and got up to take them to the sink. I pushed back from the table to help.

"Yeah. And he's a slave so I think he is saying that even though he removed himself from the really strict religious group he's still going to be Jewish because he wouldn't have it any other way," I told her with a handful of cutlery I brought from the table.

Dad came up behind us with the now empty pasta dish and said, "I like these Sharing sessions, Son. I'll admit, I thought they were a bit flaky at the beginning of the year but here you are, outside of class still discussing lyrics and the motivation behind them. I'll bet you're not the only one talking about this song with your family after the assignment is over. Good for you for broadening your musical horizons, too."

He smiled at me and then pointed at his watch.

"Better think about getting changed for the dance if we're going to get you there. Fashionably late is one thing but annoyingly late is another.

He was right. I asked Jackie if we had something non-perishable that I could bring for a food bank donation.

"Food bank? At the dance?" she asked.

"Yeah, the school is covering the cost of the DJ for this dance. I guess at the other dances there was a small fee to go but the principal asked everyone to bring a donation for the food bank," I explained.

"I don't even know where the food bank is in town. I'll have to check that out," she said while opening one of the cupboards. I watched her remove a tin of chicken noodle soup and some canned corn.

"You know, I should order in some dog food from the company I carry to donate to the food bank. I'll bet that would be helpful for people," she told me as she handed me the cans. I nodded my head and told her that was a great idea.

I headed off to my bedroom with Baxter following right behind. I had clean jeans and a plain shirt to wear. It wasn't really a T-shirt because the sleeves were longer but it still felt like one because it didn't have buttons or a collar. I wasn't even as built as the store mannequin had been as far as my chest and arm muscles went but I thought it looked alright.

"What do you think, little man?" I asked Baxter once I had changed. I held my arms out to the side to give him the full view. He tipped his round head to the side and looked so serious, as if he really was thinking about it. I wished Zagros was there to give me some support. The knowledge that I hung out with a couple of dragons gave me a boost of much needed confidence at least.

I was nervous but I was also excited to listen to loud music and watch Derek dance. I felt good that I hadn't gone all red when Gwen had caught and held my eyes earlier that day as well. It still didn't mean I was ready to even consider a girlfriend but maybe it meant I was more normal than I had thought. I decided to just give in to the idea that the night would be a surprise.

I certainly didn't expect things to turn out like they did.

NINE

Ben's parents were dropping him off in the high school parking lot just as we pulled in. Or, Ben was dropping himself off, actually, because he hopped out of the driver's side door after their vehicle had stopped. His dad came out the passenger side and walked over to Dad's window.

"Hi, Mr. Rothman. Thanks for letting me stay over tonight," I said to him. The Rothmans were a really nice family and I had been looking forward to seeing them all again. Even Cade, Ben's little brother was fun to hang out with. He could get a bit intense especially if we were playing any kind of game but it was always cool to watch him. It didn't matter if we were playing with the X-Box or outside shooting hoops; Cade's competitiveness was guaranteed to be one-hundred per cent.

"No problem, Luke. We're happy to have you. You two have fun tonight. Eleven o'clock, right?"

"Yeah, thanks, Dad. Hi, Mr.Houser," Ben called out to my Dad and we turned to walk towards the school.

Dad had been pretty funny on the drive back into town. He told me about his high school dances and that he wasn't really into them. Whoever was on the senior committee in charge of dances would hire live bands who, he said, were usually heavy metal or rock & roll. I shuddered at the thought of a bunch of guys with long hair and shiny tights screaming into microphones while teenagers danced in front of them.

He had met my mom when they were in high school, which were some of the happiest years of my mother's life. She never actually said that but whenever she talked about high school she would get a dreamy look on her face as if she was transported back to her favorite memories of all time. She had been super pretty and really popular. My mom still was really attractive and she dressed nicely. Her hair was a lot bigger when she was in high school, though, which was the one thing she didn't like about some of her high school pictures. She would probably have more of them up around her house in Vancouver if it wasn't for the big hair.

We heard music coming from the gymnasium as soon as we entered the main doors of the high school. Our school in Missing Lake didn't have metal detectors like the one in Bismarck had. All of my friends couldn't believe that when I had first told them. They were surprised that a state like North Dakota would have any issues but it was a state known for hunting and almost everyone had guns.

But then my North Dakota friends were surprised that Missing Lake's high school didn't have high level security. There was talk about getting metal detectors or hiring a security officer but there wasn't a lot of extra funding for things like that. Most of the students I knew were just happy to have the Internet.

Ben and I put our jackets in our lockers and dropped our food bank donations into a large box at the entrance to the gym. The lights were mostly off but there were some that seemed strategically aimed to highlight the scene. Someone had obviously organized a decorations committee to deck the place out.

"Who does all this?" I asked Ben as I slowly spun in a circle while looking upward. Large pastel flowers were hung at various lengths from the beams and were all over the walls and bleachers. There were spotlights trained onto a rotating silver disco ball which sent spinning light beams down onto the floor. The rays of light slowly changed colors as they spun. I chucked because it made me think of Jackie and her love of seventies music.

"Yeah, wow, they out did themselves this time," Ben answered as he, too, spun around looking upward. "I think the student council organizes the dance decorations but they have never looked this good."

Sparkly streamers were everywhere and the floor was covered with glitter. After a few moments my eyes became accustomed to the semi-darkness. I felt a bit sorry for whoever was on the clean-up committee but people probably figured that into their decorating plans. At least I hoped they had. It wouldn't be very fair to ask the school janitors to clean all of that up.

There was a small stage at the far end of the gym where a guy was set up with some fancy equipment with its own set of lights on it. I figured he was the DJ. I saw a few of the teachers standing at various areas around the gym. None of them looked overly thrilled to be there. Our assistant basketball coach, Mr.Carlson was fiddling with something in his ear. He looked like the sled dogs when they got something deep inside their ears with his head tipped to the side. I wondered if his daughter, Lily, who was a freshman was there and if that was weird for them. I scanned the dance floor, which wasn't overly crowded but didn't see her.

I followed Ben over to the bleachers where Derek and Harrison were standing.

"You made it, Houser," Derek said after he slugged me in the arm. "Our little boy is growing up."

We all cracked up. I saw Nick standing with some other guys and we nodded our heads at each other. I tried to look casual as I scanned the people coming into the gym as well as the rest who were already there.

The dance floor looked like it was mostly occupied by juniors and seniors. At least the faces I recognized from basketball were. I didn't know most of the older girls in the school but I also didn't see the ones in our grade out there. The music was fast and I had heard the song the DJ was playing but wasn't familiar with it. It was pop music, thankfully. I had been worried they would play mostly country music and that all the kids would know how to two-step. Some of the girls in Bismarck loved that and I had never known what to do. I also wasn't a huge country music fan.

"Hey, there's Karol and Jason," Ben said. He pointed towards the doorway and the box for the food bank. We watched Karol reach for his hand but Jason pulled his away.

"Whoa, what's the deal there?" I said, to nobody in particular.

"Uh oh, trouble in paradise?" said Nick, who had come over to our group. His voice had definitely changed since the school year began. He hadn't grown much in terms of height but his shoulders were wider than mine by far, which I hadn't noticed before.

"Lets not stare, guys. What if they see us?" Ben suggested.

"Good call, Ben," Derek agreed. He looked up towards the ceiling and asked, "How do you think they got those streamers up there? And all of the dangly flowers?"

We all looked upwards in silence.

"Is this one of those games where you're trying to get everyone to look up?" Bethany and Gwen had found us.

"Did you guys all remember your donation to the food bank?" Gwen asked us.

"Yeah. I almost forgot. Where is the food bank anyhow?" I asked.

"I think its next to one of the churches in town," Derek answered. Jason and Karol had slowly made their way to where we all stood.

"Hi, you guys," Karol said. I watched Gwen look down at their non-connected hands and then up at Bethany, who must have noticed the same thing. Bethany's eyes widened for the shortest of moments but then she smiled and grabbed Karol's arm.

"Come on. I love this song," she said, leading Karol out towards the DJ's stage and light show. Gwen smiled at us and followed along.

"Is that an open invite to all of us?" Derek asked.

"Derek, the dance floor itself is an open invite to you," said Harrison, laughing as he clapped his hand on his back, seemingly pushing him forward to follow the girls. Derek turned and grinned at the rest of us and almost jogged out to the center of the floor.

The song was fast with a good beat. It was something by Rhianna. I didn't know the words or anything but some of the people on the dance floor looked like they were singing along.

"Doubt we'll hear anything by the Bee Gees tonight," Ben said. It was a reference to our Sharing Sessions in English class, which Jason picked up on as well.

"What was that Joni Mitchell song we did last month? I'm still trying to figure it out," he asked as he shook his head.

"Hoo boy, I know," Ben answered. "That was the most silence we've ever had during the actual discussion. Even Luke's stepmom didn't have much for us."

"I know. If Tanner could have rolled her eyes at us once more during that class she would've strained something," I added. That had been a weird song. Something about a girl named Scarlett. The most any of us could pull together to talk about was how important a singer-songwriter Joni Mitchell was. My dad loved the fact we did one of her songs because she is Canadian but he wasn't very helpful with the song selection. He talked more about harmonies and musical changes and how Joni tried to tell a story with words and sounds but most of it had gone over my head. Ms. Tanner had looked personally insulted that none of us could make much sense of the song. Even Anne-Marie hadn't had much to say that particular day. All I remembered about the song was that the singer didn't seem to even like the main character she sang about. Something about blood red nails.

It would have been different if we were encouraged to use the internet to actually see what Joni Mitchell was trying to talk about. The song, though, hadn't seemed to resonate with any of us so nobody was motivated to look it up, even after the discussion.

"I doubt many of our Sharing songs will make tonight's play list," I said. Even if that Matisyahu guy is modern, nobody is going to be breaking it down to *Hard Way.* The rest of the guys laughed but none of us went out onto the dance floor where Derek was already surrounded by a large group of students, including Gwen, Bethany and Karol.

"He'll be out there all night, you know," Nick told me, jutting his chin out towards Derek's dance circle. "Except for the slow ones."

"Does anybody dance the slow songs here?" I asked. I felt heat creep up my neck towards my face. It was one thing to make it to the dance but I had been hoping only the older kids actually did the slow dances, as opposed to what my mom and Jackie suggested.

The guys all gave me a look like I had just asked what century we were living in.

"Well, yeah, but it doesn't have to mean anything," Harrison said, "unless you want it to." The last part of his statement sounded like a question. I looked down at my shoes and shoved my hands in my pockets.

“Derek has all these rules he’s told us this year during the dances, too, so we should maybe fill you in,” Nick said. I saw Ben nod his head and roll his eyes at the same time.

“That’s right. He told me to tell you about the slow dance rules so you wouldn’t embarrass yourself but I think his rules are stupid and I don’t generally dance the slow ones. That’s when I find it a good time to go to the can. Although its usually pretty crowded in there during the slow songs,” he told me. I realized that Harrison, Jason and Nick had moved inward to make our own smaller circle.

“Does everyone know the rules?” I stammered. My throat felt really dry. “Are they just for guys or for the girls, too?”

“Who knows with Derek? I think he’s mostly joking anyhow. You know how he likes to make people laugh,” Jason said. “Besides, the rules don’t apply to me now that I sort of have a girlfriend.” We all stopped talking and looked out towards the dance floor where Derek was flailing his arms in all directions.

I caught Ben’s eyes but hadn’t wanted to make Jason feel self-conscious. I kept my mouth shut as I waited to be told Derek’s rules of the dance floor.

“Well, the main thing is, if you kind of are into someone, like maybe a girlfriend thing, or you just think they’re really nice or you think they like you then you’re not supposed to ask them to dance the very first or second slow dance of the night,” Ben began to explain. I had to interrupt.

“How many slow songs are there?” I thought I remembered only one or two all night back in Bismarck. My palms began to feel sweaty.

“Not many,” Ben told us, “but the theory is you don’t want to look desperate. At least that’s Derek’s theory. Like I say, I go to the can.”

“Did you follow the rules with Karol?” I asked Jason. He looked a bit flushed in the face after I asked, even in the darkened gymnasium.

“Um, no, we didn’t really hook up at a dance. It was more over a bunch of lunches and then talking on the phone at night, I think,” he answered. A slight smile appeared on his face as he glanced back at the dance floor. Maybe everything was alright between them.

“How does Derek have all these rules? Does he even have a girlfriend?” I asked. Nick and Ben both laughed.

“Only in his head, Luke,” Harrison told me with a smile on his face. “And, again, these are just joke rules and that’s if you even want to slow dance. We just know if you’re out there for the first one or two slow dances it had better be with someone you are just friends with or Derek will be all over you.”

“Or me. He made me promise to tell you,” he added.

Nick leaned in and whispered in my ear in a voice loud enough everyone could hear, “I’ll be in the bathroom with Rothman.” We all laughed some more. The dance hadn’t been as uncomfortable as I had thought. Just hanging out with the guys was fun enough for me.

The song had changed to one the Black Eyed Peas had performed at a recent Super bowl half-time show. I never watched much football before I moved to the states but it was easy to get excited about the Super bowl.

Our little group stayed back and talked about where we were when we had seen that particular half-time show. Karol came up and grabbed Jason by the arm when that song ended and suddenly Justin Timberlake's voice filled the sound systems with *Can't Stop the Feeling.* Jason turned back at us with an almost-pleading look in his eyes. I looked up at Ben and shrugged my shoulder.

"Any fast dance rules?"

He smiled and said, "Nope. I just sort of move around a little and keep my eyes on Derek. He's who everyone else is watching anyhow."

Nick and Harrison joined us as we added to the growing group of people on the dance floor. I knew that was a popular song and it had a great rhythm and sound so it wasn't surprising to see the bleachers emptying as more and more students got up to dance.

I looked around as I began nodding my head and bending my knees to the beat. It looked like a safe play as I saw other guys doing the same thing. Some had their hands in their pockets so I stuffed mine back in. They just felt so loose, as if they had no purpose. At least being in my pockets gave them something to do.

Derek made a big deal during his crazy movements to point at me. He mouthed the word, "Wow" and spun around in a circle, all the while pointing at me. I figured he wanted everyone to know it was a big deal that I had made it to the dance. It was dark enough that I had hoped nobody saw the redness in my neck and cheeks.

Despite the loud music and turning lights on the ground from the disco ball above I allowed myself to drift a little bit. I silently acknowledged to myself that listening and moving to music with my friends was actually turning out alright. That it was probably some rite of passage that young people in all sorts of cultures had to go through. It had felt good to move around and smile at people.

The seniors, juniors, sophomores and freshmen all seemed to dance together, too. I had been so worried about not having enough kids in the school to have a dance but at that point it felt like we were all part of the same grade. And Derek was everyone's class clown.

I had to admire the guy. I mean, he put it all out there on the dance floor and looked like he was having the best time in the world doing it. His forehead was already beading up and shining with sweat but that grin on his face said everything. I knew I couldn't ever be that outgoing. I watched him grab random girls, mostly from the class below us and dance a few goofy steps with them. Most of the girls giggled but they honestly looked thrilled to have been chosen.

The song blended into another fast paced one and we all stayed out and danced. I caught Gwen's eyes a couple of times and smiled but then another person would dance in between us or she would turn around. The girls all moved differently from most of the guys. They seemed to do things with their hips and legs that made them look double-jointed.

It wasn't unpleasant but it almost looked painful. I kept with my left foot, right foot, knee bending thing and nobody looked overly concerned. Or different.

Until the first slow song came through the speakers.

Without a word and almost in synch, most of the student body turned and went back to the bleachers. I followed Ben and several other guys out the door to the men's bathroom. Ben had been right. It was pretty packed and nobody was talking about slow dancing with anyone. I wondered if the girl's bathroom looked the same but kept the thought to myself.

We took as long as we could to get back to the gym where Jason and Karol were slow-dancing together with a group of students that was larger than I had expected. It looked like mostly seniors with a few juniors. Of course Emily and Kyle were out there. They were moving slower than anyone else. Slower than the music, even and their foreheads were touching. Jackie and Mom hadn't said anything about that and I wasn't so sure I would be keen to be dancing that closely in front of everyone. At least they had been right about where to put your hands.

I tried not to stare or look for too long but I didn't see Gwen out there. I had no clue if I was actually going to ask her to dance if another slow song came on, or what I would say if she asked me but I surprisingly felt some sort of relief when I saw her and Bethany come back from the ladies' bathroom. Ben must have noticed as well because he nudged me in my ribs.

The dance floor filled up again after Ed Sheeran stopped singing. Ben, Harrison and I hung back by the bleachers for the first song. Karol and Jason looked pretty happy dancing together even though she was also dancing with Gwen and Bethany as well as Nick. I noticed that Trista had arrived with a couple of girls in our grade who I hadn't had many classes with. I thought their names were Maren and Lindsey. Maren was taller than most of the guys in our class, except for Ben, and she looked like she was mostly starting to dance with Nick. They made a funny couple with him being shorter. I made a mental note to try to get to know some more of the kids in our grade a little better.

"Should we?" Ben asked when the song changed again. He nodded his head in the direction of the dance floor.

"I guess. Right?" was my response. Harrison shrugged his shoulders and followed us out to where most of our friends were dancing. I didn't know if Derek had stayed out there for the slow dance. I had been consumed with the idea that I had to get out of there and hadn't noticed. He was still giving the fast songs every move he had and continued to maintain a circle of admirers around him. I watched him twirl Lily Carlson around like the old Rock and Roll style dances I had seen on TV. He actually looked like he knew what he was doing. That kind of dancing gave you something to do with your arms, at least.

We danced as a big group for another couple of songs until the second slow song of the night was played. I happened to catch Derek's eyes and he shot me a stern look as he mouthed the word, "No." I made the pilgrimage to the men's bathroom like the time before and avoided looking back.

Even if I had, I wouldn't have been able to stop what happened.

When I returned with Ben to stand with Nick, Derek and Harrison by the bleachers they all had worried looks on their faces. They each looked at me and then looked down at the gymnasium floor. Derek made a show of hanging his head and mumbled something about making a mistake and how sorry he was.

Ben looked towards the dance floor first. His only words were, "uh oh."

There, on the glittery dance floor, beneath pastel flowers and shiny streamers, with colored circles of light spinning around everything and Howie Day singing, *Collide*, was Gwen.

Slow dancing with Callum.

The coolest guy in the school.

With both of her arms up on his shoulders and his hands on either side of her waist. They looked like they were talking and laughing as they danced and I felt like someone squeezed my heart.

I didn't know why the guys looked so worried or even why I felt upset. It wasn't like Gwen and I were dating. We had never talked about it or even spent time alone together. I had that coffee date with Liz in Vancouver and hadn't felt guilty so I didn't know why seeing her dance with Callum seemed like such a shock.

"Dude, I mean it," Derek was quietly saying, "I never should have had Ben tell you the rules about anything. They're mostly a joke and clearly I have no idea about things like slow dancing."

"Guys. Relax," I managed to say in a voice I thought sounded normal. "I mean, look at the guy. If he asked me to dance I probably would have."

That made a few of them chuckle and lose their worried expressions.

I meant it, though. As cool as Callum was he looked even cooler that night on the dance floor with Gwen. His hair was perfect, his arm muscles showed beneath his black T-shirt and he had a cool leather bracelet thing on one of his wrists. How could I possibly compete with that?

Ben clapped his arm around my shoulder and shook it gently.

"Our bad, man. Our bad."

TEN

I was lying in my bed reflecting on the weekend, trying to forget about the stomach flu that had taken over my body the night before. Dad had gone into school to substitute for one of the teachers and Jackie was at her clinic. Our group consensus since I began vomiting just after midnight was that I wasn't going anywhere.

It wasn't a huge shock although it certainly was a drag to be sick. When I had spent the night at the Rothman's after the dance, Ben's younger brother, Cade hung out with us. Ben was cool about not saying anything to anyone about Gwen. In fact, we hardly talked about it ourselves. What was there to talk about? Gwen and Callum had danced the rest of the slow dances together and everybody knew it. Thankfully there were only two more of them. When we got into our sleeping bags and turned off the lights Ben asked me if I was okay.

"Yeah, man. It isn't a big deal. Besides, summer is coming up and I won't even be coming into town all that much," I had replied.

"You'll come in and shoot hoops, though, right? And then there is basketball camp in August," Ben reminded me in the darkness.

"Right. For sure I'll do that but I still won't be driving in every day and I will be helping Dad train the dogs pulling the ATV to get them into shape for next season," I told him. "And I'm not so sure I would be ready for a girlfriend situation." I paused before asking, "Are you?"

Ben sucked in a slow, dramatic amount of air and sighed.

"No, definitely not. Unless she wanted to play Playstation with me all of the time and do gaming things. Then I might be on board with a girlfriend," he answered, laughing. I had to laugh, too, as I pictured Ben and a random girl sitting next to each other on a couch with their controllers in their hands, staring at the screen in front of them.

"A girlfriend might not let you hang out with your friends as much," I added.

"Or in your case, your dogs," Ben said, which made us both laugh again.

"Well, there goes my first breakup," I said, once we had stopped laughing. "With an imaginary girlfriend I never even had."

"Best breakup with a non-existent girlfriend, ever," he said through his own laughter.

That was around the time we heard a lot of activity from upstairs in Ben's house. We were camped out in their downstairs family room where Ben had had the Christmas party a few months prior. The house had been pretty quiet after Cade had gone upstairs to go to bed but there was definitely something happening at that point.

"I heard a bunch of doors shutting just now. Did you?" Ben asked me. He got out of his sleeping bag and turned on the main light in the room. I looked up at the ceiling as I heard what sounded like water moving through the pipes when someone flushes a toilet. I couldn't make out actual words but I definitely heard a woman's voice along with Cade's.

"What do you think is going on up there?" I asked. Ben had a frown on his face.

Another flush and more water. Ben and I looked directly at each other as Thumper, their buff Cocker Spaniel sat up from the couch he was laying on. Even he looked up at the ceiling.

"Boys?" Ben's mom's voice called out to us from the stairs down to the family room. "Are you boys both alright?" She joined us wearing a flannel house coat covered in flowers that totally suited her. Her hair was a bit messy, probably because she and Ben's dad had gone to bed long before the three of us finished our game.

"Yeah, Mom, what's up?" Ben asked. He sat down on the couch and put his arm around Thumper. By that time their Golden Retriever, Wilma had also woken up.

"Oh, well, it seems that Cade has caught the flu bug. It has been going around some of the kids his age and I've been wondering if he was going to get it," she explained.

I was surprised to hear that because Cade had seemed absolutely normal when we were playing PlayStation. He felt so great he hadn't minded kicking our butts at just about everything. He didn't showboat when he beat us, though, but that didn't mean he was sick. He was just that kind of kid who didn't make you feel bad when he beat you, whether in real life or in video games. I told Mrs. Rothman that Cade didn't seem sick at all earlier that evening.

"I agree, Luke. He ate a big supper and seemed fine when you boys were at your dance. He had been looking forward to having you over, too," she said. She looked right at me and smiled as she added, "I just hope you both don't come down with this. It isn't any fun being sick during the last few days of school."

I thought I had dodged that bullet as the weekend passed. I helped Dad with some of our dog kennel fencing and a few of the dog houses that had been chewed on. Every dog was different in how they lived in their spaces. Some, like Nena, one of our leaders, were very calm about their space. She spent more time inside her dog house than most of the others and she didn't chew any of the wood. Some of the boy dogs were more likely to be chewers, at least in our kennel.

Slash had already been through two dog houses since we moved to Montana and we worked on his third over the weekend. He was a large dog, which was why we ran him in the Wheel, or rear position of the team and his sheer strength was largely a part of the dog house damage. His brothers, Axl, Gene and Kurt didn't chew or scratch their houses at all. Slash mostly did it when he was excited, like when we would be walking down from the house towards the kennel or if he saw us getting the sled out to hook them up.

Dad and I spent several hours together over the weekend but we didn't talk about the dance. I had never told him or Jackie that Bethany had told me at Ben's party that Gwen maybe liked me. I didn't want Jackie to know something like that when we all came over to her clinic whenever we had Sharing sessions to talk about. I didn't want her watching Gwen differently. Or me, for that matter.

Dad and I were close but I didn't feel comfortable talking about girls with him. Not yet, anyhow. I wondered if there would come a time when that would be a natural conversation topic between us. I had been pretty young when he was dating Jackie but I did remember that she wasn't the only woman he ever went out with after he and Mom got divorced. But I was a little kid and talking about girlfriends wasn't cool for him, or even appropriate, I figured.

I never sensed that Dad cared so much about me having girlfriends. Not like Mom, at least. I figured he was happy that I liked being a kid without a lot of grown-up things to worry about. I had a lot of responsibilities already with the dog team. Even though we weren't actively training the dogs at that time of year we still had to clean, feed and water them daily as well as play with or exercise them and inspect them. Those responsibilities were pretty grown-up so maybe I didn't need any other grown-up things going on in my life.

I was also worried that Dad would think I was losing interest in the dogs if I talked about girls that way. There was nothing further from the truth. I thought about the dogs almost as much as I thought about the dragons, which was probably why I got busted drifting during classes sometimes.

I often imagined what it would feel like running in the dark behind a full, healthy team up in Alaska, crossing the fabled arches into Nome with Dad and Jackie there to greet us. How I would be jacked up at that point despite days with minimal sleep and freezing temperatures. I had a mental image of me and the dogs completing one of the greatest, most historical mushing challenges together and the feeling that went along with the image inspired me in just about anything I was doing.

I also imagined what it would be like to see Tabitha's two eggs as they hatched. I wondered if they would hatch at the same time or days apart. I worried if one didn't hatch, what would the rest of us do? Would one dragon be developmentally behind the other if it hatched too late? What if one hatched too early? I had so many questions and not enough time to think them through and nobody to really answer them.

At least I could share these thoughts and visions with Dad. The two of us talked about dragon names and meanings when we took breaks from nailing plywood together for the dog houses.

And I had felt fine all weekend with a great appetite. Without a regular land line or Internet I wasn't able to contact Ben after he and his dad drove me home the next morning but Cade hadn't been sick since about eight o'clock that morning, Mrs. Rothman had told us. She went all out and made bacon and pancakes to go with our eggs. I didn't see Cade at all that morning.

Jackie had made a spaghetti dish with onions and black olives in it on Sunday night. It was one of her classic meals that I always tucked into but it was going to be a long time before I would be requesting that dish again. Once you have thrown up olives repeatedly through the early hours of the morning it changes a person.

I had started to feel funny during supper but not funny enough to stop devouring the chicken in its yummy sauce. Funny enough, though, to bail on Dad and Jackie for their movie night. That hadn't been a huge loss, though. It was Jackie's turn to pick the movie and she had chosen *War of the Worlds*, the remake version with Tom Cruise. As cool as the special effects were I never thought the movie's ending made much sense.

Jackie and Dad both knew that Cade had been sick the night I spent at the Rothman's, which is probably why they both gave me a look when I said I was going to head to my room and listen to music. By the time the first wave hit I could hear the alien things with stilt-like legs sucking up humans from the ground as I made my way to the bathroom.

Dad had come and stood in the bathroom doorway as I did my thing. I don't remember what he said but it was likely some type of parental concern and support. He brought me a cool cloth to put on my forehead when I made it back to bed but the second wave hit and I barely made it to the bathroom.

The rest of the night continued on much the same way. Thankfully they stopped watching the movie and retreated to their own bedroom. Both Dad and Jackie took turns checking in on me when I was up. I felt bad that they didn't get much sleep either and hoped neither of them got sick.

I remember crouching over the toilet at one point trying to think back to the last time I had been sick. I knew Jackie had helped but it still seemed like it had been years since I had the stomach flu.

My last wave had hit around five o'clock in the morning and it was mostly just me making a bunch of bizarre sounds because there couldn't have been anything else left in my stomach to revisit once again. I quietly laughed to myself when I crawled back into bed, amazed that some foods were worse than others the second time around. Black olives. Definitely black olives.

Which is how I came to be lying in bed in our otherwise empty house on Monday morning when I should have driven into school with Dad.

I did sleep most of the morning, at least, but I still felt exhausted when I got up to make an attempt at drinking some water.

I wondered if Ben had been sick, too. I hoped the guys at school didn't think I was skipping out because of what happened at the dance. It was such a small school and everybody knew everybody's business but I still held out hope that I would be able to get back there with some shred of dignity again. I didn't want Ben to be sick, too, but at least it would make my stomach flu sound more realistic. I hoped Dad would tell people what the deal was, without being too graphic. Even he had commented on not having that particular supper again for awhile thanks to the olive image. That had been during my second or third wave and I almost thought he wasn't aware that he'd said it out loud.

I slowly made my way to the kitchen and poured some water. It didn't taste very good. All I wanted to do at that moment was brush my teeth.

After I washed my face and got the teeth taken care of I felt a bit brighter. The sun was shining through the windows upstairs and it looked warm outside. Dad had left a note for me on the kitchen table that said he'd taken care of kennel chores for the morning and to just make sure I got my rest. He and Jackie took separate vehicles into town so he wrote that he would be home earlier than her.

As I was reading the note I saw something move out of the corner of my eye. I looked more directly into the living room and saw Harry lying in front of the couch, where Ella was laying. She wasn't sleeping, though. She was just staring down at Harry. I went over to them and Ella leapt off the couch but Harry didn't get up. In fact he barely lifted his head towards me.

That was extremely unusual for any of our dogs. They were always very engaged when you approached them, or even if it looked like you were going to walk in their direction. His eyes were focused on mine but then he slowly laid his head back down on his outstretched fore paws.

I didn't know why but I reached out and lifted up his upper lip. I remembered Jackie doing that when Dad thought Harry had been acting strangely and how she talked about the pink color that should be there. Harry's gums weren't pink, though. They were almost a sort of light grey. It was definitely not a healthy color and without knowing why I started to have a really bad feeling. My heart rate picked up and I muttered, "No, no, no" over and over again.

I was alone. I had no driver's license and only a satellite phone to contact anyone. The clock on the stove said it was ten o'clock in the morning so Jackie might still be doing morning surgeries even if I did get ahold of her. As far as I knew her assistant, Sherise wasn't going to be back in the clinic until later that week.

Ella never left Harry's side as I petted his forehead and made my way to my bedroom to get dressed. I wasn't sure how things were going to work out but I did feel certain that I had to get Harry into our old pickup truck and into town. My arms and legs felt funny and my stomach flip-flopped a couple of times but I leaned against a wall to steady myself. I knew I was actively making a choice to drive our windy mountain roads without a grown-up for the first time and that, technically, I was committing a crime without my Montana driver's license.

Dad's voice ran through my head. "It's all about choices, Luke."

I pictured Jackie's worried expression as she had described the hemangio-thing on the spleen. I knew enough about spleens to know that when they were leaking you had to move quickly.

Harry didn't struggle against me as I somehow carried him outside. He stood on his own and urinated, seeming barely able to lift his leg off the ground. I don't know how I did it but I managed to get him onto a blanket in the passenger seat of our old farm truck, Norm. As I fired him up and got him into gear I realized I hadn't called Jackie on the satellite phone. I sensed that time was kind of important so I made the choice to just drive. I felt bad leaving Ella inside the house by herself when clearly she had been concerned about her house mate but I didn't think I could handle the trip with both dogs to worry about.

I talked to Harry the entire time, explaining what I was doing.

"I'm going to potentially get into trouble, Harry, but we're going for a drive. Just you and me."

"Okay, big guy, I am not very strong but I'm going to lift you up and into old Norm here."

"Lets just both hope that there aren't any cops on the road today, right?"

By talking through what I was doing I was keeping myself calm. My stomach made rumbling sounds but at least I wasn't throwing up anymore. Driving along bumpy dirt roads wasn't helping but I was more concerned with how Harry felt than how I did. I had my right hand on his forehead or his back as I drove, risking the bad posture of not maintaining 'ten and two' on the steering wheel. I glanced to the right and saw that nothing had changed, Harry was still breathing alright. Maybe a little faster than normal but he was still able to hold his head up from time to time and look at me.

"I've got your back, Harry, and Jackie is going to get you fixed up, alright?"

My eyes caught sight of the new dirt driveway that was recently built and it quickly occurred to me that I might have a grown-up who could do the driving. I turned down the mysterious road and before long was parked in front of the former professional golfer with the shock of red hair. Gordon Mulder. The guy who liked his privacy and didn't seem too keen on kids.

I skidded to a stop in front of him and he jumped back. I leapt out of the cab of the pickup and rambled about how I had been sick and how my dog, Harry was sick and how we really needed to get to Jackie's veterinary clinic and how I shouldn't have been driving.

Gordon squinted his eyes at me as I spoke. I was trying desperately to make sense but I was aware of the fact most of my words were jumbled. Gordon walked over to the passenger side window and peered in as I stopped talking to catch my breath.

“Your dog? Its bad?” he asked me. I had bent forward with my hands on my knees. I was weak from being sick all night but also weak with fear. I lifted my head and nodded.

“Well, get in with him and lets get you guys to town. What’s your dog’s name?” he asked.

“Harry. He is kind of like the leader of our pack,” I told him as I made my way over to the passenger side of the truck. I climbed in, moving Harry’s arms and legs around as gently as I could. I eventually ended up with his head on my lap.

Gordon got the truck turned around and back onto the long road to the highway. He gave me a weird look when I told him he should put his seatbelt on. I remembered that Dad had implied Gordon Mulder had lived a somewhat reckless life.

“Try not to panic, Luke. Its Luke, right? We’ll get Harry to town as quickly as I can,” he told me. “I think I know where your mom’s clinic is.”

“Step-mom,” I muttered, my hand gently rubbing Harry’s forehead. “She’s my step-mom.”

ELEVEN

I can't imagine what Jackie must have thought seeing a complete stranger with Harry draped in his arms behind me as I burst through her clinic doors calling her name. My voice was hoarse from being sick all night long but I tried to be loud enough that she would hear the panic I felt.

Jackie was still in her surgical cap and scrubs but she wasn't gloved up. I figured that meant no other patients were on the operating table.

"Oh, my gosh, here, bring him in here," she told Gordon as she led him to her examination room. There was nobody else in the waiting room but I heard a tail slowly thumping in the kennel room.

"He was just down like this when I got up this morning," I explained. I leaned against the refrigerator where she kept her vaccines. "This is our neighbor, Gordon Mulder. I drove Harry to his place."

Jackie had her hands all over Harry but she looked at Gordon and said, "Thank-you, Gordon. You have no idea how important this was."

"Will Harry be alright?" Gordon asked. He had a concerned look on his face. I hadn't seen any dogs at his place but then again, I hadn't really been looking. He never mentioned having any pets but most people were pretty sympathetic when it came to animals.

"I don't know but I sure hope so," she answered. "He's bleeding internally and we need to stop that. His gums are pale and a bit tacky. I think he's going to need blood."

I knew that Jackie didn't keep any blood in her clinic for transfusions. Blood didn't last very long and Missing Lake's tiny population very rarely required transfusions in pets.

She talked as she moved, almost as if in a ballet. She kissed Harry's forehead and moved to particular drawers and cupboards, removing things in a mechanical but organized manner. Gordon stepped back as she pulled a silver tray on wheels over next to the examination table where Harry laid. Our husky's brown eyes followed her every move.

"Luke, clippers," she said to me. I got her cordless clippers from the counter and brought them to the tray along with rubbing alcohol and cotton swabs. She sat on a stool in front of the table.

"Do you think its that hemangio-thing you mentioned when we did his x-rays?" I asked. I heard a tremor in my voice that gave away my fear.

Jackie quickly looked at me and nodded her head.

"We need a big dog to donate blood. A good dog who will sit still and let us do that. Must think about big dogs. Not one on any long term medications." Jackie's sentences were spoken to nobody but herself. I watched her shave an area on Harry's right forearm and swab it up after she laid out needles and tubes and pieces of white tape on the tray next to her.

She looked up at me and asked me to hold the leg off as if we were taking a blood sample. She had taught Dad and me that back in North Dakota in case she ever wanted to take blood from our dogs at the house. I positioned myself next to Harry's right side and put my left arm over his back for comfort more than anything else. He didn't look like he had the strength to resist.

His vein didn't pop up like a lot of dogs' did when I held their arms for Jackie. I wondered if that had to do with him bleeding.

Jackie threaded an intravenous catheter into the vein after one poke, though, so she must have seen something that I hadn't. As she taped the port onto his shaved arm I suddenly remembered a patient I had met in the clinic when school had just started.

"Hercules. The Great Dane with the two little girls. Could he donate blood?" I said. My throat was dry and my stomach rumbled again. "He was pretty calm, if I remember. Didn't he just sit there with the two little girls bonking him on his head while you trimmed his nails?"

Jackie looked up at me and smiled.

"I love you, Luke. Go look them up in the computer and give them a call. Hopefully they are home," she said. As I left the exam room I heard her ask Gordon if he would help her get Harry wheeled into the surgery suite and then transferred to her operating table.

I knew how to use some of the more challenging features of Jackie's veterinary software. You could look people or their pets up by their last name, the pet's name or even their phone number. Thankfully there were only two Herculeses and one was a cat. The other was a black and white, young Great Dane. His mom was home and only too happy to bring him right to the clinic.

I quickly called my high school and left a message with the receptionist to get a message to Dad. It was almost lunchtime by then and I knew he would want to know what was going on. The school secretary asked me how I was feeling. I told her I was still pretty woozy but better than all through the night.

I made my way back to the surgery suite where Jackie was holding an oxygen mask over Harry's nose.

"Are you going to anesthetize him?" I asked. Without turning to look at me Jackie simply replied, "Just wanting to get him some extra oxygen before surgery. I'm sure he's pretty anemic from the blood loss so this is a nice start."

I told her that Hercules and his mom would be here shortly. Gordon looked at me and smiled.

"I won't knock Harry down until we get the blood from him, then," Jackie explained, still with her eyes focused on Harry. "How are you two with the sight of blood?"

"I'm fine. I've helped with surgery before," I reminded her.

"Lots of blood," she said, emphasizing the word, 'lots'. At that point she looked up at me. I nodded my head. I knew Harry needed me to be strong and that I would be fine.

"I think I'm fine. The few fights I've been in brought a fair amount of blood and I was alright," Gordon told us. "Mind you, I was drinking heavily during that stage of my life and drunk during the fights. I'm stone-cold sober right now but I think I'll be fine."

Jackie smiled and asked me to get a couple of scrub tops and hats for Gordon and me.

"I certainly don't expect you to help with this, Gordon. You have only just met me and Harry isn't your dog. I feel like I am asking a lot of you right now. Please feel free to bow out if you would like to," Jackie told him when I came back with the shirts.

"Are you kidding me? This is frigging awesome. It's the most exciting thing I've been a part of since I left the PGA tour," he said. He looked off in the distance then and added, "Well, my second divorce was definitely exciting but that was more from a lawyer's standpoint." I laughed and shook my head. He looked over at me as I handed him the scrub top and winked, adding, "She was a red head."

I had no clue what that meant but I heard Jackie chuckle.

The front door to the clinic opened and I heard young girls' voices. Hercules!

"I'm sorry I had to bring the girls, Dr.Yale-Houser," a woman's voice rang out from the waiting room. "My husband isn't home from work and it sounded like I should get here first and then worry about a babysitter later."

Jackie asked Gordon to hold the mask on Harry's face while we went to work on a blood donation. Hercules looked as calm as ever as he stood behind the two little girls. They both smiled when they saw me and one whispered to the other, "Popsicle."

"Thanks so much for bringing Hercules here for this," Jackie told her. "Harry has been with us the longest of any of our sled dogs and if we are truly going to try to save him then I know he will need some extra strength from Hercules here." She reached down and gave the big dog a rub on his forehead.

"I think, though, that the girls and I will go down to the café while you're doing this, if that's alright. I'm sure Herc will be fine with you guys. I'm just concerned that certain little people might not want to see all of this," the mother said. "Do I have to sign anything?" she asked, her hands on her daughters' backs. It looked like she was ready to usher them out of the clinic.

"Probably. But I wouldn't be able to find the form quickly. Will a verbal agreement be alright with you?" Jackie asked. She slipped a small leash around the giant dog's head and neck. It was ridiculously small compared to the size of him but he was such a well behaved dog that I knew it wouldn't matter.

"I'm fine with it. Good luck," the mother said, "is an hour enough time?"

"For Hercules' part, yes. We'll take the best care of him," Jackie replied.

They left and I followed Jackie and Hercules into the examination room.

"Do you know Harry's blood type already? What if he and Hercules aren't a match?" I asked. I had heard about people having reactions to getting blood or organs that didn't match with their own bodies. I couldn't remember where I had read or heard about those but it felt like that was just common knowledge.

Jackie was already getting another IV pole ready along with bags and more tubing.

"Dogs are pretty unique in that you get one free transfusion," she explained as she moved, once again, as if in a well-choreographed routine. "While they do have different blood types they are less reactive than humans or even cats so for a dog's first blood transfusion you can use any doggie donor."

"What about before we adopted Harry? Wasn't he used in research? Could he have had a transfusion back then?" I asked.

Jackie was already shaving an area on Hercules' arm. The big dog just let her hold his arm out while her clippers moved along his skin.

"I was mostly in charge of everything that happened with Harry so as far as I know he hasn't had any. There is more risk to him not getting the blood after we get that spleen out, though. He needs to be strong enough to survive post-operative care," she answered. Her voice was calm but I could tell she was very serious with what she was explaining.

It was a matter of minutes before she got a good-sized needle into Hercules' vein with me helping to hold the flow off. I had to use both hands because his arm was so thick but within seconds blood flowed into the human blood donation bag. I made a mental note to ask her where she got those and how long she had had them in her clinic collection of medical supplies.

Jackie had me sit with Hercules and told me to watch for any swelling at the needle site. She showed me where on the bag we were hoping to fill to and went off to check on Gordon and Harry. My stomach rumbled and I felt nauseas but I was pretty sure it was from the flu and not all of the blood I was already seeing. I wondered if Dad had got the message yet and if he would be able to come and help out, as well. I also wondered if he would tell any of my classmates what was happening just across the road from them.

I talked quietly with Hercules and thanked him for donating his blood. I told him we were trying to save one of my special friends and that I wasn't ready to lose another friend. His big eyes were trained on mine as I shared with him how we had to put my friend, Robson to sleep several months prior and how that had affected me. I also told him he was a brave dog and that I hoped I could be brave when I was grown-up and donate blood for other people who needed it.

I wasn't sure the big black and white dog with the amazing hair coat pattern understood a word I had said but it felt good sharing it all with him. It also helped to keep me focused and calm because I knew things were going to get crazy once surgery started. I was sitting on the floor next to Hercules as blood drained from his forearm and through the clear tubing into the bag. His large, floppy cheeks hung over the margin of his mouth and they puffed out to the sides when he gave a big, heavy sigh. I hoped that meant he was content. He certainly didn't seem upset by anything that had been going on.

Jackie came back to the exam room and before long we had enough blood. She said it didn't need to be refrigerated because we hoped to use it within an hour if surgery went well and "Harry was still with us." Her words startled me. Ever since we got to the clinic and found a donor and everything was in Jackie's hands I hadn't considered that Harry wouldn't make it. Jackie must have seen the horror and shock on my face because she put her hand gently on my shoulder and said, "I have to be honest, Luke. You know that."

I felt heat creep up my neck and into my cheeks and the sting of tears behind my eyes. A world without Harry wasn't going to work for me. What would Ella and even Baxter do? What would I do? Who would lead the rest of the dog pack?

"Luke, I am going to need you to be strong here. I know your mind is reeling but Harry needs us focused on him. You and Gordon are going to be clamping vessels and holding them off for me so I can get in, tie off a billion little vessels and get that spleen out as quickly as possible. I will try to talk you guys through it as we go but I'm anticipating a lot of blood in there so it might be hard to see at times. I'm sorry I threw that at you but its better now than in the middle of surgery." She paused and then asked, "Can you do this?"

I nodded as soon as the words were out of her mouth. Harry needed me. I had to be able to do it.

Dad showed up just before Gordon fainted. It was pretty remarkable timing seeing as how Jackie needed that extra pair of hands to hold off some bleeders.

"Jeez, you guys," Dad said as he burst through the clinic door and came back to the surgery suite. The three of us had caps and masks on and our scrub tops and Jackie's surgical gown all had blood splattered on them. The floor didn't look a whole lot better.

"Hon, if you could glove up we could sure use you," Jackie said. Her hands were working quickly but carefully. She had got the red, meaty spleen mostly exteriorized out of the body. We had packed sterile, moist gauze underneath it and around the opening into Harry's abdomen. A large, dark area on the spleen was where the capsule must have ruptured, she explained, and there appeared to be a mass of some sort in that area. The mass didn't look as meaty as the rest of the organ.

Once she had found the main vessels she started tying sutures around them, one by one. She talked out loud but I never once thought it was for our benefit. I figured she was talking herself through things, almost like a system of double-checking herself.

"Splenic artery. Pancreatic branch. Don't touch that. Try to keep the gastric ones. Whoop, sorry about that, Luke."

That last sentence had been when she hit a small vessel that squirted me square in the chest. It pumped with its own steady beat, which I thought meant it was an artery and not a vein.

Gordon and I had several packs of sterile gauze we were using to keep mopping things up as Jackie kept tying sutures. The main area she had to actually remove the spleen from had a bunch of little vessels that had to be tied off and they had to be tied off on both sides so that she could cut in between them. I had never seen her hands moveso quickly. Her scissors thing spun to the left, then to the right, then back to the left before she would make a quick, precise cut and move to the next spot.

I had noticed sweat on Gordon's brow and a lighter color to his face and asked him if he was alright about twenty minutes into things, before Dad had arrived.

"I think so. I'm not sure. Its weird hearing you guys talk when I can't see your mouths move," was all he said. "I think I'm better not looking at you when you talk."

"That's fine by me," Jackie had said. "I'm happy if you just keep looking at Harry."

I thought small talk might help him so I asked if he missed playing golf. He waited long enough before answering that I began to wonder if he had heard me but he finally spoke up.

"You know, I miss the game of golf. I do. I miss my driver and my putter and every club in-between. I miss the walk on a crisp Fall afternoon when the leaves are changing colors and I miss laughing with my friends or my caddie, Ralph." He paused for a moment before continuing, "But I don't miss what playing the game at the professional level and being on the road did to me. Or, what I chose to do to myself. That's how the second marriage counsellor said I should phrase it."

I saw Jackie raise her eyes to Gordon when he said that but she quickly lowered them and focused back on Harry's abdomen.

I had been in the clinic when she had done spays and neuters on dogs and cats and she usually was a bit more talkative during those procedures. I never really liked watching her neuter anything but I had helped her with a couple of big dogs that had to be spayed. Other than one small vessel one time that squirted out and nailed the gas anesthesia machine I had never seen this amount of blood during a procedure. I wondered if her silence was due to worry or if something was going wrong. I didn't ask about it.

Dad came back to the surgical suite with a cap, mask and gloves on. We had run out of men's scrub tops so he was still wearing his nice, button-up teacher shirt.

"What can I do?" he asked.

I looked up just in time to see Gordon's eyes roll back as he mumbled, "Catch me."

Dad had tried to catch him but couldn't quite get there. He pushed his back against the wall, though, and we watched Gordon slowly slither down until he was slumped on the floor. I saw Dad check his pulse in his neck then he patted his cheeks a couple of times. He had to step over Gordon to take his place at the surgery table.

I thought I heard Jackie make a snorting sound but she kept it pretty quiet.

"I don't think mister Mulder is going anywhere right now. Okay, apparently I need to hold these areas and keep blotting, right, Hon?" he asked. I could hear a smile on his face as he talked. Good old Dad. He was always able to keep things cool even in the most bizarre situations.

It occurred to me at that moment that we were an odd little scene. It couldn't be normal to have all of the members of a family standing over the open abdomen of their beloved dog, blood vessels being tied off methodically, blood being mopped up, heart monitor beeping in the background, all with Dad in his plaid shirt with button-down collars. I noticed he had taken his tie off, at least.

Jackie had Dad open a couple more suture packs as she made her little knots with the purple thread-like material. She had opened several before we even started because you had to take your gloves off and re-glove to keep things sterile if you had to get a new pack. Harry's heart rate machine beeped constantly, which was a comforting sound. At times the rate sped up and I thought that was good but the look on Jackie's face told me otherwise. As she was finally removing the bloody, meaty mass the beeping slowed down a little and I heard Jackie sigh.

Gordon had started mumbling from where he was slumped over on the floor behind Dad.

"Did I pass out? How's Harry? Is there much more blood?"

Dad, Jackie and I all caught each other's eyes. I saw the sides of Jackie's eyes wrinkle upwards. I assumed she was smiling.

"You're okay, Gordon. You just took a little nap. The wall caught you on the way down," she said as she lifted the spleen and dropped it into a silver basin. It reminded me of the basins they gave me when I had been in the hospital in case I couldn't make it to the bathroom to pee. It made a wet, plopping sound as it landed and Gordon made a grimacing expression.

I leaned over towards the basin to look at it. It was like an enormous, chunky red pancake with purple ties circling one entire side.

The blood flow had slowed dramatically as Jackie had been tying vessels off. Dad and I mostly backed off as it looked like Jackie was peeking into Harry's abdomen.

"Just want to take a quick cruise around in here to see if everything else is alright. Sometimes hemangiosarcomas like to visit the liver as well," she explained, without us asking what she was doing.

She looked up at the surgical light and then over at Dad. He nodded and, using one of the clean sterile cloths that hadn't been bloodied, reached up and tipped the big surgical light at an angle so she could see better. I stepped back to allow her to have as much room as she needed. I had no clue what she saw but she said, "Okay, I'm going to close now. Hon, if you want to help Gordon get some water and check on Hercules in the kennel room Luke can probably help out from here on in."

Dad nodded and removed his gloves and mask. His shirt had remained blood-free, which was in stark contrast to my scrub top.

I had been holding both of my gloved hands up in the air with the backs of them facing Harry and the table. Jackie had never taught me to do that but I had watched it done in movies and television shows. I wondered if doctors and veterinarians really learned to do that in school. I had seen Jackie do it during some procedures, too, but it did feel kind of silly.

Jackie flushed Harry's abdomen with a clear liquid and then began closing him in the same manner I had watched her close cat and dog spays over the years. Three layers, the final one buried so you couldn't see the stitches on the outside of the skin.

"You're good, Luke. Go ahead and scrub out. I'll have you stick around, though, in case I need more suture if that's alright," Jackie told me without looking up.

Once the drape was off Harry looked just like any other anesthetized dog lying on their back hooked up to gas anesthesia. Other than the incision, which was a long, thin, crimson line, he could have been there for a dental cleaning or a deep ear flushing. Not a hopefully life-saving emergency procedure done with untrained assistants spattered in blood.

Jackie gave Harry an injection in his hind end. She explained it was for pain control and to help him be calm as he recovered. I helped her lay him onto his side, giving more of his body access to the warming pads that were always on the surgery table.

She dialed down the gas he was inhaling and let him breathe just oxygen for several breaths. The machine controlled the animal's breathing while they were connected, too, so there were always a few moments where you had to wait for them to breathe on their own after the tubes were finally disconnected.

We waited.

The heart rate kept beeping.

And we waited.

Beep. Beep. Beep.

And Harry breathed on his own. One long inhalation and exhalation and then a few moments before another long breath.

Jackie gently removed the endotracheal tube and Harry sputtered as he breathed but he was still in sleepy-town. Dad came in and helped us lift him to the blanketed area on the ground. I hadn't even noticed Dad laying out the blankets but he must have done it while we were waiting for Harry to breathe. He had to have wiped up the blood from the tiled floor as well because it looked pretty clean. Jackie disconnected the heart monitor because Harry was breathing steadily.

"It's a matter of waiting now, you guys," Jackie said while untying her stained surgical gown. "I'll get that blood into him through his intravenous port and we will let him slowly recover through the afternoon."

"I'll just stay here, if that's okay," I told them.

"If you feel strong enough, Gordon, feel free to take our old truck back to your place. We can swing by later and get it," Dad said as he was retying his neck tie to return to school. I realized that I hadn't once asked him who was covering for his classes after lunch.

"No, I think I might grab a bite to eat at that little café down the road and hang out to see how Harry-boy does, if that's alright." Gordon was sitting on the bench in Jackie's waiting room. He had bottled water that was just about empty in one hand and the color in his face looked much more normal than it had before he hit the ground.

"Hey, dad, is Ben at school today?" I asked.

"No, actually. He got sick yesterday, too," Dad answered. He came up to me and looked me in the eye. His arm extended and we shook hands.

"Thanks, son. You did a great job in there. I'm really proud of you," he told me before wrapping me in a hug. Dad wasn't big on hugging but it felt like maybe he needed one, too. I watched him shake Gordon's hand and give Jackie a hug and a kiss before he went back to school.

Jackie hugged both Gordon and I and thanked us. She went back to the kennel room where the happy tail thump of Hercules against the steel crates told us she was thanking him, too.

Herc's mom arrived not long after Dad left and I asked her if it was alright to give the girls a Popsicle. Jackie thanked her again and told her that the next vaccines Hercules needed were on her. A thank-you gift from Harry.

"How is he doing?" she asked.

Jackie shrugged her shoulders and said, "He wouldn't be alive right now if it weren't for Luke, Mr. Mulder and Hercules so we are already doing great but it will be a matter of time before we can be sure he's got his legs back. I also have to send a sample from the spleen off to find out what kind of tumor was growing in there so we aren't out of the woods just yet."

"Oh, so it definitely was a tumor?" the lady asked. Her hand came up to her mouth when she spoke.

"Unfortunately, yes, but you can't tell if they are bad ones or good ones just by looking. All of them are bad when they cause a rupture like this but the stars must have aligned just right for Luke to be at the house this morning," Jackie explained. She turned to me and smiled.

"And for Gordon to be at his house, too," I added. I joined him on the bench and clapped my hand on his shoulder. I knew he wasn't a huge fan of kids but it seemed like the right thing to do at that moment.

"Wait a second," she said as she stared at Gordon seated next to me. "Aren't you a professional golfer? You're pretty famous, right?"

"Well ma'am, I was a golfer for sure but I don't know if that's why I was famous." He stood up and shook her hand, saying, "Gordon Mulder and I'd be just as happy if you don't announce to too many people that I live around here if that's alright."

"Fine by me. My husband doesn't watch golf anyhow. More of a baseball and football kind of guy."

"Yes, well, now me, too for that matter," Gordon told her. We all laughed.

Gordon left for the café in our old pickup truck and I went to the surgery suite where Jackie had mopped up the floors and where Harry laid covered in blankets and towels. His breathing was more steady but still slower than normal. Jackie had told me that was because of the medications he had on board. She had rigged up a second intravenous system by hanging the bag with blood from Hercules off of the bracket supports holding a shelf above where he laid. Both the red blood and the clear fluid flowed into my old friend as I sat on the ground next to him. The blood flowed in a steady stream but the clear fluid was just dripping every couple of seconds.

I had pretty much had it for bodily fluids over that twenty-four hour period. My stomach rumbled again but I wasn't hungry. I knew I would probably have to eat something later that evening but right then all I wanted to do was sit with Harry. Jackie had some frozen lunches in her freezer but I just couldn't make myself rally.

I hadn't realized how tired I must have been because it seemed like suddenly Harry was licking my hand as I was waking up.

I glanced at the clock on the wall and realized I must have been napping for a couple of hours. Harry and I were laid on the floor, both of us wrapped in blankets. I figured Jackie must have brought one in for me after I had accidentally fallen asleep.

"Hey, Sleeping Beauty," Jackie said as she came into the surgery suite. "How are you feeling?"

I had to think about her question because there was a lot to consider. My stomach flu, my anxiety, my concern and my love for Harry.

"I think I'm not bad, you know?" I answered. Harry licked my face again and I smiled. I saw that his tongue was a light pink color and asked Jackie about him.

"I haven't done too much prodding on him, to be honest," said told me, bending down to pet him and take a better look at him. I scooted along the floor so she could have more access to him. "His gum color is looking nice. I think that blood supply helped there. I'd like to keep him pretty calm still, Luke. Can you stay with him a little bit longer? I have one more vaccine appointment coming in soon."

"Sure, of course. I'm happy to sit with him. Did Dad go home from school?"

"Yes, but he stopped in first. He didn't want to wake either of you up so he was very quiet. Gordon followed him home in Norm," Jackie explained. "He brought you a ham and cheese sandwich from the café if you'd like. I can bring it to you."

I realized that I wasn't nauseas like I had been and that a sandwich sounded pretty good at that moment. Jackie must have recognized that on my face because she smiled and got up. She returned a few moments later with a brown paper bag and a bottle of water.

"That was really thoughtful of him," I said as I unwrapped my sandwich. Harry's eyes brightened and he started to sit up at either the sight or smell of my late lunch. Probably both.

"No food for Harry, though. His tummy might not be very settled after anesthesia. Not yet anyhow," Jackie told me, "and, yes, that was thoughtful. I don't know much about him but he definitely is an interesting character. I think he'll fit right in here in Missing Lake."

I wasn't sure what she meant by that so I asked in between mouthfuls.

"I don't know, Luke. It just seems like there is a collection of odd individuals here. We've talked about it before," Jackie reminded me. "How some people seem like they are hiding here. Its easy enough to do because we're not on any major highway to any major city or destination and the area doesn't get reliable cellular phone service from any one carrier so people like Gordon can easily disappear if they would like."

"Do you think he is hiding from anyone?" I asked. I figured he'd had his taste of fame and popularity. Dad once told me Gordon Mulder was a really talented golfer back when he was competing. That the media hounded him and he didn't like it. I guessed he wanted to get away from media, especially since he had made some bad decisions from the sounds of things, but I hadn't really thought about him hiding from any one person. Like one of his wives.

Jackie shook her head and answered, "I guess I don't know. I never really followed much golf but I had heard of him. More for his extra-curricular activities than his golf game, though."

"Did you pay him back for this?" I asked. The sandwich tasted really good. It had just the right amount of mayonnaise and mustard on it and a crisp, sliced dill pickle as well. I made a point to try to pace myself. It probably wasn't a good idea to overwhelm my own stomach just yet.

"No, he wouldn't take any money. He said this had been the most eventful afternoon he'd had in years," Jackie laughed. "I thanked him repeatedly for helping out and told him I was sorry we made him pass out. He seemed a bit embarrassed but I assured him he wasn't the first person to hit the floor during a surgical procedure. Maybe my first one in this clinic but not my first faint overall." She laughed out loud for a moment and then added, "And he told me it wasn't the first time he passed out in front of other people before, either."

The phone started to ring so she left Harry and me on the floor together. As groggy as he must have felt his eyes were riveted on my sandwich. He was more alert than he had been that morning at home. I took that as a good sign and slowly finished my delicious sandwich.

TWELVE

Harry slept in our laundry room which was upstairs by my bedroom. Jackie checked on him all through the night. She had given him sedatives to keep him calm and enable him to sleep. He was still hooked up to an IV that was dripping clear fluid into his arm at a pretty slow but steady rate. I checked on him through the night as well and other than the fact he was surrounded by sleeping bags and dog beds he looked like any normal sleeping Husky, on his side, legs curled inward.

I watched him stretch his back legs and then almost wince in his sleep sometime through the night. It was the second night in a row for me without much sleep but it was the end of the school year and Dad and Jackie had already told me it was up to me if I wanted to go to school or not the next day.

Dad had given me a piece of paper when Jackie and I had got home from the clinic. He made us both scrambled eggs because it was late enough and I still wasn't up for anything more challenging. I had kept the sandwich down from lunch and felt pretty good considering how horrible I had felt that morning.

Bethany had written a note at school and some of the other kids signed it. It said how sad they all were about Harry and also about the stomach flu. Derek added a note saying they all wanted to come over to the clinic but Dad suggested they let Harry relax in as quiet a place as possible. Karol, Jason, and Nick had all signed it. Gwen, too.

I was pretty tired by the time morning came around. The smell of coffee from the kitchen made my stomach flip over but I didn't stay nauseas for long.

"Hey, Trooper. What do you think about school this morning?" Dad asked. He had already finished his cereal and was loading the dishwasher.

I ran my hand through my hair and made some sort of mumbling, grumbling sound. Dad laughed.

"You look like you need a bit more time, Luke," he told me, "so why don't you come in with Jackie in a little while? She has to take out Harry's IV and wants to make sure he is kenneled in a small enough area where he won't be too active. You'll probably only miss half of your first class."

"What if she has patients at the clinic?" I asked. I tried to picture the kennel he described for Harry.

"I'm going to put a note on her door before I get to the school," he answered. I nodded and asked him to tell my friends I would see them later in the day if he ran into any of them and went to shower and get ready for school.

The ride into town with Jackie wasn't all that bad. She was on an apparent break from disco and had grabbed a greatest hits CD by Tom Petty. She and Dad both liked his music and I had grown up listening to it. Mom's husband, Frank really liked his music, too.

"You think Harry is going to be okay all day at the house?" I asked. It was a stupid question because she wouldn't have left him there if she didn't think so but I still wanted to ask about him.

"I think so, Luke. He's got some good pain medications on board and he'll probably still be pretty sore to do too much. I have a farm call first thing this morning so I wouldn't be able to watch him if he came to the clinic, plus I don't think he'd be too comfortable in my cages. I want to minimize the stress for him as much as I can so his body can focus on healing. You and your dad will probably get home before me unless you want to use the computer at my clinic."

"Yeah, I should email Mom and Sam. I haven't checked emails or anything all weekend. Maybe I'll come over and do that at lunch."

"You haven't told your mother about the dance?" Jackie asked. She had a big grin on her face and she emphasized the word, 'dance'.

I felt a bit embarrassed when she first said that but I took a deep breath and realized she was just trying to be funny. And she was right, too. It was a miracle my mom hadn't found a way to get a message to us to see if I had fallen in love on Friday night.

Something on my face must have shown how I felt because Jackie quickly added, "Sorry. I didn't mean to make fun. Its just that your mother is so focused on you getting a girlfriend."

"I know she is. She was totally hopped up about the dance," I said. I felt more comfortable just listening to the music.

You Don't. Have. To live like a refugee...

"You know, with getting the stomach flu and then everything that happened with Harry yesterday, I didn't even think about the dance. I haven't even thought about the dragons very much," I admitted. Jackie was nodding her head, her hands reliably at ten and two on the steering wheel.

"Your dad and I couldn't care less if you have a girlfriend, Luke. I hope you don't feel any pressure from us. I didn't date in high school. I had lots of guy friends but we mostly listened to music or talked about sports and things. About the dragons, I haven't talked with Oscar in a couple of days. If I get a minute at work I'll give him a call today," she said, with excitement in her voice.

When she said that, I realized I hadn't heard from Zagros in days. He knew I had the dance and that I had been kind of anxious about it. I wondered if he would have somehow known I'd been sick. He knew when I wrecked the snowmobile earlier in the winter because it was like he was somehow connected to me. It was comforting knowing that someone you cared about was attached to you in a spiritual sort of way. I had read that twin siblings had those kinds of connections, even twins who were separated at birth. They all grew up and had similar jobs and the same type of wife or husband because they were part of the same spirit. Or something like that.

"You look lost in thought," Jackie said. I jumped a little because she startled me. "You alright?"

I nodded my head and thought about my words.

"I'm good. I was just thinking about Zagros and how he and I are sort of connected. The whole Dragoneer thing, like with Tabitha and Oscar, too. How Zagros knew to come and save me when I crashed the sled and how he knew about things that happened when I went back to Vancouver." I paused before adding, "I feel like I should know more about what he does in a day or a week or how he is feeling at any given time."

Jackie smiled. She took her eyes off the road for a split second to look over at me.

"I think that's part of the magic of being a dragon, Luke. The intuition or knowledge of the humans and maybe other animal spirits they are connected to. Its not something we humans are capable of, at least not in any way we can control it. Oscar has never said he knew what was going on in Tabitha's mind. He was just as surprised about her having a boyfriend as the rest of us. Not to mention the eggs."

Jackie was right. At least about Oscar and Tabitha. The bit about humans being capable of that intuition was beyond me. I remembered Oscar and his Hawaiian Dragoneer friend, Nahele discussing the dragons and what they knew. How they had asked questions about all sorts of history but the dragons had their secrets.

Maybe it had been done that way hundreds of years before. And maybe dragons didn't even need Dragoneers back in the beginning but they could always read our minds and know our thoughts. It would have come in handy if someone was out to slay one of them. They would know to hide or move or prepare to face a dragon slayer. I had always thought those guys were kind of a joke but then I never knew dragons existed after all. I looked out the window at the trees and bare ground as Jackie slowed the truck down coming into Missing Lake.

I had so many new questions for Zagros and I felt an almost tugging-like sensation that I needed to see him. I wanted to know if he and Tabitha knew how long their dragons would stay with them before they left, if they had to leave at some point. Did he know both of his parents, like their baby dragons would? I wondered if he remembered them, and how he knew it was time to go out on his own and when that time was.

"Try not to think too much about this during school today, though. Its probably hard enough for teachers to keep you guys reigned in when the weather is this nice outside," Jackie said. "And I know you're already going to be distracted thinking about Harry."

I saw the high school coming into view and caught my breath. Jackie must have heard me because she glanced over at me with her eyebrows raised.

"You alright?"

"Yeah, of course," I lied.

The only person I had talked with about the dance was Ben and with him and I both getting sick and then Harry's emergency surgery I doubted anyone would let him and I alone together. I didn't know if the girls had all known Callum liked Gwen or not. I also didn't know if Gwen spent any time with him over the weekend or if she would still hang out with us. I hadn't realized that I was actually a bit worried until I saw the high school. I knew I could probably ask Sam some of the dating questions I had but he'd probably think I was a giant loser. A loser for not having a girlfriend by that point and a loser for not knowing how to get one.

Trust Tom Petty to put a smile on my face despite my anxiety. I chuckled as I shut the door in the school parking lot and waved to Jackie.

Even the losers. Get lucky sometimes.

"Dude. You look pretty good for being so sick," Derek said as he clasped his hand onto my shoulder. "You and Ben both hurling all night. Nice."

The memory of leaning over the toilet bowl flashed through my mind but my stomach didn't flip.

"Yeah, I didn't look so good yesterday, though," I told him. We were at my locker and Ben had just joined us.

"Oh my God, I felt like ass on Sunday night," Ben said. Derek and I both laughed. That was probably the best way to describe it.

"My dad said it will be a long time before he eats black olives again," I told them. I explained the meal we had enjoyed that night and how I felt the same about not seeing it again for awhile.

"I had milk with supper and I think it had curdled when I got to see and smell it again. That was the worst!" Ben laughed.

"Oh, gross. You guys are going to make me sick reliving your special night," Derek said. I silently agreed with him, especially after the milk comment. He looked to the left and right down the school hallways and pulled Ben and I closer towards him. He spoke in a much quieter voice when he told us that everything had been normal the day before with Gwen. That she sat with the kids in our class at lunch and he never saw her and Callum together.

"So maybe it was just a random thing, the slow dancing?" he suggested. His suggestion sounded more like a question.

"Whatever," I told him, "Its not a big deal. You know? It just , like, is what it is. I mean, whatever, and stuff, right?"

Ben had a puzzled look on his face when he said, "Luke, I have no idea what message you were just trying to convey but I don't believe it was in English."

That got the three of us laughing some more. He was right. I hadn't known what message I was trying to share, either and I was sure I hadn't sounded as nonchalant as I had hoped. Derek continued to watch me like a hawk all day when we had classes together so I figured he didn't believe me that I didn't have feelings one way or the other about what went down at the dance.

Like Derek said, though, things all kept going along normally. With it being such a small school, news of Ben's and my stomach flu had completed the rounds. Some kids were obviously avoiding both of us, which just made us laugh. Jackie had said she was pretty sure we weren't contagious anymore. The only people we could have made sick were our own parents and seeing as how Ben's were fine after Cade brought the bug home they likely were going to be fine. Dad explained that most grown-ups with children have been exposed to all sorts of viruses that cause stomach flu over the years so he and Jackie would probably be safe as well.

Lots of kids wanted the full scoop which was getting pretty gross having to describe the repeat on the olives each time. People laughed, though, which I liked. It wasn't the celebrity status I had held after my snowmobile accident and time spent in the hospital. Those questions lasted for days. This was just something new for everyone to talk about on a short-term basis.

"How is Harry doing?" Bethany grabbed my arm during lunch. "Is he at home or at the clinic?" She looked genuinely concerned. She had probably pictured her own dog, Mollie being in a similar situation when she heard about Harry.

"He's strong and so far he's doing alright," I told her. "He was actually lucky I was home. Jackie thinks he wouldn't have made it if no one was able to get him to her clinic."

"Your dad looked a bit nervous when he left but then he was smiling when he came back. Nobody said anything but he had a bit of blood on his shirt," she told me. I smiled. I hadn't noticed that when he had left the clinic.

"He was a rock when he helped out. He's always so calm in frightening situations," I said. "I was pretty freaked out. Harry is a special dog for all of us, including the rest of the dog team." I wasn't sure Bethany would understand that, with only one dog in her house. "Its as if they respect his age and the time he's spent pulling sleds," I explained, "All of the other dogs let him take over whenever we let him run in lead and there is no goofing around." I looked down at my feet and added, "I don't think we'll run him anymore but the team still needs him around. I need him around."

"I would have completely melted down if that was Mollie. I would be the one needing the hospital and I totally don't think I would be holding my stuff together as well as you are today. Or yesterday, obviously," Bethany said with a kind-looking smile on her face.

"I don't know, though. I still felt kind of sick and I was tired but I just knew Harry needed me to be strong for him. And that it wasn't about me at that moment. I bet you'd be the same," I said.

"Kind of like when people go into super human mode and they can lift a vehicle off of their kid or something, right?" Bethany asked. I wasn't sure if she was kidding about that but the look on her face had gone pretty serious so I figured that it wasn't a joke.

"Something like that, I guess, you're right."

Ben, Derek, Nick and I spent most of the lunch hour talking with the girls. We were outside beneath one of the trees on the school's front lawn. The grass was green and the sun was high and warm in the bright blue Montana sky. Kids were mostly wearing shorts and T-shirts and it felt good to not be layered up in a long-sleeved shirt, scarf and jacket. Winter was my favorite season for so many reasons but I still enjoyed feeling the sun on my bare forearms.

Everyone wanted to know what had actually happened with Harry. I didn't tell them much about Gordon Mulder, just that he was a new neighbor I had met during the winter and that he stayed to help. I didn't even tell them his first name. I had no clue if any of my friends were golf fans but you never knew. It wasn't a topic we ever discussed.

Most of my friends seemed amazed that we could take out a spleen. Only Nick had heard about a person having one done before. I was a little surprised no famous basketball player had needed one.

"Haven't there been any basketball players who get injured and need one?" I asked. Derek shrugged his shoulders and Ben shook his head.

"Not any off the top of my head. Its not supposed to be a contact sport," he answered. "I mean, guys definitely run into each other and sometimes you just wipe out and take someone down accidentally with you but we aren't slamming into each other like hockey players."

While Ben had been talking Derek got up and in his over-dramatic way did a slow-motion body check into his side, leading with his elbow. He only knocked Ben over onto his side on the grass but in the process lost his own balance during the poorly executed and illegal elbowing move and tripped over Ben. We watched, laughing, as Derek slammed into the ground. He bounced up within seconds, also laughing.

"What do you think of my stellar hockey moves, Mister Canada?" he asked as he wiped grass off of himself.

"Derek, that was elbowing and you're busted for a two minute penalty," I said. The laughter eventually died down.

"I can think of at least one NHL player and even a high school hockey player whose spleens ruptured during the game," I told them. "I think its only a big deal if you don't recognize the problem."

"Does it just keep bleeding, then?" Gwen asked. I didn't look her in the eye when I answered. I made more of a point to look at each of my friends.

"Yeah. And Jackie says the whole thing is basically full of blood. I guess the liver is kind of similar, too, but honestly, I don't really know."

"Was there a lot of blood?" Nick asked. "Your dad had a little bit on his shirt when he got back."

"You could say that," I replied, as a picture of the dark red blood pooling on the surgery suite floor flashed through my mind. As soon as I thought about the clinic I remembered that I needed to email my mom at lunch so that Dad and I could get back home to Harry after school.

Before I could say anything, though, I clearly heard Zagros' voice in my head. It came out of nowhere and had a sense of urgency to it despite the fact the voice only said one thing.

"Luke."

As soon as he said it I wondered if I had imagined it. Bethany was showing Gwen her nail polish and nobody else looked like they had heard anything. I knew then that I really had to get over to see Jackie. Zagros might have been trying to get ahold of me.

"Hey, guys, I have to run and email my mom at Jackie's clinic. Like, right now," I said as I abruptly got up from the grass. "Catch you guys later," I said, waving my hand. I glanced back at them all and everyone was smiling. Bethany and Gwen both waved back.

The more I thought about it as I crossed the highway the more I figured I hadn't heard a thing. I was just doing my space-cadet thing again and most likely imagined my dragon friend talking to me in my head. I wasn't even sure I would tell Jackie. So a quick email would take me no more than ten minutes to do and I would be back in class in no time.

Funny how that turned out.

THIRTEEN

Jackie and I were cruising in her truck a little faster than the speed limit heading north. We were going to Oscar's place. The babies were hatching!

The time since I opened the door to the clinic to that very moment in the passenger seat was a blur. My head was full of thoughts for so many individuals for so many different reasons. Would Dad worry? How was Harry? Did Jackie get home to see him that morning? How was Oscar doing? Tabitha? Zagros? Baby dragons? What would my friends think when I just didn't show up after lunch?

Jackie had been talking but I hadn't been paying attention.

Baby dragons! Two of them!

I was nervous, excited, frightened and anxious. I had to pee but figured that was probably my nerves. I became aware that I was breathing faster than normal so I made a conscious effort to slow it down. I figured that might help calm me down as well. I tried to pay attention to what Jackie was saying in her own overly excited-sounding voice.

"Jackie. Slow down, I'm not following you," I managed to say. I heard a tremor in my voice but I didn't think that had anything to do with being a teenager. Her hands were at ten and two but her fingers looked like they were tightly gripping the wheel.

We brought her basic house call kit with us but I had no clue what she would need. I had never seen a chicken hatch before, let alone a dragon.

Jackie took a deep breath and paused before speaking.

“I got ahold of your dad when I was waiting for you at the clinic. I thought you were coming right away at lunch,” she said.

“I was. I kind of forgot about emailing mom, though. We all got talking about Harry and the surgery yesterday. Did you get home to check on him this morning?”

“Actually, yes. I had a couple of cancellations so I whipped up there and he is fine. Groggy but fine. His gum color is nice and pink and he stood. Wobbly but he stood and I let him out to pee. No blood in his urine, thankfully, and he wasn’t jaundiced, although that takes time to occur and I’m not expecting anything with the liver anyhow,” she explained in a rambling sort of way. I sensed she was leaning on her veterinary knowledge to cope with the enormity of what we were going to be participating in. It made sense. I could barely keep a clear thought in my own head for more than two seconds.

“So all of that is good?” I asked when there was a break in the dialogue.

“Absolutely. Of course, this will take time but he was healthy going into surgery and lets hope he’s healthy enough to recover and be his normal self. I also mailed the histopathology off to have it looked at so we can find out what was growing on his spleen and make plans from there.”

"Did Dad want to come with us?" I asked. I knew the answer but I liked the fact we were both talking about normal things from our day to day life. Harry. Dad. Check.

"Absolutely, but he knew that it would raise flags if both of you didn't show up after lunch without a good reason."

"Do we have a good reason?" It would definitely seem strange that I wouldn't be back in class. I wondered who would be the first to notice. I had World History and Woodworking after lunch. Ben and the girls were in one class, Nick and Derek were in the other with me. Or, without me as it turned out.

"Your dad suggested a recurrence of the stomach flu. Something along the lines of you feeling nauseas when you got to the clinic so I closed up and took you home. What do you think? Believable?" she asked.

It was sort of believable but if Ben had the same bug as I had and he was still feeling fine then there would be doubt. Or everyone would just think I was more of a wuss than Ben.

I remembered how suddenly I had stood up when we were all sitting on the grass and thought that might be helpful.

"You know, I kind of left them all in a hurry so maybe I could tell them later that my stomach started churning after I had eaten lunch and I didn't want to puke in front of them. That might work," I theorized out loud just before I realized I hadn't told Jackie about hearing Zagros. It hit me just then that Zagros probably was trying to contact me if the babies were hatching. I told Jackie about hearing his voice say my name and nothing else.

“Whoa, for real?” she asked. “Wow, Luke, that’s really amazing. Kind of like what we were talking about earlier, the connection between them and us.” She paused before she added, “I didn’t hear that in my head and your dad didn’t say anything but Zagros definitely sees you as his main Dragoneer. Your dad and I are like the back-up singers.”

I chuckled.

I let my mind drift back through the previous twenty minutes. As soon as I opened her clinic door, Jackie had almost shouted at me, “LUKE! Get in the truck. We have to go.”

I remembered that I stood there, staring at her, wondering why the raised voice and where on Earth we had to go so urgently.

“Oscar called. The dragon eggs are hatching. Everyone wants us there, too, so let’s go.” She had been pulling my arm as I turned around. I caught my eye on a couple of shiny objects on a small table by the door and put them in my pocket. When Jackie locked her clinic door I saw there had already been a note taped on it explaining that she was out of the office due to illness and would be unavailable. I hadn’t even seen that when I first arrived. That gave me a good thought to go along with our story.

“Hey, your note on the clinic door said ‘due to illness’, right? If any of my friends randomly come by after school they would just think it was true that I wasn't over my stomach flu because you didn't say whose illness it was," I told Jackie. I saw her smile as she nodded her head.

"That was your dad's idea, and it was a good one," she responded.

Neither of us had turned the CD player on. This was a trip that required no background music or distractions. There was just too much to consider.

"Will they be hatched by the time we get there? It takes forever to get through that tunnel," I said. I thought I heard a bit of a whine in my voice and made as much of a mental note as I could to try to not do that again. I remembered the first time Oscar drove Jackie and I into the tunnel in his Dodge pickup truck. How it had felt like we were driving forever but it was maybe only fifteen minutes. Maybe more.

"I have no clue, Luke. I don't know how long it takes for them to hatch. Oscar said one had begun this morning and they could hear tapping from within the second egg but all of that may have changed by now. Zagros and Tabitha are there, too."

"When did Oscar call?" I asked.

"Around ten o'clock this morning. It was right after I got back from my farm call and one of my mid-morning appointments had called to cancel. I knew I would have time to get up to the house to check on Harry," Jackie explained. "The eggs could be completely hatched when we get there, which is great, too. I mean, all of this is great, right?" Her own voice cracked as she spoke.

"I don't know how I can keep my cool about this," I said. "This is something hardly anyone else in the world will ever see or even know about. Its almost overwhelming, you know?"

Jackie nodded her head, her eyes focused on the road. I had noticed she had let up on the gas pedal a bit when we started talking calmly and her hands didn't have the death-grip on the wheel like they had before.

The green trees buzzed by along the side of the road as Jackie navigated the twists and turns of the highway. I hadn't noticed many other vehicles, which was pretty common for that highway. You pretty much had to go out of your way to get to Missing Lake. It wasn't on the road to anywhere and it was a couple of hours from the closest Interstate.

The tall mountains brought a lot of snow which was great for mushers like us and people who liked to snowshoe but for families who preferred sunshine and warmth, this part of Montana wouldn't be a good fit. The mountains still had a snow line up high, including on top of spiky Mount Thuban, where we were headed.

That mountain peak kind of defined Missing Lake and was featured on all sorts of artwork and logos I had seen for some of the businesses. Not that there were many businesses. Or tourists to see the logos, for that matter.

The lonely road we drove on was one of the main reasons Oscar and Tabitha had survived in that particular part of the Rocky Mountains. Oscar had no family to speak of, as far as we knew, so there was nobody looking for him. Without cellular phone service in much of the area and no Internet access where he lived he could truly live off the grid. That was an expression I had heard Derek use one time he had talked about a camping trip he took with his family. I figured it meant nobody could find you because you didn't light up any digital blips on any screens anywhere.

"Did you say something?" Jackie asked. I had been gazing out the passenger side window and didn't mean for anything to come out of my mouth.

"The grid? Digital blips?" she asked. "If you're thinking about living where Tabitha's lair is you are correct. No blips and definitely not on any grids." I heard her laugh under her breath and felt the truck begin to slow down. We were close to the turnoff to the dirt road that led to the tunnel. It was really happening and we were really a part of it and the whole world was really going to change although hardly anyone knew. The smile on Jackie's face as she turned off the highway and looked over at me stretched from ear to ear.

"This is really happening, Luke."

My stomach flip flopped and I had to pee again.

"You are here!" Oscar said as Jackie came to a stop as far into the mountain tunnel as she could drive. The familiar orange glow off towards the lair comforted me and I felt a wave of some unknown feeling wash over me. It wasn't the happiness I felt when I played with the dogs, nor was it the pure joy I felt riding behind the dog team on the sled. It was unlike anything I had ever felt and I sensed it was going to stay with me for a long time.

“Have you been waiting long, Oscar? How did you know when we would arrive?” Jackie asked. She removed her veterinary bag from the back seat. I watched as Oscar hugged her and then came over and extended his hand to me. He had a look on his face that I couldn’t read. I wondered if his look was the same as the unusual but comforting feeling I had experienced.

“I installed a sensor at the entrance to the tunnel. It was Tabitha’s idea as a way of keeping tabs on the young dragons but it worked well for me to meet you,” Oscar answered. “Come, come, we must hurry,” he said as he led us further into the mountain towards the orange glow.

We picked up our pace and the sound of rushing water that accompanied our trips through the tunnel became louder. During that first trip we hadn’t had any idea what that sound was being made by. I actually fully expected to see real water and not a crimson dragon in the largest set of animal stocks I had ever seen. I remembered that Tabitha had snorted at us as she breathed out, which had created the sound. Back then I had felt a bit of anxiety, or even fear because we didn’t know Oscar very well and he had been pretty elusive about his injured mystery pet. Those feelings were long gone as we rounded a bend into the dragon’s lair. My eyes had to slowly adapt to the lack of daylight deep within the mountain but with time they adjusted and I felt more comfortable moving forward.

I sensed Zagros' presence before I saw him. It was comforting to me. I hoped he felt the same way about me.

"I do," his deep voice rang through my head. "We are glad you are here."

I ran ahead of Jackie and Oscar, around stacked boxes and piles of shiny objects. I saw the set of stocks that weren't needed anymore had been moved to a far side of the lair. I was pretty sure Zagros would have been the one to move them because I doubted Oscar would have been able to. And not like he could have hired a bunch of high school kids to do it for him.

I hadn't been that far into the lair before and I wasn't even sure where I was going. I just followed the sense of Zagros. I noticed the body of a shiny old bicycle that I hadn't seen before. Its wheels were missing but the frame was in good shape. It even had a basket between the handle bars.

"A gift for Tabitha," said the voice. I thought about the shiny objects in the pocket of my coat and knew they didn't compare to the bike but I hadn't had much time to plan ahead. There was a good chance that no gift would ever be appropriate. What did you give your dragon friends when their babies hatched?

Zagros peered around a pile of what looked like blankets and bedding. His sinewy silver neck reflected the orange glow from the fire that burned off on the other side of the tremendous cave. His black eyes sparkled in the crackling light as he leaned down so I could embrace his neck.

"You are a little late," he told me without speaking any words out loud. He slowly raised his neck and gently guided me with his forearm around the blanket pile so I could see what he was looking at. Tabitha was next to him and she bent down so I could hug her neck, too.

"It is good you are here, Luke," she told me. I didn't always hear Tabitha or feel her presence as strongly as I did with Zagros. She was mostly bonded to Oscar, of course, which was understandable. When we met Zagros he had been without a Dragoneer of his own which was how I got selected, or chosen, or whatever had happened. I smiled at the memory of meeting my giant silver friend.

My eyes finally settled on what was in front of us and I heard Jackie and Oscar coming up to that area as well.

I didn't have to force myself to believe that what was in front of me was real, like when we first saw Tabitha. That feeling was gone but, for the first time, I truly felt the magic of what was happening in our secret little world. Right there, in front of us, lying on thick blankets was what appeared to be a perfectly formed, golden baby dragon. It was a complete miniature version of the dragons who stood on either side of me, right down to the spike at the end of its tail. It was shorter than I was which I hadn't been expecting.

"What did you expect?" I heard Zagros ask me in my head.

"Nothing, I guess," I said out loud.

The baby golden dragon was moving its little arms while his tails swished across the floor. Tabitha reached out to him and the two held their forearms out to each other. I noticed a claw-like object on the ground along with what must have been egg shells.

"We have cleared most of the shell away while we await his sibling," Zagros silently explained.

"It's a boy!" I nearly shouted as I turned to Zagros and instinctively smacked at him, as if he was Ben or Derek and the most incredible thought in the world had just occurred to me.

"Oh, my God," came Jackie's voice from behind Zagros. "He's perfect," she added, and I had to agree.

A tapping sound was becoming louder and louder from behind where the golden baby was. He had a heavy stack of blankets behind him that Jackie, Oscar and I moved around to get to the source of the tapping. The second egg!

It stood upright but was moving and the tapping definitely came from within.

"Is it okay?" I asked, to nobody in particular.

"This is how the golden one hatched so I believe so," said Oscar in a hushed voice.

"We are moments away now," I heard Zagros tell me.

I kept looking back at Tabitha and her baby but I wanted to watch the egg. Two life-changing spectacles were happening in slightly different areas and I didn't know which one to focus on. At that point, Jackie grabbed onto my arm which brought my attention back to the wobbling egg.

An indentation towards the top appeared and the tapping sounded a little different. Without any warning a spike or claw-like point burst through the shell and the three of us jumped back. I tripped on the edge of a blanket and landed on my butt but never once took my eyes off the egg.

The claw tip disappeared back into the egg and then reappeared through the opening in the shell, jamming at it to enlarge it. It repeated that a couple more times before the final jamming broke open a huge hole and suddenly there was a baby dragon's head covered in a glossy, sticky-looking membrane peeking out of the cracked shell. I saw the claw-like object that had been doing the jamming fall off the dragon's nose area. We all watched as the dragon used its claws to destroy what remained of the egg and the entire world changed yet again.

A shimmering dragon had just hatched itself in front of me and my step-mom. I briefly felt sad that Dad had missed it but we would have, too, if we had waited for him to finish work. And we couldn't risk the questions that would have arisen if he, too, suddenly had to leave that afternoon.

There was, truly, too much at stake.

Jackie, Oscar and I stood back as Tabitha went to the new dragon and gently helped clean itm off with more blankets. I turned around and saw the golden dragon rubbing his head against Zagros' abdomen. I wondered what the two dragons were sharing in their secret mind language.

“We are thrilled and overjoyed right now,” Zagros answered for me. I smiled and turned back to the new baby, who, when getting dried, looked almost black in color. I wasn’t sure if dragons changed colors as they grew or if how they were born was how they remained.

“They might molt to a lighter or darker version of what you see but, generally they stay the same,” was the answer I got from Zagros. I never got over how weird it was that he knew all of my thoughts but I was alright with the weirdness.

“I have never seen anything like this in my entire life,” Oscar whispered to all of us. “I cannot wait to talk with Nahele and Kenji. This is a crucial part in history for the dragons around the world and we have been a part of this.”

I looked at Jackie who had tears streaming down her cheeks. They glistened in the orange firelight and she smiled back at me.

Slowly the darker baby dragon was dried off and we watched it take a few tentative-looking, wobbly steps towards us. We backed away further so that the babies could see each other. Without any hesitation they both moved towards one another and reached their arms outward, as if they were long lost friends who hadn’t seen one another in years.

“She is green,” I heard Tabitha’s voice.

“She?” Jackie asked. Her voice squeaked as more tears streamed down her face.

“A green that is almost black is a good color for a dragon. They are a symbol of rebirth and life. Of spring and of the Earth,” Zagros’ voice told me. I told Jackie and Oscar what he had said.

“What about the golden color?” Jackie asked.

I looked at Zagros and saw the sides of his mouth turn upwards in what I always figured was a smile.

“They have strong attachments to the sun. Another excellent color for the strength and future and hope for our survival,” Zagros told me. I shared that with the others.

We watched the baby dragons in verbal silence although my head was spinning with questions. I knew that Zagros could hear and understand me but he didn’t say much. I noticed that the darker dragon’s forehead horn was shorter than her brother’s. Her body was a bit smaller, as well, but not by much. I felt like I had just watched my own little twin siblings being born. There was no feeling like it and I knew I would treasure the opportunity to share in it forever.

I wouldn’t be able to share those feelings with anyone other than Dad and Jackie, though. I mean, I wanted to run through the halls of the school shouting the news of their birth, or hatching. I wanted to take pictures and post them all over social media and create web pages that would follow every aspect of their growth and development but that was just ridiculous.

I also wanted to remain in the lair forever but we had to get back to Missing Lake. An image of Harry wrapped in blankets passed through my mind when Jackie put her hand on my shoulder and said, "We should go. Its been a couple of hours already."

I had no clue that much time had passed. It felt like we had just turned off the highway only moments before. I had to be gently tugged away by Jackie as Oscar joined us on our way back through the lair. Zagros followed for a short distance but then stopped. I did, too.

"You will be back very soon, I hope," Zagros asked me. I nodded my head.

"Absolutely. I would rather just stay, if you really want to know."

"I do know," he said, and I smiled because he was right. "You all must help with names for the babies. The names are important because they will carry them for many, many years. They must be dignified and strong, like we hope they both grow to be. They must be distinct and unique. Some dragons will be part of history and their names have to stand the test of time. Tabitha and I have already chosen one for our golden colored son."

I gasped.

Zagros bent his face down to mine and looked me in the eyes as he silently said, "His name will be Helios."

FOURTEEN

Hey, Luke. How's it going? Big Joe's tail is good. How was your dance? We had our spring dance the other night. Kristi and I are kind of taking a break 'cause she wants to hang out with her girlfriends more and my parents thought that was a good idea for me, too. We weren't serious or anything, I don't think. We still text all the time but at lunch I hang out more with the guys again. Its been fun, actually. Alex got a job at Papa John's pizza and I want to get a job, too. What about you, or are there any places to work for kids our age? Good luck with your permit next week. My parents actually like me being able to drive. They send me to do their errands and stuff. You should come and visit this summer. We could do some pick up hockey, too! If you remember how to play... Later,

Sam

I desperately wanted to write back to Sam to tell him about the dragons. I wanted to share their incredible existence and now the babies hatching with someone my own age. Dad and Jackie were great but they were adults. I knew it could never happen but I also knew Sam would love the dragons.

Dad, Jackie and I had talked about names. We all agreed that Helios was just about the coolest name for the boy. Dad had sort of freaked out when we got home that first night and told him.

"Helios? The Greek Titan? I love it," he said. "Helios drove the chariot of the sun across the sky each day."

"Whoa, a sun chariot?" I asked. I hadn't taken many classes that taught about Greek history or anything like that.

"Oh, wow," Jackie had responded. We hadn't even taken our shoes off after returning from the dragon's lair. Dad began hitting us with questions as soon as we were in the door.

Did the dragons make sounds? Were their wings developed? Did Jackie examine them? How did Oscar handle it? What do you mean a claw to help break open the shell? Did you touch them? Were they big? They're not mammals so they didn't nurse, right? What do you feed a baby dragon?

Oscar told Jackie that birds like turkeys or geese were going to be a large part of their diet for maybe a full year. He had bought a new freezer to store some in but said Zagros would happily be bringing some back for them. I didn't know how Zagros was going to hunt wild birds but if anyone could do it, that big silver dragon could. If we had been in North Dakota there would be a lot of pheasants around but the hunters might notice the population decreasing.

The next few days were a bit of a blur. I tried to focus on my school work and my friends, knowing I wouldn't see most of them for the rest of the summer but it was difficult. I often got busted staring out the windows in class or drifting off when anyone was talking to me. I wanted to go to the clinic at lunch every day to see what Oscar's updates were but Jackie and I agreed that might look suspicious. Or that my friends might want to come, too.

At least my little white lie about having to rush to Jackie's clinic seemed to work. Nobody questioned it so I felt good that I didn't have to continue to lie. Or make up more lies. It was hard enough keeping the real truth and the secret truth apart. I always had to be on my toes to try to be one step ahead of even myself because it was so free and easy at home or in the truck to talk with Dad or Jackie about the dragons. If I let my guard down or didn't think before I spoke at school it would be terrible.

It hadn't helped that the weather was amazing that week. The sun had real heat to it and everyone was wearing shorts and even sandals to school. The sun in our part of Montana never heated up like it did in Bismarck. I remembered a few of us from hockey getting together to help a friend's folks get hay bales off the ground one summer when a guy's dad was deployed overseas. It had to be the hottest day they chose to do it and you couldn't drink enough water to stay hydrated. It was as if our bodies were crying sweat, which matched how we all felt. That was the hottest I had ever been in my entire life and I never wanted to feel like that again.

Ben told me he saw Gwen and Callum sitting on some benches together after school one day. It hadn't bothered me at all. My brain was too full of dragons. I knew, as well, that I wasn't ready for a girlfriend. Sam's note seemed to emphasize that for me. I thought it was interesting that his folks preferred him being single when all my mother wanted was for me to be going out with someone.

"Yo, Luke, are you still in there?" Derek asked. One of our final days of school had arrived and we had been sitting under the tree out front again at lunch. We'd all eaten from the cafeteria because the school was selling hot dogs and hamburgers super cheap to get rid of them before summer break.

Most of the kids who lived in town would still be able to hang out but until I had my actual driver's license I wouldn't be in that much. Jackie had asked if I wanted to assist her a few days a week so that Sherise could have time off to go horseback riding. Dad and I figured that was a good idea and it would give me something to focus on all summer other than just the dragons and dogs.

"Yeah, just thinking about the summer, sorry," I stammered as I looked at my hands.

"I think its great you're going to work at the clinic," Ben said, excitedly. "We can hang out over your lunch break and I can keep tabs on Dr.Yale-Houser and make sure she's not getting into any trouble." I had to laugh. You had to admire Ben's alleged crush on Jackie.

"Dude, she's my step-mom. That's creepy," I told him.

"Not when I picture it," he said, with a dopey look on his face that made us all crack up.

"If we have to bring Mollie in for her shots or nail trims I'll make sure it's a day when you're working so we can catch up, too," Bethany told me.

"Yeah, I'm going to need regular updates on Mollie now that we don't have Sharing Sessions for a couple of months," I said. Everyone laughed and nodded. "Dad also told me we're going to be getting cellular service up at our place because of a new tower going in somewhere."

"That's awesome," Ben said. "Finally you can get back in touch with the world."

I was looking forward to being able to connect again. Dad told me that our generation would do well to be off-line like we had been living. That we expected instant gratification because of cel phones and the world of social media. He wasn't necessarily referring to me, though. It was more the kids in high school that he taught who used their phones a lot of the time. He knew that I learned a bit about patience and working hard over time for something because of the training we did with our sled dogs.

"If you guys come to the café at lunch you'll hopefully see me," Gwen said, "and I expect a decent tip."

"Is Jackie actually paying you to work there or is it just part of being her step-son?" Bethany asked.

"She wants to pay me by the hour, so, yeah," I answered.

"Will you be answering phones or helping in surgeries, or what?" Nick asked. We all enjoyed Nick hanging around with us more. He seemed like he had a level head and usually had neat things to say. Nobody commented on the black eye he had shown up to school with, though. I didn't feel like I knew him enough to ask about it. I figured if he got it doing something funny or stupid he would have told us. It wasn't like it was subtle.

I had noticed it the first class we had together that morning but quickly forgot when my mind drifted back to the dragons. It looked like one of those bruises that was going to change a million different colors before it went back to normal. Kind of like some of mine when I had wrecked the snowmobile.

"All of those things. Its helpful to have someone other than the owners to hold the pets when they get their vaccines and Jackie has taught me the correct ways to hold the pets so they don't freak out and they aren't able to bite her." I said, making sure I didn't look right at Nick when I answered. I didn't want him to think I was staring at his eye.

"Hey, sometimes you need more hands, like when we helped with x-rays with Harry so make sure you call Ben in for that," Derek said, wearing his traditional grin. Ben gave a thumbs-up.

"Are you doing anything special for your birthday next week, Luke?" Gwen asked. "I mean, other than getting your permit in Missoula."

"Ben is going to come up and spend the night and then come to Missoula with us," I told my friends. Ben thrust another thumbs-up into our little circle.

"That will be fun. Even if you don't have Playstation," Ben said before adding, "and, hey, nothing with olives in it for supper, okay?" Everyone laughed again.

"Or milk."

Karol-with-a-K and Jason joined us and we spent the rest of the lunch hour telling each other about any summer plans or jobs we had lined up. It felt almost like we were grown up, talking about things like that. A couple of nasty new pimples had appeared on my cheeks after the dragons had hatched so even though we were talking like adults, physically I wasn't feeling it.

I liked having a group of girl and guy friends who all talked about their plans and lives. Even Nick, who didn't talk about his family or home life much sounded excited for the summer. I felt pretty lucky that a collection of kids who had almost all grown up together and been in school together for so long had accepted me into their group. I still missed having Josh around. He was the other new kid in our grade and we had always felt connected by that. I wondered how he was doing and if he had made some new friends to sit under a tree with and talk about his upcoming break. I didn't know if he was allowed to work or if his mom would be even more restrictive with him after they had to move again.

"Are you alright, Luke? You look lost in thought," Karol asked me.

"He's been like that all week. You just learn to live with it and remember to wake him up every now and then," Derek explained. I smiled and nodded my head.

"I was just thinking about Josh, actually and wondering if he's made some new friends."

"I think about him a lot," Gwen said. "He was just starting to open up and laugh more." There were several 'mm-hmms' and head nods.

"Yeah. I know. That was just weird, him having to leave so suddenly," Ben said, voicing what all of us were probably thinking.

"Did any of you ever meet his family? They were so private and he never talked about them," Bethany said.

"Jackie saw his mom in the clinic a few times. She said she was really kind and sort of soft-spoken. I think those were the words she used," I said.

Our group fell silent and several of us lowered our heads. It was like being in a movie scene where someone just mentioned a person who had died. Maybe it did feel a bit like that when Josh and his mom and sisters had to leave. Usually when people moved you had some notice. Their house would be for sale, you'd see the signs, and you knew they were making plans. It would take days to pack things up and lots of people would be around to help. And then when they left you had an email or mailing address, like Sam had for me when we came to Montana. But in Josh's case it was as if he was a part of a tragic, unexpected accident and just like that he was gone.

I looked over at Nick who looked a bit uncomfortable. I wondered if he didn't like us talking about how private Josh and his family were. Somehow everyone always had a clue about what was happening in Nick's home between him and his father even though Nick didn't ever seem to say anything. At least not to me. I felt a need to change the subject but the only other thing that came to my mind were two infant dragons up the highway in the middle of a mountain.

"What made you laugh there, Luke?" Gwen asked me. I hadn't meant to laugh out loud. I wasn't even aware that I had.

"Oh, um," I sputtered. I couldn't think of what to say.

"Dude probably pictured Ben camped out on the veterinary clinic's front door every morning this summer with a coffee for Jackie," Derek said. Everyone laughed again and I felt appreciative for our class clown's attempt to make people smile.

"Where did that come from?" Ben asked with an exaggerated innocent expression on his face. After the laughter died down a bit it picked right back up when he leaned over to me and asked, "Does she like cream or sugar?"

FIFTEEN

We drove to the mountain that weekend so Dad could meet Helios and his sister. Zagros' voice had been in my head a couple of times that week telling me everything was fine and that the little ones were already growing and making noises. I was never one hundred per cent sure it was really him or my imagination when I couldn't see him but the messages had given me comfort. They still hadn't picked out a name for their dark green daughter. The three of us tossed some ideas around during the drive up to the mountain.

"What about Midori?" Dad suggested. "It is the color, green, in Japanese."

"A little on the nose, isn't it, Hon?" Jackie asked from the passenger seat. I heard Dad chuckle quietly.

"You're probably right. So the Japanese word for dragon is out, too?"

"Yes, I think so," she replied, smiling at him.

"I was looking up some things at the clinic the other day and the name, Aviva, means spring and innocent. What do you think?" I asked.

"It has a pretty sound to it," Jackie said. "It's a nice meaning, too."

"I don't know about the innocent thing, though. Zagros said the names have to have strong meanings so he might not like the connection to innocence," Dad said. I wasn't sure what he meant by that so I asked.

“I think when you call someone innocent it implies a lack of worldliness and maybe even maturity,” he explained.

“But doesn’t it also mean you’re clear, like a clean slate or a new beginning? The whole green dragon thing and Earth and rebirth could be a good connection to innocence,” I responded.

Dad looked like he gave that some thought before saying, “You could be right, Son. We’ll run Aviva by the dragons for sure.”

“How can we possibly choose a name for a being we don’t really know, whose personality will change as she develops when she will also outlive us? Who knows what the world will be like one hundred years down the road. Maybe innocence will be valued as a strength then,” Jackie said. She sounded a little bit frustrated, like when she was spaying a large breed dog and was having trouble plucking the first thing she had to pluck. I knew it had to do with the ovaries but I never wanted to know much more than that.

“I was so surprised that Zagros came up with the name, Helios, so quickly,” I said. “I’m pretty sure he hadn’t planned that, either, because they didn’t know what color the dragons would be. I like it, though. It sounds cool.”

“If we had another litter of sled dogs to name…,” Dad began but Jackie cut him off mid-sentence.

“There won’t be any sled dog litters to name in the foreseeable future, gentlemen.” We all laughed at that, knowing Jackie’s rule about everyone being spayed or neutered on the farm.

"Seriously, though," I began as a thought raced through my mind, "what a great idea for a litter. We could name them all of the dragon names we know and nobody would know why."

"Yes, but then what would we say if people asked about them? You know how some mushers are nosy about things like that," Dad replied. I gave that some thought and had to agree with him although most of the mushers I knew didn't care all that much. Some litter names were pretty obvious, like the litter our friend in Minnesota had where she named them all after flower parts. Even the boy dogs. Rose, Petal, Leaf, Stem. And others used letters of the alphabet for individual litters where each pup's name began with the letter, 'A'. Then there were some where you had no clue what the theme was, if there was a theme at all. Also, many dogs didn't stay with their littermates their entire life so you could have a Tabitha on your team with a bunch of Kennedys, Reagans and Lincolns.

"Aurora is a pretty name," Dad said. "Your mom and I were going to name you that, Luke, if you had been a girl. We always wanted it to be a surprise so we had to have a backup name or two and then we had to see which ones suited you after you were born. We liked Ivy, too, but Aurora was our first choice."

"Really?" I asked. Mom had never told me that. I began to wonder what life would have been like if I had been a girl. If I had been Aurora Houser instead of Luke. I wasn't sure if Mom would have let a daughter go to live the sled dog life with Dad in the prairies. I knew a few junior mushers who were girls and they were just as into it as I was. There were also a lot of women mushers, maybe as many as there were men.

You had to have mental toughness to do long distance races and lots of women definitely had that.

Gwen's parents were divorced and she lived with her mom. I wasn't sure if that was her choice or her parents'. It sounded like she had a good relationship with her dad, maybe like my relationship with my own mother.

Would I have liked spending time with my step-mom as much if I had been a girl? I wasn't sure about that. In that case, I probably never would have met the dragons and been chosen by Tabitha to be a Dragoneer for Zagros.

After having given it some thought I came to the conclusion that it was a good thing I was a boy. I was pretty glad the way things had turned out.

Oscar knew we were coming out and he was once again ready at the far point of where you could drive in the tunnel. He shook Dad's and my hand and Jackie gave him a big hug. He couldn't hide the obvious enthusiasm in his voice as he told us about the baby dragons' first week after hatching.

"The hatchlings are developing their own personalities as each day progresses! Helios may turn out to be a bit mischievous as he grows into an adult. He is very curious and wants to explore everything. Tabitha is concerned, of course, but so far we have all been able to keep him contained within the lair," he told us.

"What kinds of things has he been exploring?" I asked.

"He has been into every stash of shiny objects Tabitha has in there and he is trying to learn how to use his limbs more and more each day. At first they could not really grasp onto objects but the strength in his hands seems to increase every day. Their hindlimbs are already strong and they can move faster than I was expecting."

I tried to picture a golden dragon running around like I had seen toddlers do, wobbling and teetering side to side on chubby little legs. I couldn't come up with anything other than cartoon images in my mind.

"Do they speak yet?" Jackie asked.

"No," Oscar replied, "but they do make verbal sounds. They will need weeks if not months to learn how to share their thoughts and eventually words with humans but Tabitha and Zagros both can hear some private gibberish type of language from them. The female seems to be more vocal, making sounds, apparently, much more of the time than Helios does."

I looked over at Dad, who had an enormous grin on his face. We were making our way towards where the dragons had hatched. My eyes were once again adjusting to the orange glow and the lack of daylight but I could see that some things had been moved around.

"Will you need to build a wall or a gate in the tunnel, perhaps?" I asked, "For when they're moving around a lot more and learning how to fly?"

"We have considered that, yes," Oscar said. "Tabitha says Zagros definitely wants one, which might not to be too difficult to construct. He has told her he can bring trees that have fallen from the various mountain forests around the area and we can fashion a type of rope or something to latch them together for a gate. The area where your truck is parked would be a logical place."

"It would also provide one more level of security in general," Dad said, glancing back to where we had come from. "You know, just in case?"

Before anyone could answer a burst of flame shot out in front of us from behind more objects that were laid about the lair. A loud, WHOOSH sound accompanied it and I felt some warmth on my face. It retreated as swiftly as it had occurred and the four of us stopped in our tracks. Dad's arm was extended in front of me, like a police barrier or forelimb seat belt. I hadn't noticed he'd done that.

"What the Hell was that?" Jackie asked. We stood frozen, my arms positioned mid-swing from my pace. Oscar looked over at Jackie. Dad looked back at me. I looked at Oscar. It was one of those moments when one of us should have known what to say or do but apparently nobody did. It was one thing for a fifteen year-old to be speechless but they were grown-ups!

"Do you think..." Dad began but he never finished his thought.

"I don't know what to think but you all saw and felt that, right?" I asked.

I scanned the area that the arm of flame reached but didn't see anything burning. It had all happened so quickly I wasn't sure the flame touched anything.

I sniffed the air.

"Guys, I smell smoke," Jackie said, sharing the exact same thought that went through my own mind.

Dad started moving forward, his arm still outstretched in front of me. The rest of us followed but before we could see where the flame came from I heard the unmistakable deep voice of Zagros in my head.

"We are fine, Luke. Come quickly."

I told Oscar and the four of us picked up the pace. I wasn't sure what we were going to find. The expressions on Jackie's and Oscar's faces read the same way.

As we moved forward I started to hear a crackling sound, like the sound of a campfire. The smoky smell grew more pronounced and there was more of a glow in the area where the dragons had hatched. Louder crackling and a brighter glow led us around stacks of objects and blankets and we finally arrived at the source of the flame.

Helios stood facing us with ash down the front of his golden neck and chest. Tabitha was trying to wipe it off. The young golden dragon looked directly at me and I could have sworn he smirked. I saw Zagros sitting off to the side with the young female dragon. He looked towards us and told me, "Helios is learning some of the many things he can do." I thought I heard him sigh heavily.

Dad jumped back as he brushed up against a smoldering stack of blankets. The smoke smelled unnatural, like something that shouldn't be burning. Dad and Oscar whacked at it several times to smother the flame. I glanced around and saw several scorched areas along the walls as my eyes grew accustomed to the glowing light.

"That's quite the learning curve there, young Helios," Jackie said, moving forward towards Tabitha and her son. The young dragon took a step backwards but then looked up at Tabitha as if she was communicating with him. She must have instilled some trust in him because he stood still as Jackie approached and touched his neck and chest. His little arms pulled upwards as if it tickled when she did that and he made a strange vocal sound that was like a combination between a squeal and a grunt. It was like nothing I had ever heard before.

Jackie slid her hands up to his chin-area and slowly tipped his head upwards. Helios looked like he wasn't resisting at all. Dad and Oscar had stopped whacking at the blankets and the lair grew quiet.

I wondered if it had been possible for a dragon of that size to have blown fire such a distance. It had to have been seventy feet. I tried to remember what that would be in meters but the conversion eluded me. There was way too much going on in my head to try to grab onto any recollection of the metric system.

"I believe his skin and scales look alright," Jackie said out loud. "I'm amazed he isn't burned given the force of that flame."

I heard Zagros sigh again.

“It is not the first time he has experimented,” said the voice in my head. “We are trying to teach him to control it but he is just young and thinks this is all great fun from what we can tell.”

I looked over at Dad and I watched the amazement wash over his face as he finally had a good look at the hatchlings.

“They’re spectacular,” he said. “I mean, simply spectacular.” His voice was almost a whisper and he didn’t seem to be talking to anyone in particular but I understood that. We were looking at a family of dragons after all.

As Dad was staring at her, the little dark green dragon extended her neck towards him. A sound like bubble wrap popping came out of her and she took a step towards him. Zagros didn’t hold her back but his black eyes were riveted on her.

“They are curious, Luke,” he told me. “And they remember things. She knows she hasn’t seen your father yet.”

“What is she thinking?” I asked out loud. She took another step. And then another. Dad stood still, which I thought was a good thing because it might have been less intimidating. Less predatory. Who knew what the young dragons thought of humans?

“They are trusting because they are young and because Tabitha and I trust you all. We must teach them as they grow older to be wary, though, and that only the Dragoneers of the world can approach us like this.”

“Tabitha has told me in the past that dragons can tell Dragoneers apart from other humans. That’s how they know who to avoid,” Oscar said. “And how they knew to choose you.”

“There must only be a handful of us around the world, I would suppose,” Dad said. He stayed facing the young female who had stopped advancing toward him. She cocked her head to the side as she stared at him and an image of Baxter and his goofy black and white head flashed through my mind. I laughed out loud at the similarity but my voice chose that moment to change into more of a loud croak that was far louder than I had expected. I saw Dad jump at the same time the young green dragon almost leapt backwards. She made the same squeaky-grunt sound her brother had.

“Sorry, sorry,” I apologized. I was pretty sure she couldn’t understand my words but I tried to look concerned and truly sorry. I didn’t want to start our relationship with her being scared of me. I looked at Zagros, who didn’t seem very concerned at all. Before I could consider anything else I felt a shove from behind and lost my footing, tumbling forward onto the ground.

Everyone stepped back and I was pretty sure I heard Zagros sigh another time. A line from our Sharing song ran through my head, *‘I’m learning this the hard way.’*

I turned around from where I laid on the ground to see a golden dragon standing above me, his chubby forearms dangling at his sides. I tried to make my brain think happy, friendly, non-threatening thoughts even if

Helios couldn't understand our language. I hoped he could understand my feelings.

"He is very protective of Cassiel already," I heard Tabitha's pretty voice in my head. "As all brothers are of their sisters."

I looked over at my crimson dragon friend and saw her and Zagros share a look.

"You've named her!" Jackie exclaimed. She clapped her hands together in front of her, a gesture that usually embarrassed me but that time I was more focused on the fact I had been tackled by a dragon. In hockey, that was an illegal checking-from-behind kind of move and you got penalty time and maybe even a game suspension for that.

"Cassiel," Dad said slowly, clearly enunciating each syllable. He was still facing her with a smile on his face. "That's lovely."

As I wondered if I was safe to stand up I heard Zagros' voice in my head saying it was. He also told me that Oscar and Tabitha had made the final decision on her name but he had been hoping for Cassiel.

"We liked Aurora as well but I knew it could have been your name and that did not seem appropriate," he added silently. The thought that the dragons knew things about me before I was even born flashed through my mind but I tried to brush it away. It was too big of a concept and there was already a lot happening in the dragon's lair that needed my attention.

I got to my feet and brushed off my pants. Nothing hurt. I had been able to block my fall with my hands even though that was a dangerous way to go down. When I had first learned how to skate as a little kid in Canada, before I played hockey, the coaches taught us all how to fall down safely on the ice. On our butts. I remembered our coach having us do it over and over and we were just little kids, laughing in our puffy snow suits practicing how to wipe out.

I also remembered hearing one of the parents asking Mom why they paid a bunch of money for us to learn how to fall down as they took our skates off on the bleachers after the lesson. Mom had explained that falling was a big part of skating because ice is slippery. And that we needed to learn how to fall correctly so that when we fell countless times we wouldn't hurt ourselves and we would still enjoy skating. She explained that we were less likely to hurt anyone else around us if we learned the correct technique right from the beginning. Even as a little kid I thought my mom was pretty smart.

I pictured Tabitha and Zagros teaching their dragon-kids how to do things. Obviously the fire-breathing thing needed to be worked on. And even though it wasn't learning how to skate, they would still have to learn some basics so that when they became more advanced with flying and the whole dramatic landing thing they wouldn't hurt themselves. Or anyone else around them.

I looked at Tabitha who had Helios back by her side. It was his turn to scrutinize me just as Cassiel had done to my dad. His head cocked forty-five degrees to one side and then slowly to the other. His eyes never left mine.

"He likes you, Luke," Zagros told me. "I believe he looks at you differently from the others because of your size."

"In a good way?" I asked out loud. Dad, Oscar and Jackie turned to me when I spoke. They hadn't been aware of the private conversation in my head. I would have to explain all of that on the drive back home.

"Yes, in a good way."

"What about Cassiel?" I asked, once again out loud. We all turned to look at the dark green dragon. She had moved towards where Zagros stood, having stepped back after I startled her. Her features were more feminine than her brother's, even at such a young age. Her dark eyes had more of a teardrop shape than her brother's and her scales had a shimmer to them that changed depending on which angle you looked at her. I thought then that she was going to be very beautiful.

She curled her thick tail around the front of her legs and I could see that the pointed tip was more narrow than the tip of Helios' tail. Her forehead horns were shorter as well.

"She likes you all," the voice said. "She is very intelligent. It may take her longer to fully trust humans but she will. And, yes, she is very beautiful."

The sides of Zagros' mouth curled upwards into that sort-of smile. Or at least a sensation of happiness.

In the orange glow of the still smoky-smelling lair I looked at the expressions on everyone's faces. Dad's smile was incredulous. His eyes glistened with what I figured were tears. Oscar looked as if his heart was in his hands. He looked emotional and proud, the way I had seen parents look at high school graduations. I chuckled to myself thinking it was the same look my own mother would have on her face if I brought a girlfriend home to meet her.

"Your mother only wants what is natural for you, Luke," Zagros told me. "You do not have a hundred years to find a mate like we do."

Yeah, but give me more than fifteen, I silently said in my own head. It was a brief, more personal conversation between Zagros and me because I didn't want anyone else to hear. I didn't want to talk about Mom on the drive home with Jackie and Dad when there was clearly so much more to discuss in our lives.

There was a twinkle in those black eyes and that same smile on my silver dragon friend's face.

"Fair enough, Luke. Fair enough."

SIXTEEN

The school days that remained passed in a blur. Most of the teachers hadn't assigned homework and, in fact, seemed just as anxious as the student body to start enjoying our summer break. There was a graduation ceremony for the seniors that Dad and Jackie went to but I chose to stay at home to visit with the dogs. I didn't really know any of the seniors that well, even the guys on the basketball team because my own season had been cut short after my accident. Even if it hadn't, I doubted I would have got to know any of the guys. The most information I had on any of the graduating class was gossip that Bethany would share with us from time to time.

I wasn't sure what to expect with summer break as far as my friends went. The high school in Missing Lake was so small compared to any school I had ever attended. The fact I saw the same kids every single day in the hallways or classrooms was strange enough. I wondered if I would actually miss that. I knew I would keep busy with caring for the dogs, training them with the four-wheeler and helping out at Jackie's veterinary clinic but I honestly had no idea how the summer would go.

As far as the dogs went, Jackie brought home Harry's final histopathology report on the section of his spleen that she sent in after he had his emergency surgery. She hadn't been able to hide her enthusiasm over the good news.

"You guys, we have wonderful news about Harry!" she had shouted to us. Dad and I were in the kitchen and school had just ended. He was showing me how to make his chili and we were just about to add some canned corn. Jackie came running up the stairs without taking her shoes and jacket off, waving a single piece of paper at us.

"Its benign," she began, "Benign. Just a hemangioma, which I don't mean to imply isn't a bad thing on its own when I say, 'just' because, obviously it wasn't benign or harmless in what it did to poor Harry and he could have died had he kept bleeding but its not a Hemangiosarcoma, which would have been a grave diagnosis and I'm just so happy for the really good news for our special guy."

Dad and I just stood there. I had to catch my own breath after she finished. Jackie usually didn't ramble but she was obviously trying hard to get the information out. It was like being with Bethany at the start of a new Sharing session only in her case it was a spaniel, Mollie, and in Jackie's case it was a husky, Harry.

"Do you guys get it?" she asked.

"So Harry is going to be okay?" I finally asked after I let a lot of what she said sink in.

"Yes, that's exactly what this means. He's as good as any senior husky can be. I mean, he is almost thirteen so we have to be aware of that but this particular tumor isn't going to be the end of our old boy."

"Oh, Hon, that's wonderful news," Dad said, taking his hand off the wooden spoon he'd been using so he could give her a hug. He clasped his hand on my shoulder after and said, "This is wonderful news, Luke. I'm so happy for all of us but mostly for Harry."

Harry had done well after his ordeal. Jackie told us that reactions to blood transfusions could still occur up to two weeks afterwards if his immune system rejected the blood. We had all watched for any loss of appetite or that pale color returning to his gums. Jackie was going to do one more blood panel on him to see where his cells were and how they were reacting but she had wanted to wait until the report came back.

That night after we had cleaned up after supper I made sure to get in some extra cuddling with Harry. Ella seemed fine with being up on the couch but I sat on the floor with our big husky, my arm draped over him. He had ended up laying against my legs and I felt lucky that we weren't automatically going to lose him to some nasty cancer.

Jackie had explained that if it was the bad form of the cancer then Harry might only have about one month to live and he would have to go on steroids to give him a good quality of life. In Harry's case, while it was still cancer, it was a good cancer in that it wasn't going to take over his body. It only took over his spleen but we took care of that in the surgical suite.

I couldn't quite wrap my brain around good versus bad cancer. I had always thought cancer was always bad. The "big C" I had heard it called. I didn't know a lot of people personally who had gone through cancer but I always heard about other family members of friends who had it. Jackie said there were several different types of cancer that all mammals could get. I learned a lot when our husky, Robson became ill. His type of cancer was very different from Harry's type and his had taken over so quickly. I hoped it would be a long, long time before I had to go through anything like that with any of our pets again.

I hadn't ignored the fact that Harry was almost thirteen. That was considered old for most dogs let alone one who had worked hard a lot of his life. We had never had to put one of own dogs down due to old age and I wasn't looking forward to it. I wondered how you would know when it was the right time if nothing was specifically wrong with them.

Over the years I had heard Jackie counseling pet owners about that but she usually shut the door and made it a private conversation. I never chose to stick around in the exam room if I ever sensed a discussion was heading that direction. The few times I had been in the clinic when a euthanasia was scheduled were pretty heavy and sad. I usually tried not to look people in the eyes when they came out of the room and it seemed like most folks kept their heads down.

I was happy, at least, that it wasn't something we had to think about for the time being. At that point I allowed myself to think about how things were going to change with school being out and how my days were going to shape up. I wasn't sure how often we would get up to see the dragons or how often they wanted us there. I hoped Zagros would let me know somehow.

It was our first full summer in Missing Lake. The year prior we had moved there and had been so busy packing up in North Dakota, driving everything to Montana and then setting up our new house and Jackie's clinic.

As stressful as moving a normal house and family is, moving a kennel with several dogs, their crates, their food, their bedding, our sleds and mushing equipment made it an entirely different deal. I was always thankful that my dad was a pretty calm person who methodically got everything prepared and loaded and didn't panic. The move hadn't been as big of a deal as it could have been. At least, that was how I remembered it.

The first couple of weeks of summer vacation flew by. I turned sixteen on June ninth and Ben joined us for supper and to spend the night. Jackie had made a really good German Chocolate cake. Ben ate two pieces himself, which Dad bugged him about all night.

I didn't feel any different being sixteen. I certainly didn't feel older or smarter and my own body was working hard to remind me I wasn't any closer to being an adult. The day after school had ended it was as if someone took a pimple paint-brush and swooshed it across my face, my left chin to my right forehead. It itched and then it felt raw if I scratched it.

Dad tried to take the blame for it by telling me how bad his acne had been as a teenager. It was unusual for him and me to talk about things like that. Generally we kept that kind of thing to ourselves. Jackie didn't comment, which I appreciated. I knew she'd had great skin when she was younger and admittedly couldn't relate. If I lived with my Mom she might have found some cream or lotion or something to help.

"I think there are a few different products out there, Luke, if you want to see a family doctor," Dad said quietly one morning when Jackie was out of the kitchen. "Its not like you eat a ton of junk food but you do have certain stressors in your life that are unusual for kids your age."

"Like the dragons?" He nodded his head.

"Dragons, being a Dragoneer, even having a team of sled dogs we're responsible for can be added stress and stress can definitely have an impact on your skin."

I had said thanks for the offer of the doctor's appointment but didn't want to deal with that. I had the whole summer ahead of me and I had hoped that my stress levels would decrease because I wouldn't have to lie to my friends pretty much every day of my life. I knew I would still see them at times but it wouldn't be a daily struggle to keep my two lives separate without blurting something out, like, "Oh my God you guys, the dragon babies are here and they're so cool!"

Dad said he would look into what products were available online and do some research. I knew he just wanted to help and for me to feel good. I didn't freak out too much because I knew I would only be seeing Ben and that they wouldn't take my picture for the learner's permit. It was just a little piece of paper saying I was legitimate to drive with an adult for the following few months.

Ben came with my family to Missoula after my birthday and I took and passed my learner's permit. After the exam we all went to the mall before hitting up Costco. Everyone in Missing Lake joked about the fact you would see others from town on the same route. One of the big grocery stores, a sporting goods store, one of the big building stores, the mall and Costco. They were all places to buy things we couldn't otherwise get in Missing Lake unless you shopped online.

Ben's mom had given him a small grocery list that Jackie helped him fill. Dad treated us to lunch at a quirky restaurant in the older, downtown section of town. Missoula had some old buildings like the ones I always saw in downtown Bismarck and also downtown Vancouver. The restaurant was in one of those and our lunch was great. The place had a bit of a hippie vibe. Ben and I joked about Ms.Tanner probably being a regular. Even Dad chuckled at that.

I drove the four of us home, with Ben in the front seat. I wasn't thrilled about driving on the fast, busy Interstate but, thankfully, we turned off towards the mountains of Missing Lake before long. Dad and Jackie even let me choose the music, which was more annoying than I had anticipated. I was extremely aware of the fact one of my best friends was in the car, along with my folks and that everyone's lives were in my hands. And cars were going fast and passing me and the music was more distracting than anything. I wondered how Jackie did it on our windy roads all winter with snow and ice and disco sounds but I kept that question to myself.

Before long we settled into a summer routine at our house. Dad had coffee ready in the mornings and on the days I went into town with Jackie to help at her clinic I got to drive. Usually we had leftovers or sandwiches for lunch but our first day at the clinic together Jackie took us to the new café in town. Where Gwen was our server.

"Hey, Luke and Doctor Jackie. Its great to see you guys," she had said when she brought us our water. Her hair was pulled off of her face in a pony-tail with a white ribbon wrapped around it. She had pretty pearl earrings in her ears and her bangs looked like they had been curled because they were more curvy than I had seen. She had makeup on that matched the Silver Bullet top she wore.

"Have you been keeping busy since we got out of school?" she asked me as she handed us menus.

"Uh, yeah," I stammered, my voice cracking a little. "I got my driver's permit and today is my first day at the vet clinic."

"Oh, cool. I'm working here three to four days a week. It might change but they are hoping to hire another person to help out. We're, like, really busy," Gwen said.

"That's good because it helps the time pass, right?" Jackie asked. She had a big smile on her face. It made me wonder if she missed having us all come over to see her for help with our Sharing Sessions all year.

"Yeah, exactly," Gwen said, sounding excited. "I'll get drinks for you guys and let you look at the menu. Our soup is chicken noodle and our special is a hot turkey sandwich but I can't remember how much it costs." She giggled and gave a little wave before she went off in a different direction, taking empty plates off of another table as she walked by.

"Gwen sounds happy with her new job," Jackie said to me as we both looked at our menus. I had liked the sandwich Gordon Mulder had brought me after we did Harry's surgery but there were lots of different things to pick from.

"Yeah, she does," was all I had to say to that. I didn't think Jackie had ever known about the supposed thing between Gwen and me. As the days had gone on I wasn't so sure there even was a thing. All I had to go on was Bethany's word during the winter that Gwen liked me and then the guys always said she was looking at me. It hadn't helped when Derek always busted me looking at Gwen, either but I had never said anything to Jackie or Dad.

And I especially hadn't said anything after the spring dance fiasco.

As we ate our sandwiches, Jackie told me about the afternoon appointments and how one of the clients was a bit of a difficult one. Our morning had been pretty calm that day with two cats to spay and a few telephone calls to handle. The cats both did really well and were resting in crates at the clinic as we ate our lunch.

"What is so difficult about this guy?" I asked. I took a bite out of my enormous French Dip sandwich that I was glad I had ordered.

I watched as Jackie finished chewing. Her eyes drifted up and off to the side like they did when she was thinking about how to say or explain something. She had done that a lot during our Sharing Session visits over the year.

"Well, he's just odd. I mean, he's nice and his dog is really sweet but he asks me human medical questions that sometimes creep me out," she said.

"Oh, gross. Does he always do that? Why not ask his doctor?" I took another mouthful of yummy sandwich.

"I don't know if he has one. He's like one of those people I suspect are maybe hiding out here. He never has anyone with him, there's no wedding ring and he's just... odd."

Jackie had paused before saying, 'odd'. That could mean so many things, I thought at the time. Ms.Tanner was odd. I sometimes thought my step-dad, Frank was odd. You could even say our dog, Baxter was odd with his snorting sounds and weird breathing and funny head tilts.

"I know he lives north of town and I suspect he doesn't get out to see many people, if you know what I mean," she said. I asked if he was a hermit and she shook her head and said, "no, not quite. He speaks well enough and seems to know normal social skills but there is some sort of disconnect there as well."

"Disconnect?" I asked. The French Dip continued to disappear.

"I guess you'll see for yourself, Luke. Again, he's nice enough and I'm sure you'll like his dog, Charlie. He's a cute little beagle."

Jackie smiled and went back to her lunch. Most beagles I had met that far were nice dogs. Jackie used to say to people if they asked about them as a breed that they were truly a 'nose-to-the-ground' type of dog, which could get them into trouble if they were allowed to wander. That usually led to one of her 'reason-to-neuter' conversations as well. She had a few of those.

"Have you seen anyone else from school yet?" Gwen asked as she cleaned the plates off our table.

"No, I've mostly been up at the house but now that I'm coming into town with Jackie regularly I'm sure I'll run into some. Have you?" I asked, suddenly very aware of the pimple rash on my face. I hadn't given it any thought until then. I resisted the urge to bring my hand up to my right cheek.

“Bethany and I email every day. I mean, its only been just over a week, right?” Gwen laughed, adding, “You guys could all coordinate one day and come in while I’m working maybe. Or we could all come here when I’m not so that way I could visit with you guys, too. There just aren’t any other places to go out to eat, really.” As she talked, her pony-tail bobbed up and down. I realized it was more curly than it used to be, too. It looked like Gwen put a lot of work into her hair and makeup and the sudden realization that maybe Callum would be visiting her hit me like a punch in the stomach.

“Going to where you work on your day off isn’t always fun but you guys would probably all make the most of it,” Jackie said. She had sounded motherly when she said that but I couldn’t explain why.

“Yeah, okay, that sounds good,” I said as I nodded my head. I wondered if she and Callum had lunch dates together as well. I watched Jackie write out a check and before long we were out the door. I knew Jackie didn’t like to leave recovering pets in the crates for long without someone being there, even though most of them were still really sleepy until mid to late afternoon after surgery.

I told Jackie I should email my mom before patients started showing up and she left me alone in the main waiting room at the computer. Mom and I had talked on my birthday and I had emailed since then but I knew she liked more frequent updates.

Hi, Mom. I've started working today at Jackie's clinic and we're just finishing up our lunch break. It's great because I can practice driving with someone else in the truck both in and out of town on the days I work. When I'm here her assistant, who has the pot-bellied pig and the horses, takes the day off so I might get to do some cool things. Cat surgeries this morning. They were good. One of my friends from school works at the new café I told you about. We just had lunch there. It wasn't anything like that amazing Greek place you guys took me to. That has to be one of my favorite places to eat.

Part of me had wanted to tell her about Gwen because I knew it would interest her but most of me knew it would sound like I had a crush on her. Then I would have to tell her that Gwen was dating the most popular guy at school and that wasn't somewhere I wanted to go.

We haven't worked the dogs much yet, they're kind of on break right now. Pretty soon Dad will be able to hook them up to the ATV, though. I can't believe its almost been a year since we moved here. I know you miss me but I'm really happy we are here. We go hiking in the forest around our place and its just so beautiful and peaceful. I think you would like it but you might get bored. The closest mall is in Missoula and it takes a couple of hours to get there.

I'd better get ready to help with appointments but I wanted to say hi and let you know that everything is going well. Say hi to Frank, too. I love you!

I made sure to add the exclamation mark after 'I love you' because it would make her happy. It was a pretty boring email but she told me she wouldn't care if I didn't have anything to write about. She just wanted me to write frequently.

I tried not to think about it too much but Mom probably had it rough with me wanting to live with Dad and then us all living in the States. Her life was good and she seemed happy and successful with lots of friends and parties to go to but I wasn't sure if it went the way she had planned. At least she seemed happy with Frank.

And even though Frank could be considered a bit odd by some people, he didn't hold a candle to the client Jackie had warned me about who was scheduled for two o'clock that afternoon.

"And who might you be?" asked the tall, bearded client we had been anticipating.

He had looked startled when he first came in the waiting room of the clinic and saw me sitting at the front desk. He had probably been expecting to see Sherise. The man had glasses and an old-fashioned looking hat and he was holding onto the leash attached to his little dog.

"I'm Luke Houser, Jackie's step-son. I'm going to be helping out a couple of days a week here now that school is out for the summer," I said as I stood up. I extended my arm for a handshake but the guy initially just looked at my hand and made a grimace. After an awkward moment he finally shook my hand but it wasn't a strong, confidant handshake. It was more like the ones little old ladies gave you. He made a grunting sound at the same time and then said, "Mr.Stewart here with Charlie."

I peered over the desk to see a cute little beagle attached to the leash. He had floppy ears and was nicely marked in a tri-colored hair coat with big brown eyes that looked right up at me. I smiled at the dog and told Mr. Stewart I would go to get Jackie. I was pretty sure she had heard him come in because her clinic really wasn't very big. Sometimes, though, she was working on notes on her laptop in the exam room and didn't pay attention to the voices out front.

"You don't call her Mother, or Doctor Yale-Houser?" Mr.Stewart asked me as I walked past him towards the exam room. He grimaced again. I sensed that he was one of those adults who didn't think too highly of teenagers.

"No, I have a mom who doesn't live here. And I guess I slipped up on the doctor part." I had tried to be friendly and apologetic but he just kept sneering at me. He was right, though, and I made a mental note to myself to try to remember to not call her 'Jackie' in front of clients.

Thankfully, Jackie had me bring Mr.Stewart and Charlie back right away. I hadn't been looking forward to being alone with him in the waiting room.

"Do you need a hand with anything?" I asked.

"Not just yet. Maybe when its time to do Charlie's toe nails but I'll call you in for that. Thanks, Luke," Jackie said as she closed the exam room door. As it was closing I heard Mr.Stewart's voice ask, "Can I tell you anything and you have to keep it confidential, like a real doctor?" I wondered what kind of a question that was to ask your veterinarian. I hustled back to the main desk and secretly hoped they wouldn't need me. The guy gave off a weird vibe.

I answered a phone call and made an appointment before, unfortunately, Jackie asked if I could help out.

"I'll just have you hold Charlie, Luke. He is being a perfect gentleman but he does wiggle a bit. I think his paws are ticklish," she told me when I joined them in the exam room. Mr.Stewart stood back from the table. He looked almost uncomfortable.

"Just doing the toe nails right?" I asked. Toe nail trims generally didn't make owners uncomfortable.

Jackie nodded her head and I did my assistant hold on the cute little dog. Charlie nestled up against me as I held him and he showed me his big brown eyes again. I couldn't help but wonder how his personality fit with his owner's.

"Are you holding him too tight? Don't hold him too tight," Mr.Stewart said before Jackie had finished the first paw.

"I don't think I am but I'll be careful, Mr.Stewart," I said. I definitely hadn't been holding the dog tightly but I tried to make it look like I was loosening my arms.

"I think he's nervous. Or maybe scared. I think Charlie is afraid of you, like he doesn't trust you," Mr.Stewart said. His voice went up a pitch but Charlie just continued to calmly lean against me.

"I think Charlie is doing fine, Mr.Stewart. Luke has held countless rambunctious dogs and cats for me before and we're only going to be a few more seconds," Jackie told him without looking up. I was thankful she could trim toe nails quickly.

"Are you certified to do this, young man?" he asked. It was pretty clear that anything I did with his dog was going to be questioned or unacceptable. Charlie seemed fine the entire time. He never tried to pull his feet away or shivered or seemed upset and yet his owner was being a total jerk about it.

"How can you tell you aren't hurting him? I don't think I like how you're holding him," he added before letting Jackie or I comment on the certification question.

"Charlie and Luke are doing just fine, Mr.Stewart, and besides, we have finished our manicure and pedicure for this month," Jackie said in calm, controlled, lowered voice. She often talked like that when people started to freak out. She told me one time that she thought it helped calm the other person down when she did that. As she placed Charlie back on the floor she said, "Luke has been helping me for a couple of years and does an excellent job of holding animals and helping everyone stay safe. He actually has a gift with dogs and they seem to calm down in his presence."

The look on Mr.Stewart's face told me he didn't agree with her assessment. He hooked Charlie back up to his leash and rubbed his back. I was glad to see him being affectionate towards his dog, at least. I made my way out of the room with the full intention of hiding in the surgery suite so Mr.Stewart wouldn't have to grimace at me anymore but I made sure to say, "it was nice meeting you," before I closed the exam room door behind me.

I felt touched that Jackie stood up for me like she had. Mr.Stewart was a paying client and she needed as many of those as she could get in such a tiny community. I had never heard her say I had a gift with dogs. It might have been something she just said to try to comfort the guy, though, too.

If that was my first day on the job that summer I wondered what else would be in store and did I want to meet all of the people in the area who Jackie figured were hiding from reality. Or, at least, their realities. That made me think of Josh and his family who were hiding out from his dad but not necessarily from the real world. I hoped once the baby dragons were a bit older that Zagros would be able to check on my friend again sometime. Not only did I like hearing that Josh was alright, I also liked the fact Zagros wanted to check on him. There was something special about knowing a dragon had your back.

SEVENTEEN

"Hi, Luke. Is Jackie having lunch with you, too?"

I was back at the café a couple of weeks later and fully immersed in my new summer life. The job at the clinic had way more normal and friendly people than Mr.Stewart, and I had been enjoying driving Jackie's truck when we came into town. The weather was warming up and there was hardly any snow visible up high in the mountains. It stayed light pretty late into the evening so I could go out and visit the dogs in their kennel longer than in the winter.

Dad had set up a bon fire pit behind our house and we had been enjoying sitting there with Baxter, Harry and Ella at night as the huge sky slowly lit up with stars. A clear night sky in rural Montana was unlike anything I had ever seen. There are no big city lights for hundreds of miles and the stars twinkled and looked like a sparkly costume a figure skater would wear. Some looked closer than I could have imagined and others shone with a fierce intensity.

Mom used to say that we could always feel close if we looked up at the stars, knowing we were looking at the same ones but the stars above Montana were nothing like the stars above Vancouver at night. Vancouver was such a huge city that sparkled with its own light show but it muted the night sky. Mom might have been looking up to the sky and maybe they were the same stars but it sure was a different, more spectacular view from our farm in Montana.

I had been able to email Mom and Sam more regularly and it was great having more of a conversational feel to our communication. Sam was still single and had got a job at one of the golf courses in Bismarck. I told him about Gordon Mulder because I figured Sam would be pretty safe living way over in another state. He was impressed that I knew the guy and that he helped us out with Harry. Sam said his dad told him that Gordon Mulder was known as kind of an angry guy after he chose to end his professional career.

We had figured out a great way for me to get out at lunch on my clinic days when Dad suggested I take my bike in and leave it in town. It wasn't like I biked on our forest trails up at the house. It was a regular mountain bike and for the trails around our place you probably needed a Fat tire bike.

But in town my mountain bike was a super way for me to go to get the mail or even grab lunch if Jackie had paperwork, which is why I was in the café that day.

"No, actually, I'll take ours to go today if that's okay," I said. Gwen had her curly bangs and pony-tail going on again. Her eye makeup was a pretty pink color and I thought she wore lipstick. I didn't remember her wearing lipstick in school. She smiled and took my order for a couple of turkey and bacon sandwiches. I asked her if they ever hired another helper for her because the place looked fairly busy.

"Yes, actually. Do you know Lindsey Grant from school?"

"Um, brown hair, glasses? I think she was in a couple of my classes," I said. I could picture her but I didn't know much about her. She had been at the spring dance and looked like she knew everyone. In our home room she sat on the opposite side of the room and I had never had much of an occasion to talk to her.

“Yeah, you’d know her if you saw her. She starts tomorrow. It will be neat to get to know her a bit,” Gwen told me before she paused to write our order down on her little note pad.

“If you want, just have a seat and I’ll bring it out when its ready,” she told me. I glanced around the café which must have had a dozen people in it.

Including Anne-Marie.

Who happened to look up and catch my eye at the same moment I saw her sitting by herself at a small table by the window. I quickly looked at my feet and immediately felt guilty for doing so. I glanced in her direction again and saw that she, too had looked away.

It looked like she was there alone. There were no other knapsacks or handbags or even jackets around her. The idea of eating alone at a busy restaurant made me feel uncomfortable. Figuring I had nothing to lose and knowing I wouldn’t be there for long, I walked over to her table and asked if I could join her.

“I’m taking lunch back to the veterinary clinic for my step-mom and myself but if you don’t mind I can wait here with you,” I offered.

For the first time since I had met her, I saw a genuine smile come over Anne-Marie’s face. Not her smirky, smug, I’m-better-than-you smile, either. This one had a look of relief in it by the way the sides of her eyes and the corners of her mouth tilted upwards. It was similar to the tilt at the corner of the dragons mouths when I felt like they were expressing a happy emotion.

"Sure, Luke. I'm, um, just having a salad," she said in a voice much quieter than the one she used in her Sharing sessions in school. "My dad was supposed to join me but his meetings went later than normal today so I figured I'd try this place out."

"I like their French dip a lot but its too messy to carry back on my bike," I said, nodding my head in the direction out front where I had stood my bike up against the building. I had no idea how to have a conversation with her but it had gone well up to that point so I kept going.

"Where does your dad work?"

Anne-Marie finished chewing her forkful of salad and told me he was the manager at the local bank. I laughed out loud and admitted I didn't even know we had a bank in town. My laughter must have been louder than normal, probably because I was a bit nervous talking to Anne-Marie. Everyone in the café, including Gwen seemed to stop what they were doing to look over at our table. It might have been more in my imagination but that's how it felt at the time.

"You and your step-mom are pretty close, it sounds like," she said, once the normal murmur came back to the café. "You guys always went over there with our English assignments."

"Yeah, I guess so. I'm close with my dad, too and Jackie is pretty cool. She loves our dogs, which is important to me and she likes music and hockey, too. She makes my dad happy and that's the biggest thing," I told her. Her plate of salad had bright green leafy bits throughout that looked like all sorts of different types of lettuce. The cucumbers crunched as she ate them and it looked like there was feta cheese scattered throughout.

"Did you want some?" she asked, pushing her plate towards me a little bit. She must have seen me staring at her lunch.

I thanked her but declined, chuckling at the different things we all notice about people.

"My mom and I are pretty close, I guess. I think that's weird for teenaged girls and their mothers but its alright," she told me. "She kind of struggles with depression from time to time and I feel sorry for her because I know she doesn't have a lot of lady friends in town."

I asked her why that was and she said, in what Dad would call a very matter-of-fact way that it was because they were rich.

"People see our big house and fancy cars and we take all these incredible trips and of course dad manages the bank so they just assume its all easy street for us. I know I'm pretty spoiled and I know you know that so don't pretend otherwise, Luke Houser." She took another forkful of salad and looked off to the side as she ate it.

I smiled and said, "Well, everyone knows you have lots of nice things."

"I do and I'm very lucky but you know, I don't always even ask for these things. My parents just sometimes show up out of the blue with things so I try really hard to be the perfect student for them and a friend for my mom when she gets depressed."

"I guess I don't know anyone who gets seriously depressed. Do you mean, like, just super sad or more like the real depression they talk about on TV?" I asked. I wasn't sure if I was crossing a personal-space line but she had been the one to bring it up.

"Clinical depression for sure. She takes meds when she needs to, which is most of the time, and Dad and I just try to keep things happy. It isn't so bad but I just feel sorry for her sometimes. That's what Dad and I were going to talk about at lunch. Maybe a weekend away to lift her spirits right now. She gets pretty sad at the beginning of summer each year."

Anne-Marie paused as if she was second-guessing disclosing all of that about her family to me. It felt a bit like when Josh used to confide in me about his feelings. Maybe because I hadn't grown up with everyone she felt like her story was brand new to me. That I had fewer preconceptions about her than kids she'd known forever. I hadn't expected her to share the reason for her mom's depression though. What she told me next had me speechless.

"I had, or I guess I have, or, no, maybe its had an older brother who died right after I was born. He was barely two years old and it was summertime and my mom has never been the same since."

What did you do when someone you barely knew dropped that out in front of you?

"Oh my God, Anne-Marie," I said, almost stammering to get the words out. She sighed and looked directly at me from across the little table.

"Its not something I talk about and I don't actually know why I just told you but that's the truth about my family and maybe why we keep to ourselves and stick so tightly together. Its also why I don't do a lot with the other kids outside of school because Mom likes to know where I am and I don't mind that for now."

I nodded my head because I didn't know what else to do. I was thankful that she continued to talk so that there was no uncomfortable silence. If there had ever been a time where things could have felt uncomfortable, that was it.

"And I know most of the kids at school think I'm a bitch and maybe I am. I don't want to be like everyone else here and stick around a small town. Its good for my mom because she doesn't have to deal with a lot of city noise and traffic and the mountains and scenery are very calming to both my parents but once we graduate I'm out of here. Bright lights, big city time for me," she said.

"But, your parents," I said, but it sounded more like a question. I was confused. "You just said how close you all were. How will that work?"

"I don't know but I hope they visit me a lot and that I can visit them. In all truth, I hope my mom can get over her depression and want to live in a city again with me and then they would have all of their fancy restaurants and plays and events to go to. They used to have that before..." She paused before saying, "Well, before Victor got sick."

We both looked down. At least she had her food to look at. All I had were my hands and fingers that were entwined in themselves. I hadn't realized I had been wringing my hands as she spoke and wasn't sure what that said about me. I hoped she hadn't noticed.

"Hi, guys," Gwen's voice chirped from behind me. "Your lunch is ready, Luke. I'm going to go on break pretty quickly but you can just pay up front if you'd like." She handed me a brown-paper bag and smiled at both Anne-Marie and myself.

As I tried to stand up to take the bag I knocked my chair backwards and had to grab at it before it hit the floor which led to my elbow bumping up underneath the table causing all of the plates and cups to rattle loudly. The pepper shaker tipped over and pepper spilled out over the clean napkins and cutlery at my seat. Anne-Marie held onto her plate and kept it from falling. She raised her eyebrows at me.

"You alright?" she asked, with a smaller version of her real smile on her face.

Gwen laughed and helped me get my chair back on its legs. She waved at us both and walked off back towards the kitchen area shaking her head. I turned to Anne-Marie and said, "I guess I'll get going." That didn't seem like enough so I added, "And I'm really sorry about your family's loss. I totally can't imagine what that would be like. My mother would probably be the same way. And its great you have some big goals, too. I admire that, even though I'm not sure what I'm doing tomorrow let alone after graduation."

That made her laugh, which was a first. I didn't think I had ever heard Anne-Marie laugh before. It was a high-pitched laugh that reminded me of Christmas bells, but not in a bad way. I thought to myself that maybe once you got past the outer image that she wanted everyone to think she was that she was actually a nice, normal kid.

I wondered briefly what outer image I portrayed. Apparently it was a trustworthy one or that of a good listener. Maybe a bit distracted at times but that was only because the real truth about me could never be shared. That two of my best friends were dragons and I was responsible for one of them.

I was busy thinking about outer appearances and dragons and how good my sandwich was going to taste when I glanced outside the window by our table and saw Gwen standing on the curb. With Callum. And they kissed. Gwen had to stand up on her tippy toes to do it but there it was right in front of the café, immediately next to my bike. I noticed that Gwen's eyes were closed.

Heat rose up my neck and onto my cheeks as I stood there staring at them from the other side of the glass. I turned away and caught Anne-Marie's eyes.

They looked a bit sad, like perhaps she was watching me as much as I had been watching her. That maybe we all had our external sides we wanted everyone to think was the real us but the internal sides were much different. Or just more vulnerable.

I held her gaze long enough to see her mouth the words, "I'm sorry."

That night we were getting set up around the bon fire pit and I shared my lunch conversation with Anne-Marie with Jackie and Dad. Dad knew all of the kids in school because he had done substitute teaching throughout the year for all of the grades. He said Anne-Marie was a top-notch student as far as her grades and work went.

"She is very bright and mature for her age, no question," he said, poking at the fire with a long stick he'd found.

"It was a bit weird for her to share all of that seriously personal stuff, though, don't you think?" I asked.

"Maybe she wanted to tell somebody, instead of just keeping it as a family secret," Jackie suggested.

"Oh, like keeping our secret lives as Dragoneers between the three of us?" Dad asked. He poked around a little more and then leaned back into his lawn chair.

"When you say it like that then I totally understand her wanting to say something but in Anne-Marie's case she won't endanger anyone by telling me," I said. "In our case we would jeopardize every single dragon that exists if we shared outside of our family."

The three of us sat silently as the fire popped and crackled in front of us. The sky wasn't completely black yet but the blanket of stars had begun popping out. I could still make out the mountain silhouettes off in the distance but just barely.

After what seemed like a long time Jackie finally spoke up.

"In our case we do have other Dragoneers to talk to. I know they're all mostly older than you, Luke, but there are young ones we will eventually connect with. Nahele's son is around your age and it sounds like he might be someone whose company you would enjoy. If he's anything like his father he will have an excellent sense of humor."

We all laughed and agreed. I pictured our large Hawaiian friend in his brightly-colored floral print shirts he always wore when he visited. I had never seen him without a friendly smile on his face and I hoped his son would have the same personality.

"There are veterinary conferences in Hawaii we could look into," Jackie said, adding, "there is one every year in the fall, right before you guys get heavily involved in the dog training."

"We can't just leave the dogs for several days, though, Hon," Dad said, staring at the fire. "And we don't know anyone enough up here who could take care of them. We live so far from town that it would be a big inconvenience for anyone to come up twice a day and I can't picture anyone staying out here for several days."

I thought about suggesting our neighbor, Gordon Mulder but I wasn't sure about asking him to take on that much responsibility. At least he had been concerned about Harry so I thought that might mean he liked dogs or animals in general.

I knew Ben would probably want to care for the dogs but it was one thing to help out once or twice when he spent the night but it was way too much to ask someone, especially when we would be back in school at that time.

"I could ask Mom," I jokingly suggested. I wasn't anticipating Dad to react so hilariously but he spit out whatever drink he'd been sipping from his steel mug and burst out laughing. When he did that one or two of the dogs down at the kennel must have heard us because it got a few of them howling, which led to the entire kennel howling. They had different sounds to their voices and the howls echoed off the nearby hills and trees and sounded like a bizarre canine symphony. It was a clear night and I wondered if Gordon Mulder would be hearing it all. I was used to the dogs all getting going whenever they saw us approaching the kennel yard but hearing them almost barking and howling through the near-blackness with a crackling orange glow in front of us made it all seem magical.

Sonny's bark was as goofy as he was and easily identified in the noise. He gave high-pitched, short barks that almost sounded like a little kid screaming. He was one of our pups, as we still called the litter that we bought and raised. None of his siblings sounded or even looked anything like Sonny with his loud-colored red and white coat. We had other red heads but nothing like Sonny. I laughed as I realized Gordon Mulder might like Sonny, too, if he had a thing for red heads.

The barking and howling stopped abruptly, though, which was pretty unusual. Generally one or two dogs would keep at it, needing to be the last one to speak. I figured it was Jackson, one of our lead dogs or big Slash who usually had the most to say when they kept barking long after everyone else settled down but nobody kept barking. The dog yard was silent. Dad, Jackie and I all exchanged glances.

At that point the stars in the sky all seemed to vanish as something even darker than the sky floated over us. An intense sound of rushing air blew over our heads loudly and almost knocked me off the bench I had been perched on. As quickly as the stars had disappeared they reappeared in all of their sparkly glory and there was a subtle shaking of the ground that we could feel from off in the distance.

Zagros!

"I am here," said the familiar voice in my head.

Jackie, Dad and I all stood up and faced the sound of trees being brushed aside as Zagros walked past the house and towards our campfire. It had always been an impressive thing to see my silver friend move towards me but with the dark night sky and the crackling orange glow from the fire the image looked almost surreal.

"That is a little fire," he told me, which made me laugh. I told Dad and Jackie what he had said. I wondered if Zagros would ever allow them to hear his voice and realized, as I always did, that he was listening to my thoughts.

"If it needs to happen, they will hear me."

"How are Helios and Cassiel?" I asked out loud so that Dad and Jackie could try to follow our conversation. By that time Zagros had come right up to our fire and sat opposite from where I was. The ground shook a little once again and he made a fairly loud 'thump'. Sometimes I hugged him when we first saw one another but it didn't seem quite right with there being others around, even if they were obviously on board with the dragons.

"Its so good to see you, Zagros," Jackie started to say. I quickly turned to her and said Zagros was talking. She smiled in the orange glow and said, "Well, lets give you guys some time together." She stood up and put her hand on Dad's shoulder.

"They do not have to leave," Zagros silently said as they both walked off towards the house. Jackie had touched Zagros on his side as she passed him and told him to give the young ones a nice touch or embrace from her when he got home.

"You guys don't have to go," I called towards them but Dad called back that it was fine and to keep the fire stoked.

"The young dragons are doing well, I believe. I have no other reference but I think they are developing as they should," he shared. His voice, as always, sounded crystal clear in my head as though he was actually making sounds out loud but his mouth never moved once. His eyes were focused on my own across the glowing fire pit.

"Is Helios still working on breathing fire?" I asked him.

"Not as much. Tabitha and I have worked with him to show him how powerful but also how dangerous our fires can be. It is challenging to know if he understands but he is not making his fire much at all now."

"Did his sister try the fire-breathing thing?"

"No. She is an interesting creature. She watches and observes everything. Her eyes are always moving. I believe she learned by watching her brother and that this seems to be a pattern with the two of them. It is very interesting and makes me think it might have been different if I had a twin to grow up with." When he said that, Zagros took his eyes from mine and moved his head. It was like he looked off into the distance.

"I used to think it would have been cool to have a sibling to experience things with," I told the enormous dragon sitting across the fire. "But it is what it is and instead of a brother or sister I have my friends and family to talk to and go through life with."

Zagros' eyes were once again locked onto mine as he asked, "Do you think of me as your friend?"

"Of course," I said without hesitation.

"I do, as well," the voice told me. We didn't speak for a few moments as I grabbed a couple of pieces of wood that Dad had split and stacked over by his empty lawn chair. I placed them onto the dwindling fire and used his long stick to poke around to get the fire going again. Zagros seemed to be watching me intently.

"I have plans to check on your friend, Josh again soon but the timing of the skies must be just right for me to travel. I also want to make sure the wyrns are a little bit older and that Tabitha is alright on her own."

I didn't hold back the excitement I felt and told him that I would always wonder about Josh and his family. I also told him that I believed Josh would always be my friend even if I never saw him again. Zagros agreed.

He also told me that dragons had relationships the same as humans and that they could feel emotions about seeing or being with one another.

I wondered if he ever thought about or missed his first Dragoneer, Lawrence, which he heard from my silent thoughts.

"I do but it comes to me surprisingly sometimes. I am so busy with Tabitha and the young ones and we are often preoccupied with maintaining our hidden presence in the world that I do not choose to think about him. The thoughts just are there." He paused before adding, "I believe he would have been pleased with Helios and Cassiel. He came from a long line of Dragoneers."

I poked around a little more at the fire with a smile on my face.

"If you have children, Luke, will you let them know about us?"

I stopped prodding with the stick and sat up. I had never really given it much thought up until that moment. I hadn't thought about having kids in general until later on in life. I knew I would always have dogs around me, hopefully a team or two of huskies but I didn't know about the whole having kids thing. I couldn't even keep a girl interested in me so the idea of a family was unbelievable at that point.

"You know how things went with Gwen, Zagros, so I don't really know about girls or wives, let alone children. Its hard to look that far ahead for me, to be honest," I told him. I went back to digging around the fire until it really picked up into a bit of a blaze once again.

"Gwen is only one girl and you are young. I believe you will find a partner one day and she will make you very happy," Zagros said. He sounded so confident about my future it made me smile.

"If I was close enough to a girl to want to be with her forever and to even consider having children with her then I would definitely share you guys with them. That's only if you wanted it, too. You dragons seem to have a better grip on a lot of people than humans do. I might need you to help me in that department if I ever got close enough to someone," I said. As always, I continued to speak out loud during our conversations. It would look crazy if you were watching from afar but probably no more crazy than me having a bon fire with a big silver dragon.

"Humans spend much of their time over analyzing each other and their situations. Most people have lost the ability to sense things about other creatures although there are several who still can. I believe you have some of that within you and it will serve you well in life. It is one of the reasons Tabitha knew you would be a good Dragoneer for me."

I smiled again.

"Thanks, Man. That means a lot," I said.

"Other humans see it within you, which is why they tell you things that are very personal. It is why Josh connected with you and why Anne-Marie shared her story."

I sat up feeling a bit startled that he knew about my time at the café earlier that day. And yet it shouldn't have surprised me by then that he knew everything about my world. He knew what happened when I was in Vancouver so why wouldn't he know about my activities in Missing Lake?

"How come you know everything about me but I can't see into your world every day, Zagros?" I asked.

Even with just the fire light between us I could see his black eyes sparkle and the sides of his mouth turn upwards.

"There is already plenty of information for you to process about being a Dragoneer, Luke on top of your own daily events. The very last thing you need is to know what happens within my own mind," he explained.

I couldn't argue with him on that. I was distracted enough as it was with our two worlds without knowing everything about his. I probably couldn't handle the hunting he had to do to keep his family fed and didn't want to picture how any of that went down. It occurred to me it would be amazing to see Josh through his eyes, though.

"It is something that could happen, my friend," his voice buzzed through my head. "But only in time."

EIGHTEEN

I had been looking forward to a relatively calm day at home by myself. Dad had left early to go to a one-day teacher's meeting in Missoula and Jackie was at work with Sherise. While Sherise liked having a few days off to go horseback riding that summer she also wanted to keep her job and I didn't mind the days off. I missed having instant access to the Internet during the day but I was hoping to spend time with each of the dogs.

I had also begun experimenting in the kitchen with Dad's guidance. Not that I would be graduating from high school anytime soon but it always impressed me when my friends knew how to do more than heat up some soup and make toast.

The coffee that was left in the pot was still hot by the time I got up so I treated myself to some and began to work on scrambling some eggs. Dad and Jackie had debated the process. He claimed you heat the pan up pretty high, beat the heck out of the eggs, get them in the pan and keep moving from the outside in. He called them 'diner style scrambled eggs.' Jackie's version involved milk and less heat and less movement. I figured Dad's recipe involved less ingredients and less fuss so I went for it and they were actually pretty good with some salt and pepper on top. They had a different, more smooth but still lumpy texture than when Jackie made them but it felt good to be in charge of my fine dining.

I loaded the dishwasher and was getting ready to head out to the dog yard when the unmistakable voice of Zagros suddenly came into my head loud and clear.

"Luke," was all he said. No instructions, no indication of what he wanted, just my name. The voice had what sounded like concern to it, which made me freeze in place in my bedroom. I glanced down at Baxter and Cooper who were both lying on my bed and asked out loud if either of them had heard anything.

Baxter cocked his round head to the side like he always did when I asked him a question. Cooper, at the opposite end of the bed, started kneading my bedspread. Just as I started to think that I had imagined it, Zagros said it again only with more urgency than before.

"LUKE!"

I had no clue what to do but I definitely knew I was supposed to get to him wherever he was calling me from. But how? I only had our farm pickup, Norm and I still didn't have a driver's license. I also couldn't go to Gordon Mulder's house and explain the situation without giving away the dragons. As much as I thought Mr.Mulder would probably leap at the chance to meet them it wasn't worth the risk.

I knew I would have to drive to Jackie's clinic on my own. It was risky, even though I had been driving to and from the clinic every day I worked there but legally speaking I wasn't allowed to. If I got in an accident it would be really, really bad and Dad's insurance would probably go up and every single person in town would know. And even if that all happened I would somehow have to explain what was so important that I chose to break the law when there was no clear reason to do so.

I wondered how I would ever explain my choice, even to Dad or Jackie if something happened. The only thing that would make any ounce of sense would be if I claimed that I had made the extremely bad choice to take a joy ride. It wasn't like Zagros was with me when he called for me. It was merely his voice in my mind. His booming voice. The voice that had sounded like something was very wrong and that he needed me.

I had to go.

It was one of the only times I knew, without a shadow of a doubt, what to do. For most of my teen years up to that point I had questioned just about every single thing that I did and every choice I made. But at that point the decision making was clear.

"I have to go," I said to Baxter, who was still watching me with his sideways head. He barked. I took that as a sign that I was right and that Zagros was calling for me.

As always, the keys were on the front seat of our old pickup truck. He fired up perfectly and I buckled up and adjusted the seat. The radio kicked on from a station in Bozeman. I listened to it for a moment as the broadcaster talked about the price of grain within the state before I turned it off. I knew I couldn't afford to have any distractions. Zagros hadn't said my name again but I figured if he always knew what I was up to then he'd know I was on my way.

I glanced at Norm's gauges to get my bearings. The truck was a lot different from Jackie's newer ride. Even though I had driven Norm a lot it had been awhile and I wanted to feel as comfortable as possible on my illegal ride to town. I was glad to see that Dad had left him with nearly a full tank of gas.

I was also thankful it wasn't raining. The sun was climbing up into the bright blue summer sky and already the world was heating up. I knew Norm didn't have air conditioning but I could roll down the windows if I wanted. I contemplated doing that before I even put him in gear. It would be one less distraction.

I thought, for the most part, that nobody other than Mr.Mulder usually drove on our roads but tourist season had begun and there was a lake many miles past our home that some die-hard hikers liked to go to. I tried to make myself as tall as possible in the driver's seat but then I had trouble reaching the pedals. I just had to go for it.

I drove slowly with the window partly rolled down. I braked often as our gravel road wound its way through the forest. I was mimicking Jackie's 'ten and two' hand hold on the wheel. The only time my eyes left the road in front of me was to briefly glance down Mr.Mulder's gravel driveway. I didn't see any action or movement. I felt a sense of relief that he was a private kind of person and continued on my cautious way.

I got passed by a couple of other vehicles once I was on the highway. There weren't many straight stretches or passing zones but I was going slow enough that the folks behind me had a lot of time to get by. I knew I couldn't go too slowly, though, because you could get reported for that. Not that we had a huge police force in town but the Missoula highway patrol sometimes drove around Missing Lake.

As much as I had focused on the road I also tried to think of what I would say to Jackie to get her to come with me to the dragon's lair. Sherise would be there, too. She would probably make a comment or judgement about my choice to drive to the clinic with just my learner's permit and no licensed adult but I couldn't worry about that.

I hoped Jackie would understand. I hadn't heard any more from Zagros but I just knew within my gut that something was wrong. Something had happened. It could even be one of the twins. I realized I had sweat on my forehead that had nothing to do with the warm sunshine outside.

I eventually, cautiously pulled into a parking area at the veterinary clinic that was mostly hidden from the main highway that went through town. I wasn't sure if Ben would recognize the truck from our farm but on the off-chance he or his family drove by I didn't want them to worry.

I turned Norm off and peeled my fingers from the steering wheel. Before I even opened the door Jackie was there, right outside the driver's side of the truck. She had a serious expression on her face so I figured I was going to get a lecture.

"Jackie, I can explain," I began to say when I finally got out but she cut me off.

"We have to go, Luke. It's the dragons. Something is wrong."

"I know. That's why I'm here," I said. I didn't try to hide the confusion in my voice but I was glad I wasn't receiving a lecture on illegal driving and poor choices.

"Don't ask me how I know but Zagros communicated with me and I knew you would come here. Don't ever do it again but I secretly wanted you to drive Norm down the hill," she said. I followed her into the clinic where we appeared to be alone.

"Where's Sherise?" I asked as I peeked into each of the rooms. Jackie's veterinary bag and several boxes were on her desk. It reminded me of the very first time we went to the mountain to meet Tabitha. It was a bizarre collection of things that a vet would possibly need for a variety of procedures.

"Do you know what's wrong?" I asked without waiting for an answer on Sherise.

"Lets just get this all loaded into my truck and hit the road. I don't know if your dad knows anything. He's in meetings all day so I don't think I can get ahold of him. Did you leave a note at home for him?"

That was one thing I hadn't thought to do. I just knew I had to get into town and get up to the dragons. I grabbed one of the boxes and followed Jackie out to her truck. We loaded everything in and she stopped and stood, staring at the clinic one more time. She went back inside and came out with two scrub tops and her coveralls. It looked like she had packed up half of her clinic already so why not empty out her closet as well, I figured.

I jumped into the passenger seat, not even wanting to practice driving at that point. Jackie hadn't offered, either. She could drive aggressively at times and I wasn't comfortable driving that quickly on curvy mountain roads. With both of us sensing that time was of the essence, I was happy she got behind the wheel.

"I have no clue, Luke, before you ask. All I know is that it's very important that we get up there with some medical supplies," she told me once we were on the highway.

"Did Oscar call you?" I asked.

"No. I was just sort of summoned, you could say." She had a look of uncertainty on her face. "By Zagros."

"Me, too, but I can't explain how I knew that something serious had happened," I told her. My stomach took a nose dive when I said that. I regretted the cup of coffee I had enjoyed that morning.

"Yeah. I know what you mean," she agreed, nodding her head. My body pulled backwards as I felt the truck accelerate with her increased pressure on the gas pedal. The CD player remained as quiet as we did as we headed north on our mission. Little did we know how important a mission it was for the future of the baby dragons.

The funny thing about experiences like those ones, looking back, is that they help make you into the grown-up you're supposed to be. Even if you didn't know it at the time. And even if things look really bad or they're really scary, you are going to be better off for having survived the ordeal.

And for having done everything you could do to try to save one of the most important, special creatures you would ever dream of knowing because you're the only person who can.

I learned that fear was a pretty good motivator for me, like it had been when Harry was pale and collapsed in our living room. If nobody else was around to help then I could just sit there and watch everything end or I could dive in to try to help.

That's not to say that things always work out. Harry might not have lived. I might not have made the successful, solo drive to Jackie's clinic that day. But I know I tried. Not that I didn't get lectures from Dad and Jackie about driving without my real license. I knew they had to be parents, regardless of the reasoning behind my actions. And Jackie had fully admitted she secretly hoped I would come to town in Norm. When I asked her what she was going to do if I hadn't shown up when I did she told me she would have gone to the dragon's lair on her own.

We were both glad she hadn't, though. It turned out she needed me.

We knew right away from the blanched, worried look on Oscar's face as he met us where Jackie parked her truck in the tunnel. He was waiting in what I assumed was a golf cart, although I had never seen it before and nobody asked questions about it. I noticed that one of the sides was pushed inward, as if it had been under some great pressure. I didn't know much about golf but I guessed golf carts could be in accidents like regular cars.

All of the boxes fit onto the cart and the three of us squeezed into the bench seat together with Jackie's medical bag on her lap. Before driving us down the tortuous dark pathway Oscar turned to us and said, "There is a lot of blood. We must hurry. Hold on."

The little cart lurched forward and Jackie grasped onto the metal railings attached to the cart's flimsy-looking roof. I tried to anticipate how the cart would weave as we drove through the narrow tunnel and its headlights illuminated the crowded path. The orange glow was up ahead as always and the stacked boxes and piles of random objects weren't disturbed but it looked as if someone had moved things more to the side. Oscar had probably done that to get the golf cart to fit.

The headlights illuminated our dragon family in the distance but the cart wouldn't fit much further and Oscar turned it, and our bright light source off. I sucked in my breath quickly when I saw that all four dragons were present but they were all huddled together so I couldn't see what was going on.

I grabbed one of the boxes that looked like it had bandage material in it and Jackie had her medical bag. She pointed at another box of tubing for Oscar to bring. We moved as quickly as we could towards our dragon friends. As we approached them, Zagros moved slowly aside to show us what we were facing.

Or what we had to try to figure out we were facing. It was impossible for me to tell with how Tabitha had her arms around Helios who was seated on the ground in front of her. Blood was on her arms and all around the young golden dragon. His twin sister's eyes peeked out from behind Tabitha at me and glistened in the orange light.

"He was climbing, and fell," Zagros said without sound. Jackie nodded her head so I figured he had been communicating with both of us.

Jackie moved quickly and kneeled immediately in front of Tabitha and Helios. His eyes were half-open, as if he was partly sleeping.

"Tabitha, you are doing a great job holding off the wound," Jackie said out loud. She turned back and asked me to bring the box of bandages I had brought. I did and helped her dig out several packs of her four by four gauze pads. I still hadn't figured out where the blood was coming from and wasn't so sure Jackie knew, either.

"The wound is in his abdomen, as far as I can tell," Oscar told us. Jackie never took her eyes off of Tabitha's hands as she unwrapped the gauze packaging.

"I'm going to have you slide your hands off of Helios so that I can try to see the wound and then we will use the gauze on it but you need to stay right here to hold your boy, alright?" she asked the crimson dragon.

I didn't hear anything in my own head but it looked as if Tabitha and Jackie communicated something.

"You have trusted me with your own body before. I will do everything I possibly know how, my friend," Jackie responded.

Tabitha's hands moved slowly away from the young dragon's upper abdomen. A hole about the size of a baseball appeared through the blood and I could see the shimmer of new blood being released. Jackie immediately applied what I hoped was gentle but firm enough pressure with her gauze pads.

I looked over at Zagros, who stood next to Tabitha. I saw Cassiel slowly move behind Tabitha and her brother and almost snuggle up against her father. She was staring at her brother the entire time she moved. Zagros' large silver hand moved to her shoulder and pulled her towards him. It was then that he looked at me and his black eyes twinkled with what could only have been moisture.

"Thank-you, Luke," he said within my head.

Before I could say or think anything, Jackie said, "Luke, I need a bag of intravenous fluids and more gauze. Can you also please grab a suture kit and my head lamp? It is in the box that Oscar carried."

Oscar, himself searched for and retrieved the flashlight while I got a sterile, wrapped surgical kit and the requested bag of fluids. I noted that Jackie had brought the fluid bags she used for horses, that were at least four times as large as the ones she hooked up for small animals, like Harry.

Jackie had me douse the wound area several times as she tried to assess the wound itself. Each time she removed the gauze pads more blood would seep out. It wasn't pumping like that one vessel on Harry's spleen had done. I allowed myself some hope when I noticed that and it seemed as though Zagros felt that from me. I sensed the tiniest bit of lightness to his mood since the first time he called out for me back at the house.

Jackie's head lamp shone into the wound every time she peeked at it while I rinsed but her head blocked whatever she was looking at. Not that I wanted to look into a baby dragon's abdomen. Harry's abdomen had been enough for my lifetime as far as I had been concerned.

Little Helios made a moaning type of sound as she kept applying gauze to try to stop the bleeding. As this continued I didn't think as much blood was coming out but that could have been all the flushing I had been doing.

Jackie opened her surgical kit without saying anything out loud. I wondered if she and Tabitha were having a thought-conversation about what she was seeing.

"They are, Luke. Jackie is explaining everything," I heard Zagros tell me. Oscar hadn't said much the entire time. I glanced over at him and he looked worried. He was wringing his hands and rubbing his chin. His grey hair looked more wild than ever as he watched the medical drama happening in front of him. With his dragons.

Jackie opened her surgical pack and everything fell into place perfectly. She had tried to train me how to wrap the packs each time before we sterilized them so that all of the tools and sutures would be in exactly the same place each time. I hadn't mastered that skill yet but was glad that she or Sherise had. I realized then why it was so important to have the tools right where you needed them in the case of emergency surgeries.

"I'm going to get these skin bleeders sutured off and close this wound, guys," Jackie said without turning around. "I'm pretty sure the blood is mostly coming from here and nothing on the inside." She paused before adding, "Thank God."

She still needed me to rinse as she worked and Tabitha was able to hold gauze along edges of the wound that were bleeding.

"Its too large to just close together so I'm going to make a little flap, which will bleed a bit more," she said, presumably to all of us.

"Luke, in Oscar's box there is a bottle of lidocaine. Crack the top and pour it over the entire area, please," she told me. I put the fluid bag down gently and did as she said.

"Can I overdo it?" I asked, spraying lidocaine all over Helios' abdomen where the wound was. Jackie shook her head from side to side. I caught Tabitha's eyes as I was leaning in and they looked so tender and soft. She was worried, I could tell, but I felt her trust as well.

"I didn't have time to grab you anything shiny," I told her.

"Next time," her pretty voice told me.

"He has lost so much blood, Jackie. He looks weak already," Oscar finally spoke. His voice sounded fragile and worried.

"I know, Oscar, but we have to close the wound," she said. "Trust me?" Her last words sounded more like a question than a confidant statement.

"She can stitch things up pretty quickly, Oscar," I said.

“I trust you both,” Zagros said. Jackie paused and glanced towards Zagros and Cassiel and gave what looked like a brave smile before saying, “Thank you.”

With all of us huddled close together and the warmth of the lair itself I started to feel a bit clammy. I knew I had sweat on my brow but it took both hands to hold the bag of fluids.

We all watched her make a flap through his skin, avoiding or going around scales as she had to. With some strange scissor action beneath his skin the flap seemed to move forwards towards the opposite side of the hole. I wondered if young dragons had softer scales than adults, even though golden dragon scales were supposed to be pretty tough. When I got no response in my head I realized that Zagros didn’t know the answer, either.

As she worked, the head lamp on Jackie’s head bobbed up and down and despite my routine flushing I really couldn’t see much. I heard Helios make the moaning sound again and he rolled his head to the side. He righted it again, but I wasn’t sure how aware he was of everything going on. I hoped the lidocaine helped with the pain. Jackie’s needle was rapidly moving in and out, darting left and right and making the fast circles when she tied her knots.

Jackie sewed. Helios made random sounds. Oscar paced. I rinsed. Tabitha dabbed the gauze. Zagros held onto Cassiel, who never took her eyes off her brother. Our little surgical team repeated the moves over and over in the dimly lit lair with the light of the headlamp bobbing up and down until the wound slowly came together.

I sensed worry and concern from Zagros although we barely spoke during the surgery. It occurred to me that he had either let his guard down or he had chosen to let me inside and allow me to share his feelings. Any parent would be concerned for their young one in such a situation but I was acutely aware of his exact feelings. Maybe that was why words weren't necessary.

The wound was closed and the bleeding had stopped. Jackie reached out and gently rubbed the sleepy golden dragon's forehead, above his eyes and below the first spines that followed down his spine. It felt like all of us within the lair exhaled a sigh of relief even though we were all still so quiet.

I was just about to exclaim how excited I was to see the wound closed when Jackie announced to all of us that our work wasn't over and we had to get busy.

"Helios needs a blood transfusion."

NINETEEN

"Do you know if they are compatible? Do you know how much to give? What if he reacts to the transfusion?"

Oscar was a wealth of questions. His own brow was shining from being covered in sweat and his voice had a tone of panic in it.

"I don't know, Oscar," Jackie said. She stopped grabbing supplies from one of the boxes and turned to face him. "The amount of blood that Helios lost is too much for his young body. If it were one of the adult dragons I believe they would be fine but Helios probably won't survive if we don't try this. He is already half-way into shock and even though the bleeding has stopped he is going to need some healthy blood from one of his parents."

Nobody could argue about the amount of blood within the dragon's lair. And, looking at the little guy almost slumped in Tabitha's arms, leaning up against her, I had to agree that he looked pretty weak.

"Do whatever you need to do, please," came Tabitha's voice. Oscar, Jackie and I all turned to her when she spoke without saying a word out loud. "Not only are they the future of our species, they are our children and our love for them is immense."

I saw movement where Zagros stood. Cassiel was peeking out from beside her father. He had her wrapped in his arms and looked down at her when she moved. I saw her shiny eyes blink as she stared at me and while she didn't communicate with words I completely felt her plea. The young dragon had only met us a handful of times, including when she had hatched, but she must have sensed that she could trust us. Or maybe she knew her parents trusted us and that something frightening had been going down but we were trying to stop it.

She had to know how hurt her brother was. He hadn't moved much since we had arrived and there was all the blood. I didn't know if the two of them were able to communicate with each other yet, before the accident, but I suspected they were.

"Yes, they can communicate with each other and they are beginning to with us as well," said the voice of Zagros in my head. "She is trying to reach you now, too."

I nodded my head up and down and was aware that Jackie and Oscar were watching me.

"I know," I told them all. "I can feel her. She's asking us to fix him." I turned back to Jackie and Oscar and said, "She needs us to fix her brother."

"Is she speaking in English inside your head?" Jackie asked.

I turned back to Cassiel and Zagros and the young dragon's eyes locked onto mine once more. They sparkled and widened as the pleading sensation I felt from her intensified within my body. It was as if I was locked onto or into her very being as she made it crystal clear how she felt about her brother. There was love and friendship. It was a sense of togetherness or of them being part of each other. I was frozen in place, locked into a baby dragon's gaze and we had a big job to do. A sense of absolute purity and beauty washed through me as she was somehow able to show me her soul, possibly without even knowing she had.

The hairs on the back of my neck stood up and I shuddered briefly and uncontrollably.

I knew, instantly, that I wasn't going to be able to comprehend or process much of what had occurred and that I would have to revisit this afternoon in the lair many times in the future. Something amazing and unbelievable had just happened but I also felt a release and knew it had ended. Cassiel lowered her eyes from mine.

I moved towards Jackie and Oscar and said, "Lets get going, you guys. Cassiel needs this as much as Helios."

I held my hands out and Jackie started handing me intravenous tubing and supplies. I heard both Tabitha and Zagros in my mind, thanking me. I thought, "You're welcome," and hoped they got the message.

"Zagros, I'd like to use you for the donor, if that is alright. I really don't want to move Tabitha and Helios right now and you're the largest one here with the most blood to spare," Jackie said to him as we carried our equipment over towards him and his daughter.

"Do you have collection bags for his blood?" I asked, looking around at what was in our hands. Oscar stood a few steps behind Jackie, also holding supplies. I didn't see anything that resembled the blood bag we had used during Harry's transfusion weeks prior.

"Nope. I don't have a centrifuge to spin blood down, I don't have a collection bag and I don't know if blood from one dragon is compatible with that of another but we're going to wing it, Luke," Jackie said. She had sounded businesslike but not necessarily upset or angry.

"I am honored to give my blood to help Helios," Zagros said. He looked at Cassiel for a moment. He must have communicated something to her because she moved slowly over towards where Tabitha and Helios were seated. I watched her sit down by Tabitha's thick tail.

"We are basically going to go right from Zagros into Helios, so I should be alright without heparin," Jackie said. I figured she was talking primarily to herself, like she did sometimes during surgeries and procedures. "Unless dragons clot differently, of course," she added.

"Let me get a line going on Helios, guys," she said, moving over towards him. As she passed Oscar she grabbed an IV catheter about the size we had used for Harry and some bandage materials. I joined her, figuring she might want me to hold off a vein.

"I'm going to go on the assumption that dragon vessels are aligned like most animals'," Jackie said out loud. "It worked when we first met Tabitha and it needs to work now."

"I trust you both," Tabitha said.

I watched as Jackie lifted the forearm of the weakened dragon. As she turned it over slowly from side to side Helios opened his eyes and looked directly into my own. It wasn't anything like the connection I'd had with his sister. I figured that might have been due to his blood loss and lack of strength. I still tried to convey feelings of friendship and trust. The memory of him shoving me to the ground flashed through my mind but I tried to push it aside.

“There’s a vein here,” Jackie said, “but his pressure is low. Tabitha, Helios, I apologize if I have to poke around a little bit to get good access.” She had knelt down in front of him and his mother.

I saw that she had the small bag of fluids by her feet, ready to connect to the port once she got a line going. It always amazed me how she knew where to poke. Looking at his arm I couldn’t see a single thing that stood out as being different from any other area. She was also holding his arm off with her own left hand. I didn’t ask why but figured maybe she had more control that way.

Without hesitation, Jackie poked and I saw the flash of blood at the tip of the needle. She had used an area on the underside of his arm where it appeared there were less scales. She removed the gauge from within the catheter and hooked the bag of fluids up.

“Oscar, can you hold this bag higher than his arm? I just want to get a bit of blood pressure going and then we’ll get his father’s blood into him. Luke, I’m going to need you to come with me.”

Cassiel was looking over Tabitha’s arm at her brother. She looked concerned but didn’t take her eyes off of him. It seemed already that she had intense observation and concentration skills. I admired that and smiled, knowing that my own lack of concentration and focus was the joke of all of my friends.

"She watches and sees everything," Zagros said as we went back towards him.

"Yeah, I get it," I said out loud. Jackie just turned and raised her eyebrows at me.

"Get what?" she asked.

"Nothing. Just thinking about Cassiel and how observant she is."

Jackie nodded her head and said, "I've noticed that, too. She's incredible, really. It was like she had you in a trance earlier."

She explained to Zagros that his part of the deal would pretty much be the same thing only we would be removing blood from him with a syringe. Jackie would draw out blood and then block his vascular port, then immediately go and give it to Helios through a side port in his tubing, bypassing the clear fluids that he was already getting.

With Zagros she needed my help. His forearms were almost too round for me they were so muscular. I had to use both hands to do my best to wrap around it and it still wasn't a full circle. Jackie had me hold it all as tightly as I could as close to where she wanted to poke. I hoped I wasn't hurting him.

"I am not in discomfort," he said. I wasn't sure if he was making a bit of a joke about how weak I must have seemed compared to him. It was a great way to feel inadequate, comparing my wimpy adolescent self to a dragon.

“I am not making fun of you, Luke. You will have great physical strength to match your inner strength. All in good time,” the voice told me. I couldn’t help but smile.

Jackie had to poke a couple of times with Zagros. I figured it was because I probably wasn’t able to hold off the vein very well but she eventually found it. She immediately blocked the flow with a cap and then wrapped her vet wrap and tape around his forearm to secure the line.

Over what seemed like hours, Jackie would pull blood from Zagros into a syringe and then immediately go and inject it into the line going into Helios’ arm. Oscar and I took turns with the slowly dripping bag of fluids that had to be held above him. She methodically would cap off the port for Zagros and then block the flow of fluids into Helios, remembering to reverse each step after each injection.

Cassiel stayed by her mother’s tail the entire time. She had eventually stopped staring right at her brother but her eyes followed Jackie’s every move, each step of the way.

I didn’t want to talk and get her distracted. She kept mumbling things to herself that sounded like math equations. They were probably important things so I talked within my head to Zagros when I wasn’t holding the fluid bag.

“I’ll bet my dad is panicking right now,” I told him. Zagros assured me he had got word to him, though, and that he knew Jackie and I were helping in a scary situation.

“He is back at your house waiting for your return,” he said. “I have sent him the news that you are both helping to take care of things.”

“Do you know what Helios fell on?” I asked. “Were you here?”

“No. And, yes. He has been climbing the boxes and furniture and piles of things that are within the lair. He wants to fly already but is far too young.”

“Oh, man, did he leap off of something?” I asked. The image of Helios hurling himself off some elevation came to mind before he crash-landed on the ground.

“It was something like that, yes,” Zagros said. I had forgotten he could see images I pictured as well as the words that I thought.

“Jackie will probably want to give antibiotics to him with a big wound like that,” I suggested. “That’s what she did to Tabitha the first time we met her.”

I pictured how she had been in the enormous stocks during our first meeting, which Oscar had done for us, but not because she needed them. Jackie and I had no clue what kind of creature Tabitha was going to be back then and Oscar had no way of knowing how we would react to seeing her.

“You know,” I silently told my friend, “I kind of thought Tabitha might have been a Sasquatch.”

“That’s ridiculous,” he said, looking me right in the eye. “Sasquatches don’t exist.”

I couldn't help but laugh out loud when Zagros said that. Oscar and Jackie both looked over at us because my laughter had been high-pitched and uncontrolled. Part of that might have been a release from the extreme tension and stress we had all been under that day but I hadn't been expecting him to crack a joke.

Eventually Jackie decided the amount of blood was enough. I didn't ask what she based that on largely because I didn't want to sound like I doubted her. We all watched her draw up an injectable antibiotic I had seen her use on cats in the clinic. She injected it into an area by Helios' tail. The sleepy golden dragon didn't even flinch.

Oscar looked less freaked out when she removed both intravenous ports from Zagros and Helios and started to clean up her supplies.

"What do we do now?" he asked. We all looked over towards Tabitha and her dragon children.

"We wait," Jackie said. And we did.

We waited for half an hour, until little Helios lifted his head up and almost pulled away from Tabitha. His energy and strength must have caught her off guard but he was too weak to resist her hold and slumped back into her body.

"This is good, yes?" we heard Zagros ask.

"Yes, absolutely. But it is all a waiting game as to whether his body responds and then whether his body tolerates the new blood or not," Jackie explained out loud.

Jackie glanced down at her watch and told me it was already six o'clock in the evening. I didn't know if I was surprised to hear that or not. Sometimes the moments had passed so slowly and other times there hadn't seemed to be time to stop to think that day.

"How would you feel about staying the night with the dragons, Luke?" she asked me.

"Oh, um, wow," I stammered. "I mean, yeah, right? That's the best idea because then I can help make sure Helios is doing well kind of like how we had to watch Harry." I heard the excitement in my own voice at having a sleep over with the dragon family and tried to keep that down.

We all discussed it and everyone agreed it was the best thing. Oscar said he would get some food and water and bedding for me at his house and Jackie would get home to see Dad.

"What about work tomorrow, though. You have appointments and its one of Sherise's days off," I remembered.

"Actually, that works out well because your dad and I can come into town and he can help me with the one surgery I have booked. If anything else looks too challenging to do myself I'll have him stay, otherwise he can drive up here to see how things are. Then you two can drive back home afterwards. " Jackie said.

Adults always amazed me at how they could plan ahead so many things all at one time. How their brains could picture two, three and four steps ahead of the first step I hadn't even considered.

Helios began moving a bit more and Tabitha allowed him to step away from her arms. He didn't go very far and sat back down on his own. Cassiel went to him and sat next to him. She watched her brother slowly lay down and she joined him, both curling their tails around their limbs. They reminded me of how some of our dogs slept, curled up next to one another. I sometimes laid in the snow with our dog team. It always gave me a feeling of camaraderie curled up with my team, not to mention the physical warmth. It was always better if we had hay or straw to lie on, of course. I had been looking forward to camping out with our team with Dad when I had my snowmobile wreck that winter.

"That was your first time sleeping in a dragon's lair," Zagros said and I smiled. He had been inside my head watching the same memory with me.

Jackie waited for a little while longer before she and Oscar left.

"You sure you're going to be alright?" she asked one more time.

"See, this is how I know you're not my real mom," I told her and she laughed,

"What the heck does that mean?" she asked.

"No real mother would let her only child have a sleepover with four dragons in a secret mountain lair in the middle of nowhere," I said.

"You're right, Luke. I'm not your mom," she said, laughing again. Jackie reached out and tousled my hair. Tabitha finally moved away from the cave wall and left her sleeping young dragons for a moment as she,

Zagros and I watched Jackie and Oscar fire the golf cart up and back up to where they could turn around.

“Are you scared?” Tabitha silently asked me.

“No. Not anymore. How could I be scared with you guys here?”

Tabitha leaned her head against Zagros’ shoulder and sighed. I felt hungry and exhausted and yet all I wanted to do was stand there with my two grown-up dragon friends. We had crossed species lines again as a team and I didn’t want the moment to end. Maybe I was going to be a more important team player after all.

TWENTY

My night in the dragon's lair was a far cry from most of the sleepovers I had ever been to. For starters, I hadn't been to many with my human friends. We always lived out of town and without my driver's license I had to ask Dad or Jackie to drag me back and forth. When I was younger, in Vancouver, I remembered a friend from hockey spent the night at our place because his parents worked early in the morning and couldn't take him to practice before school started. I couldn't even remember that kid's name.

It seemed to me that guys didn't do the sleepover thing as much as girls did. Sure, Ben and I had slept over that year at each other's house but that was largely so other things could happen the next day without four parents being involved. Like the spring dance. And taking my learner's exam in Missoula.

It wasn't like I didn't enjoy sleeping over and talking late at night with my friends. It was fun playing video games late into the night and sleeping in sleeping bags on family room floors. Sam and Alec and I and maybe one or two other guys on the junior varsity hockey team had slept over at each other's houses to watch hockey games or celebrate birthdays. It was different playing hockey in the states, though, because we played it for the high school. Most of the kids in Canada, as far as I knew, played for their community and themselves.

We were all still a team, it just wasn't a school sport. So our parents had to get us to practices and all around the city for games. Vancouver had a ton of ice rinks, too. You could be driving for two hours just to get up to Squamish or out to Hope to play in a tournament and none of it was covered by the school. When I started playing high school hockey in Bismarck I was pretty shocked that the school covered our travel and some of our uniforms. It seemed strange to show up to an ice rink in a school bus. Dad still had to pay for my skates and my stick but it was a completely different set of circumstances and one that didn't apply anymore with us living in Missing Lake.

As we all watched the young dragons sleep that night, Zagros and Tabitha asked a lot of questions about hockey and sports in general. Zagros found it humorous that we would put on "body armor" to slam into one another when we weren't born with any serious body protection of our own.

"It is one thing to have mighty strength, long claws and tough scales all over our bodies," he tried to explain to me, "but to apply these protective items that appear uncomfortable and bulky all in order to protect yourself from something you were not born to do seems preposterous."

Tabitha had questions about the ice rink and why we would choose to make a dangerous situation even more difficult.

"You are wearing this unnatural, heavy armor that must slow you down and you force yourself to chase objects on a slippery surface?" she asked as the night time passed.

"And you can use physical force to get others out of the way so that you can retrieve the object?" Zagros asked inside my head. Neither of them spoke out loud but I had been. I had thought that if the baby dragons were even slightly awake they could get used to the sound of my voice.

"How is this even remotely fair when you are at an age of such change," Tabitha continued with what felt like an inquisition. "Some of your peers must be twice your size and then you will be twice another person's size. The physical differences could lead to serious consequences." She had sounded confused inside my head.

"Well, yeah, that's a good point," I said, nodding my head. The three of us were seated where we could face Helios and Cassiel as they continued to sleep side by side where Helios had received his transfusion a few hours prior.

"I didn't mature as quickly as some guys my age so when we got to the checking, or the physical force part of the game, I took some pretty big falls until I learned to get out of the way faster."

I had a very clear memory of my fist huge wipe-out back in Bismarck, where a kid who looked like he had been shaving for years locked eyes with me seconds before I felt the blow. I had possession of the puck and was carrying it down the boards, hoping to find Sam or someone else to pass it to. I had a feeling the giant from the other team was barreling down on me and I lifted my eyes from the puck for one second. My eyes locked onto his and I saw him smile through his face mask. That, and the sensation that I had been hit by a bus, was all I remembered about the hit. Or at least, the initial contact from the other player was clear in my mind but there was a second sensation of crash-landing, as if from leaping off of a speeding train that was also firmly embedded in my memory. And the fact they blew the whistle because I hadn't got up in an acceptable amount of time.

I remembered Sam kneeling over me and seeing his mouth move. It took a moment before the ringing in my ears quieted down and I heard him say, "Dude, you had serious air time. You got frigging clobbered." I shook my head and chuckled at the memory, which hadn't been very humorous at the time. Coach benched me for the rest of that period and the school medic had to check me out before they let me back on the ice afterwards.

They had asked all the usual concussion questions like what my name was and did I know what day it was. I had answered everything well enough to be allowed to play in the third period. The ringing in my ears had lasted a full day, though. Not that I had told anyone that.

"Until now," Zagros' voice came through.

"Did you revisit that hit with me just now?" I asked, a bit hopeful that they had seen me in what was a type of athletic combat but more embarrassed at how my side of the story ended.

"I think you humans have a different type of bravery than we do, Luke," Tabitha said. I saw Zagros tip his head to the side like Baxter did, in an almost curious way.

"Well," I said to both of them, "I didn't feel especially brave that game but I didn't cry, at least." I laughed to myself again when I recalled some of the other players on the bench who watched my hit told me they wanted to cry when my body slammed into the ice.

"Humans and their interest in dangerous sporting events fascinates me," Zagros said. "Tabitha and I have discussed this before."

"Yes," she silently agreed. "We wonder if we are all of similar spirit but we dragons have to fight for survival. For our food, for our hidden existence, for our shelter and for any family that we can bring to the world."

As she spoke she looked towards Helios and Cassiel. She raised her hand and pointed towards them, saying, "It is what we must do in order to keep our species and ourselves alive. Perhaps the humans have an innate need to continue to fight and struggle for their kingdoms and families, even if it is done for game or sport instead of pure survival. Your kingdom is your team and you fight valiantly to preserve honor, and thus, survive."

I tried to wrap my brain around what she said and the fact she and Zagros probably had given that a lot of thought. We did fight hard so that our team technically survived, or hopefully made the final top tier of the playoffs. But we weren't doing it to survive for all of eternity. There would be plenty of other hockey players and teams from every city in every country in many parts of the world.

"I don't think there's a whole lot to compare there, Tabitha," I said. "Part of your guys' struggle to survive comes from the fact that you have to hide from us humans who took over the place. Hockey players don't have to hide in the daylight and come out to darkened ice rinks buried in the center of mountains to duke it out all in the name of

Century High School's kingdom." I paused before adding, "What we do is just hockey. What you do is try to stay alive."

Before Zagros or Tabitha could weigh in on the already heavy discussion we heard the baby dragons making soft, almost chirping sounds to each other. They hadn't moved from their sleeping positions but they were both chirping quietly, out loud, in the dim orange light of the lair.

We watched little Cassiel open her eyes and raise her head. She reached out with her short forearms and touched her brother, who then opened his own eyes. The chirping and tweeting sounds continued. I imagined it was similar to the sounds of the birds in the high tree top canopies of an African jungle or a rain forest. I wondered if their parents could understand the language.

"Not yet," Tabitha's voice rang through my head.

"But we are learning to understand each other slowly through gestures and our thoughts," added Zagros. I looked at the enormous silver dragon seated next to me. His scales glistened with beams of light flickering off various ones at different angles all over his body. I caught a glimpse of some of the jagged edges on certain scales and one larger area that took up several scales along his shoulder area. It looked like a scar. Suit of armor, indeed.

"I should check to see how his gum color looks, if that's okay," I said, getting to my feet. Jackie had given me a sparkly green, small flashlight that read, 'Missing Lake Veterinary' on it. I figured she was adding to her advertising goodies she liked to give out to people while feeding her sparkly needs at the same time. I clicked the little flashlight on and made my way to the young dragons. Neither Zagros nor Tabitha tried to stop me and even Cassiel continued to lie next to her brother as I approached.

"Hi, guys, I'm just going to check on our patient here," I said. I knew they wouldn't be able to understand what I was saying or doing but I hoped the tone of my voice would keep them calm. I also had hoped how I talked would also keep me calm.

I kneeled down slowly in front of them and reached my hand out to Cassiel's face. Her dewy eyes were glued to my face as she leaned forward slightly and sniffed at me. I hoped she wouldn't pull another Jedi Mind Trick but I held her gaze anyhow. She turned to look at Helios, almost as if she knew why I was there. I wasn't sure what I smelled like, having not had a chance to wash up after all of the blood and anxiety and stress from earlier but she didn't pull away after sniffing me.

I held my hand to her brother's face. His eyes were open although they weren't as alert-looking as his sister's. Still, they held my gaze and I heard him sniff my scent. I knew he could smell a lot more of me than just my hand and I couldn't remember if I had applied deodorant that morning or not. It seemed like days or even weeks had passed since I woke up and leisurely enjoyed coffee alone at our house that morning.

"I'm going to touch your mouth, Helios," I said, "and I'm going to shine this light in there. I just want to see how your body is doing with your dad's blood inside you." I wasn't sure if that was too much information or not. What did one tell a baby dragon when you were going to examine his gums for their color?

Nobody moved and I heard nothing from Zagros and Tabitha so I lifted the round, blue beam of the flashlight and shone it into his mouth. With my other hand I lifted what must have been his cheek and leaned in close so I could try to assess things. The gums felt moist. I remembered that was a good thing. They also looked a much brighter pink than I had noticed before. I wasn't sure what color dragon mucus membranes were supposed to be but I figured I would have something to report to Jackie in the morning, at least.

I applied a tiny amount of pressure with my fingertip to the gums and watched it blanch, then unblanch and return to the bright pink color almost immediately. I knew that three seconds was the general rule for most animals and a healthy vascular system but I wasn't sure about dragons. Again, it was something reportable and hopefully a sign that his body was not rejecting Zagros' blood.

"Let us hope so, Luke," came the voice of my friend, Zagros. I thought he sounded a bit relieved but I wasn't sure if that was because he was inside my head or because I was inside their lair.

"It is both," he added.

That was about as crazy as our sleepover got that night. Oscar had brought a pillow and there were plenty of blankets in the lair so I made a sort of bed area for myself by Helios and Cassiel. Zagros and Tabitha were nearby but I don't think either of them slept much at all that night. As for myself, I don't even remember shutting my eyes.

...

Oscar came to the lair before I was even awake. I was aware of his voice during my dream, though, and eventually I realized where I was and what had happened the night before. I sat up faster than I should have and felt a swirling, dizzy sensation. I also caused Cassiel to stir. The three of us were still huddled close together. The golden tail of Helios was draped over my feet.

"Oh, hey, good morning, pretty girl," I said to the dragon whose scales appeared more green than black. I wondered if they would seem to change color throughout her long life or if it had something to do with the time of day.

I made the effort to move more slowly and reached around the blankets to find my shiny green flashlight. By that time Helios started to stir. They did their jibber-jabber thing back and forth with the chirping and tweeting, always in hushed tones. Their lips moved around the sounds they made and they even looked at me from time to time, as if I could understand them.

"I'm going to do the mouth thing again, if that's okay," I said while raising my hand towards Helios. His eyes looked more sharp and bright than they had the night before. He pulled his face back a little bit but eventually let me lift his cheek and shine the light again inside his mouth. Moist. Pink. Quick refill time on the gum blanching. Before I could explain myself to Oscar or the dragon parents his golden arm jutted out from where he laid and within seconds he somehow had his pointy claws in my own mouth. His eyes narrowed and as I was recoiling backwards to try to get my feet beneath me both baby dragons began a high-pitched chirping that could only be described as hysterical laughter.

Finally on my feet, I looked back towards Zagros.

"I think he feels better, Luke," I heard him say.

"You think?" I called back.

Oscar had brought a couple of hard boiled eggs for me with cold toast that I devoured. Helios was moving all four limbs and would stand for a few minutes every now and then before he would sit down again. Cassiel never left his side all morning.

I told Oscar that I had checked on him through the night and everything looked like it was supposed to. At least, as far as I knew. I explained that when Harry had his transfusion, Jackie mostly wanted him to be calm and quiet and not move around much for the first few days. I wanted them all to try to keep Helios from being active because we weren't out of the woods for several days, if not weeks yet. I had no clue how long a dragon with a blood transfusion needed before you declared them safe. I also knew he had a boat load of sutures in his abdomen that had to hold and that any vigorous activity would definitely strain them.

"I understand what you are saying better than how you are saying it, Luke," Zagros told me. I wasn't sure if that was a compliment or not.

Dad showed up later that morning and we told him everything about how the night had gone, including the suturing and the blood transfusion. He wanted to know as much as he could about it all even though he'd said Jackie had told him about the entire event when she got home. Zagros showed him where he had sat and where we got the intravenous catheter into his arm. I assumed he was inside of Dad's head because Dad was answering out loud to a dragon who was silent on the outside. He was also silent in my own head during their discussion.

Dad sat with Cassiel and Helios, who seemed wary of him at first. By that time Helios was walking several steps in a row and seemed much more his bright, energetic self. That worried me and I silently sent that concern to both Tabitha and Zagros.

"We know, Luke. We'll try to restrict his activity," Tabitha replied.

Dad and I made our rounds with Oscar and each of the dragons as we got ready to head back to Missing Lake and then to our home. It felt like it had been a long time since I had been there and I missed our animal companions. Dad told me Baxter and the cats had all slept on my bed, almost as if they were waiting for me.

Oscar and Dad headed to the golf cart but before I joined them I went to my crimson friend, my first dragon friend ever, and dug into my pocket to retrieve a little gift for her. Her eyes sparkled like always whenever I offered her something special.

"I forgot about this little guy," I said, as I placed the shiny green flashlight into the palm of her upturned hand. She snorted and warm air rushed towards me which blew my hair back from my head. We locked eyes and the sides of her mouth turned upwards as her amber-colored eyes sparkled yet again.

TWENTY-ONE

"You must be starving," Dad said as we took a seat at a table by the window in the café in Missing Lake. It was already the middle of the afternoon by the time we got back to town and traded vehicles at Jackie's clinic. She wasn't overly busy and had already had lunch so Dad and I decided to grab a sandwich before we drove back home.

Gwen had smiled and waved at me when we first came in but a different person took our order. I realized, as I was asking for a club house with fries, that it was Lindsey from school. She and I never interacted that much during the school year but she seemed to know all about me. The few conversations I had ever had with her usually involved horses. She might have even known Sherise, Jackie's assistant. I wondered if Gwen had said anything about me. Lindsey's long brown hair was pulled back in a headband which made her green eyes stand out. I'd never noticed them before.

"So, how are your dogs doing this summer, Luke?" she asked before Dad ordered. I saw a quick smirk flash across his face but chose to ignore it.

"Good, although I think they miss the snow," I told her. I had no clue how much she knew about me.

"I don't miss the snow. Did the one do alright after the emergency surgery you helped with?" she asked, with a genuine look of concern on her face.

"Yes, that's Harry. He's doing really well. How did you know about that?" I couldn't help but ask.

Lindsey laughed and said, "Luke, everyone knows everything about each other in our school." Dad and I both joined her in laughing.

"I believe the entire community operates that way," Dad said and we laughed some more.

"Don't you have horses?" I asked, with a bit of hesitation in my voice. I hoped I hadn't got her confused with someone else because that would sound worse than if I didn't ask at all. Luckily a big smile appeared on her face and she nodded her head.

"Yes, we have five horses. Mostly Quarter Horses because I do barrels," she excitedly told us. I must have had a blank look on my face because she giggled and added, "They're a rodeo type of horse and I'm a barrel racer, where we compete against the clock running around barrels."

"Doesn't sound any more insane than riding a sled behind a dozen dogs," I said and we all laughed again.

Dad ordered the same thing as me and when the food arrived we both agreed it was an excellent choice. Crispy, meaty bacon and turkey were exactly what I needed after the stress and lack of sleep the day and night before. With a few tables around us we didn't talk much about the dragons but we were able to discuss a few things without giving them away.

"How many stitches do you think Jackie used?" Dad asked me in his normal, non-hushed voice. That was a completely acceptable question because if people knew Jackie was the veterinarian they probably knew I helped her out from time to time.

"Oh, man, there were a lot. As many as with Harry's spleen and even then I lost count," I told him between mouthfuls of tasty sandwich. I looked down at my fries and secretly wished they were coated in thick, brown gravy before I added, "She told me she used more than was probably necessary but she didn't know how active he would be afterwards and wanted to make sure the wound stayed closed."

Dad was silent as he ate his sandwich. Just as it looked like he was going to say something, Gwen stopped by our table.

"Hi, Mr. Houser. Hi, Luke. How are you guys doing today?"

I made sure to swallow what I had been chewing before answering.

"Great, we're both great. How is work going for you?" I asked. "I see Lindsey has started. Has that helped?"

"Totally," she answered with an exaggerated voice. "We don't work every shift together but she's really funny and helpful and she is doing a great job. Its kind of nice getting to know her a bit, too."

"I don't really know her all that well, myself," I said.

"I know. I think how weird it is in our little school that some of us don't know each other very well."

I nodded my head and suggested we make a point next year to socialize with more kids. I flashed back to my short visit with Anne-Marie and how little we knew about people even when we did talk with them regularly. Gwen agreed but couldn't stay because a customer at another table was trying to catch her attention.

"Hope you liked your lunch. I have to go," she said. I watched her pony tail bound around in little circles as she quickly walked off to the guy who was waving at her.

After a few silent moments where we continued to work on our sandwiches Dad asked, out of nowhere, "Is there something between you and Gwen?" He didn't lift his eyes from his sandwich or even stop eating after he asked it. I looked down at my own fries as I felt that all-too-common flush of uncomfortable heat rise up my neck and chin. That wasn't really like Dad. He never usually asked about my friends. Especially not girlfriends.

"Um, well, uh," I stammered. What could I say? That I sort of, kind of, maybe liked her and that maybe Bethany had suggested one time that Gwen liked me but obviously she didn't because she was suddenly slow dancing with the best looking, most popular, older guy in our school? And that I had seen them kissing in front of the café this summer?

"Hey, I'm just bugging you, son," Dad said. His forehead was wrinkled which made him look slightly worried. He must have seen the redness in my skin. "You two seem very relaxed with each other, like you have a nice rapport. I shouldn't have said that. I don't want to be like your mom and push you into having girlfriends at your age."

"No, its okay, Dad," I told him. I watched him pour even more ketchup over his fries, which made me laugh a little, breaking up the anxiety I had felt. The ketchup bottle squeaked as he squeezed every last drop of it onto his plate.

I decided to leave myself out of the question altogether when I told him, "Gwen is dating Callum, who will be a senior next year."

Dad looked surprised but all he said, in a questioning tone, was "Callum?"

That, thankfully, was all Dad ever said about Gwen and girlfriends unless I brought it up.

We spent the rest of the afternoon in the dog yard, poop-scooping and visiting with each of the dogs. I had a clipboard that I carried while I followed Dad around to each pen where he examined each dog. We took notes on their eyes, their teeth, their body condition, their hair coats, their attitudes and energy levels, and even how their poop looked.

Jackie was more fixated on the poop thing than either of us but over the years we had learned she was right that sometimes a dog's poop could tell you a story or two about the pooper.

As we were examining one of the newest dogs, Candy, with her sister, Lucy, Dad commented that their hair coats were coming in really nicely. The four black and white littermates that had come to the kennel together had all looked tough when winter was coming to a close. They had been blowing their hair coats in thick tufts. That, in itself, wasn't unusual for sled dogs in the springtime. You never wanted to have Chap Stick on your lips around any shedding Husky that time of year. But

Candy, Lucy and their brothers, Martin and Burnett had all looked particularly tough with clumps of dry hair coming out by the handful.

At the time I had asked Dad about their deworming status and he couldn't remember what the previous owner had said. Whenever new dogs joined the kennel, though, Jackie always went over their vaccination records and took care of any breeding potential within days of their arrival. She had agreed with us that their hair coats looked particularly rough back in the early spring and had suggested changing our dewormer for the entire kennel.

She ordered a huge bottle of a thick, yellow liquid that the dogs didn't seem to mind tasting when we syringed it into them one weekend. Half of the dogs got a bit loose for a day or two which wasn't much fun given the warmer temperatures outside but in the end it appeared to have done the trick. Candy's hair coat was thick and lush and it looked like it glistened in the late afternoon summer sunshine. Her blue eyes looked like they sparkled. They were striking surrounded by her black hair. Jackie had told us that their lush-looking hair coats probably had as much to do with the timing of the year as anything else. Huskies loved to shed their winter coats every spring.

Burnett, who was mostly black except for the tips of his bushy tail and his front paws shone like I imagined hot lava would.

The four dogs had come from a musher who lived up by the Canadian border. They were very active and seemed to feel fantastic. Their body condition was also terrific with a nice curve to their waistlines when we looked from above.

I always enjoyed spending time with the dogs. Even doing things like routine physical exams and making records of it all was enjoyable. Every single experience was just another part of building our team and increasing our trust in each other. I hadn't been able to really focus completely on the dogs since Helios and Cassiel had hatched, particularly when I was in school but it was great to make and spend the time keeping track of our kennel.

The dogs helped ground me after a crazy, incredible twenty-four hours that seemed unbelievable when my mind drifted back to the lair. I relished spreading my fingers and rubbing my hands slowly through thick hair coats and making notes on their physical conditions.

I enjoyed watching how the dogs interacted, especially when we weren't in their pens. Some dogs watched us, usually with barks punctuating the air, while others seemed to try to get our attention. It was important to know and stay current on the many personalities of our various dogs. The more time you spent with them, the more you saw differences or unique qualities. And it was easier to know if something was wrong if there was a change in their particular personalities as well.

Like Jackson, one of our leaders, who spun in continuous circles when we were paying attention to him. He managed a straight line when hooked up to the sled but on his own if you even looked at him from across the dog yard the spinning begun. He always spun to the left, too, which cracked me up every single time he got going. Sometimes he would spin so quickly his body looked almost horizontal in the air.

That day he was putting on a spinning clinic for the rest of the dogs. Most of them seemed to ignore him, while a few watched. I always wondered what went through their heads when they saw him pulling Louies like that.

Goofy, red-headed Sonny was a funny dog. He and his littermates had come to our kennel as puppies and he stood out for his personality and his looks. None of his siblings had the same bright orange hair coat and none of the others were as silly and happy in their behavior. Dad had feared that Sonny would never be a successful runner because he seemed content being a pet or a companion. However, by the end of winter he was running well with a smaller team which had made both of us pretty happy.

Sonny's sister, Raven, was all about business and had been training with Dad's main team early that winter. Sonny had taken longer than the others to learn just about everything but we just let him mature and develop at his own rate. He seemed to always try to get our attention right away and we didn't discourage his behavior. If there was one thing you wanted in your dog team it was trust. A little affection didn't hurt much, either.

Nena, as expected, was her calm, demure, elegant self. She sat on top of her dog box and seemed to observe the handling and visiting Dad and I had been doing. Nena had been depressed after we lost Robson soon after moving to Montana. She hadn't been the only one, I thought to myself as I recalled how distracted and upset I had been about Robson.

I was surprised to feel moisture in both of my eyes when I reflected back on Robson's death. I hadn't thought about it much and certainly hadn't cried about him in months. I had never lost one of our dogs before that and it must have stuck with me in a deeper place than I'd imagined.

"You alright, Luke?" Dad asked, pausing from rubbing his hands along Nena's spine.

"Yeah," I answered. I looked up at the blue sky and tried to will the tears away. "I just got thinking about Robson and how close he and Nena were."

Dad stood up and clapped his hand on my shoulder and said, "I think about our old friend now and then, too and I miss him. He was a great dog and those two made a great pair of leaders but we had to do what we did for his sake, son. There was nothing more we could do because of his cancer. Saying goodbye was a kindness. Like our last gift to our special friend."

I swallowed hard against the lump in my throat. I knew Dad was just trying to make me feel better but it just made the tears fall out of my eyes and down onto my shirt. There weren't many of them and I managed to wipe them away quickly but I was pretty sure Dad saw them. We didn't comment on it because I saw him wipe a few away, too.

TWENTY-TWO

Days passed with Oscar updating Jackie over the telephone at the clinic as to how young Helios had been doing. The hardest part about his recovery had been keeping him still. According to Oscar, Zagros and he had built a cage-like area within the main part of their lair where they would contain him for a few hours each day. Cassiel joined him, apparently, but both dragons were obviously bored from what Tabitha told him.

I tried picturing a play pen large enough to hold two young dragons and it made me smile. Probably most sixteen year olds were picturing cool cars or video games or musical concerts and there I was picturing two dragons, one gold and one green, driving their parents nuts.

Jackie became more and more confidant that he was going to be alright with each passing day and each new phone call. I was at the clinic when Oscar called a couple of times and the relief on Jackie's face was unmistakable. It was probably the same on mine.

We had a full surgery schedule one morning with two dogs to neuter and a lump to remove on a third. Thankfully Jackie didn't need any help with the neuters other than to help hold them while they were being anesthetized. They were already partly sedated so it wasn't difficult and both were medium-sized dogs anyhow. I watched the lump removal and was fascinated by how the tissue was so shiny and slippery looking. Jackie said the lump was a lipoma, or a tumor made of fat. Her gloved hands looked like they had been handling raw bacon by the time she was finished and the dog went to the kennel room to recover.

I offered to bike to the café to grab us lunch and Jackie happily accepted. I enjoyed getting out into the fresh, warm air and get a bit of exercise. The café had become a fun routine for all of us.

As I pedaled through town towards the café I saw an unmistakable blue pickup truck parked immediately out front. It was Callum's truck, Baby. I had no desire to see him and Gwen kiss out front again so I ducked into the small alley immediately next to the building to park my bike but ended up just about slamming into Callum and Gwen. Kissing.

Only, Gwen's back was to me and her long brown hair wasn't in a pony-tail. And she was taller. In fact, it wasn't Gwen at all. My embarrassing near-collision and even more embarrassing discovery brought their make out session to a rapid halt and I lowered my eyes and started to turn my bike around. My face felt hotter than ever.

"Hey, uh, Luke, uh..." stammered Callum as he stepped away from the brown haired girl.

"No biggie, just going to get out of here," I said, with an obvious quiver in my voice. I looked up past Callum and saw Lindsey's bright green eyes looking back at me. We both quickly looked away.

"Luke," Callum said but I made a point to interrupt him. Almost slamming into people you know with your bike was one thing but while they were kissing? I was mortified.

"I didn't know you and Gwen broke up, I'm just getting lunch," I stammered.

I suddenly felt Callum's strong hand clasp down on my shoulder. I felt like the ninety-eight pound weakling from the comic books because I almost winced when he did it but more from being startled than anything else. I was still looking at the ground.

"Look, that's the thing, buddy. Gwen doesn't know," he said.

An image of Gwen with her pony-tail flipping around her freckly face with a ribbon and makeup that matched her outfit flashed through my mind. I looked up at Callum.

"This just accidentally happened," he told me.

Not having any experience with girlfriends or kissing I wasn't going to say much although I was fairly certain you didn't just accidentally go to the alley to kiss your girlfriend's co-worker. I was also pretty sure that I was supposed to wind up and punch Callum in the face to defend my friend's honor but that wasn't going to happen. As quickly as the thought came to my mind I got rid of it, having pictured what it would look like for me to pretend to know how to punch someone. I would have to jump in the air to do it, too, which sealed the fate for that move.

I glanced back towards the café, wondering how I would face Gwen with my little discovery running around inside my head. Callum must have sensed that.

"She's not working today, you don't have to see her," he told me.

I bent my knees and slowly pulled out from under his hand and started to back up.

"Okay. I'm just going to get my lunch and forget about this if that's cool with you two," I said. My voice had more of its normal sound to it, thankfully.

"You're not going to say anything, are you, Luke?" Lindsey asked from behind Callum. She hadn't moved since I busted them and she looked back at the ground as soon as she had asked the question.

"I'm not saying anything," I said, shaking my head. "That's Callum's job."

I looked directly at the high school heartthrob who everyone adored. The bright, talented athlete with the cool truck, the great name and the mature physique who was admired by teachers, coaches, team-mates and classmates. The guy we all wanted to be and the one all the girls wanted to be with. And even though I got to the café on my bike, with my skinny arms and legs and a bit of acne on my forehead that morning and several dog and cat hairs on my jacket, I was just fine not being him.

It was better to be me.

It was Callum's turn to lower his head and look uncomfortable.

"Yeah, man, of course," he said, his voice much quieter than I had ever heard it before.

I picked up my pace and backed my bike out of the alley. I ended up leaving it out front, by Callum's famous truck. As hungry as I had been riding down there I didn't have the same feeling when I went inside to order but I still did. I knew I would want to eat by the time I got back to the clinic. I gave my order to a guy behind the cash register and let my eyes wander around the busy café. Another woman was serving tables who looked much older than Gwen or Lindsey. I wondered if she was the owner and made a mental note to ask Gwen sometime. I just hoped it wouldn't be any time in the near future.

Something was waving in the background from a table by the window. I tried to ignore it, assuming it wasn't anyone trying to get my attention but it turned out to be Anne-Marie, seated with who must have been her parents. I smiled and waved back at her. She didn't invite me over and I didn't want to intrude so I just turned back towards the kitchen and waited for our lunches.

There was no sign of Callum's truck, him or Lindsey when I left the café.

As I peddled back to the clinic I wrestled with whether to tell Jackie about the Gwen and Callum thing or not. She had never asked about my friends' personal lives and I appreciated that. I figured if I told her then that might invite future questions about things and I wasn't comfortable with that. It wasn't like I wanted to ask Gwen out. I hadn't even been sure I was going to ask her to slow dance we me but I still felt bad for her as her friend.

I partly wanted to tell Jackie so that I wouldn't have to explain if I acted differently the next time we saw Gwen. We had been enjoying our summer of lunches from the café and if we went there and she served us it could be really strange, especially if Gwen ever found out that I knew about Callum and Lindsey before she did.

I didn't want to mention it to Dad because of how I reacted when he had asked me about Gwen. I couldn't call Ben up or email it to him. That felt like gossip and it wasn't my place to tell our friends anything about any of them. It was reasonable to think that Gwen would eventually tell Bethany but girls told girls things like that more than guys did. At least they did on the television shows.

I hoped Gwen never found out that I came up on Callum and Lindsey like that in the alley. It had been embarrassing for all of us. I didn't care about Callum or Lindsay being ashamed because they should have been. I didn't want her to think about how awkward and uncomfortable the whole situation had been for me.

I wanted to talk to someone about it but the only person I could trust was Zagros. And he was pretty busy with dragons in play pens up inside the belly of a mountain. At least Baxter and the cats would hear me out.

Like so many times, though, Zagros had heard my thoughts in that strange, mysterious way we were connected and he showed up in the backyard as I was cleaning up our small bonfire that night.

Bonfire season was coming to a close for those of us who lived in rural western Montana. As summer continued the trees and ground would be drying out and lightning strikes or careless campers made the threat of forest fires a very real thing. We had a nice, rock-rimmed fire pit but the three of us had agreed to not push our luck. We were completely surrounded by forest and the thought of a fire being our fault was daunting.

I had been shoving the last few glowing embers and branches around in the ashes when I felt his presence. I hadn't heard or felt him whoosh above my head so he must have flown in from another direction. Even before seeing him in the smoky, dim light I knew he was there. And I felt comforted by his presence.

"Today was awkward for you," his voice said.

I smiled and laughed a little, saying, "You could say that," out loud.

His giant figure appeared from the trees to the side of the house. Further beyond that was the meadow where I had first met Zagros months prior. Where he had impatiently lit a tree on fire while waiting for me.

"It was done to get your attention," the voice said.

I got up from my chair and walked over and hugged him. We hadn't done that in a long time and even though I had turned sixteen it was something I still needed. His arms wrapped around me and I felt him hold on as well. Maybe he had needed it, too.

It never ceased to amaze me how my large dragon friend with claws and scales and ability to eat an entire elk could be gentle with me when we were together.

"Parenting is exhausting, Luke. There is so much pressure and difficulty. I am worried all of the time and I do not sleep as much as I should," he told me as we let go and I went back to sit down. I grabbed a couple of smaller logs from behind my chair and put them on the fire, moving things around to try to encourage it to build up again so I could see my friend better.

"I can't imagine what its like, Zagros," I said, "especially when Helios got hurt."

"My heart fell to pieces. I did not know what to do or what could be done. Tabitha was very frightened, as was Cassiel."

"I know, man, so were we."

He paused before silently saying how in the old days, Helios would have died. That Dragoneers weren't always connected to the dragons in the early centuries and there would have been too much blood loss for him to survive. He told me that Oscar had cried when he first saw injured Helios because he knew the significance of losing even one dragon. He was also frightened and sad because he had feelings for all of them.

"I'm just glad you were able to get a message to Jackie and me. I just hope that if you ever have to do that again its after I have my driver's license," I said. The fire crackled and popped and came a little more to life.

"Will you tell your friend about what you saw today?" he asked me.

"No," I thought immediately before actually saying, "It isn't my place to do that. It would be mean, I think, for me to tell her about it. That has to come from the guy himself."

"Yes, I believe you are right, Luke."

We sat in verbal silence but I knew Zagros was inside my head, watching me replay the bicycle incident over in my mind.

Finally, his deep voice came through.

"Are you sad for your friend, Gwen?"

"Maybe. I mean, I'm sad if she is sad because I think she really liked Callum. I thought he really liked her, too, but its not like we ever talked about it. I just don't like it when my friends are unhappy or they have their feelings hurt," I answered.

"Like your friend, Josh?" he asked.

Sparks flew upward from the small fire between us and I said, "Exactly, only in his case I never knew his dad or the things that happened to him and his family before I ever met him. I always knew there was some big secret to Josh and his world but I would have been fine to never learn what it actually was. I would be happy to have him back here in Missing Lake."

"I will need to travel for food purposes soon, Luke. I will try to check on Josh and his family for you," Zagros said. I smiled at my silver friend. After the strange events of that day the thought of hearing any news about Josh gave me comfort.

"Although your friend may be sad by today's events, I want to tell you that you spoke well to Callum today. I believe words can be very powerful for your species. That, perhaps they can be as dangerous and damaging as other means of combat," he added.

“You are totally right about that, Zagros,” I agreed. “Words for humans can cause every single emotion, good or bad and they have just as many consequences as other ways of fighting or negotiating.”

I thought about what we both had just said and asked, “What about in your non-verbal world, though?”

“What do you mean? We communicate with one another all of the time.”

“You said that words are powerful for our species, even in combat. What about for dragons?”

I knew the sides of his mouth had turned upwards and that there would be a twinkle in his eye by the way he replied, “Have you ever tried breathing fire?”

TWENTY-THREE

"You just have to hold still a little while longer, Helios," Jackie said. It had been two weeks and we were taking his sutures out. The young golden dragon had survived and was squirming around in the lair as Jackie tried to maneuver her little scissor-like suture removers beneath the tiny threads. The tip of the blade was tiny and the suture itself was also thin so any movement made it challenging to get the blade where it needed to go without stabbing Helios in the abdomen.

"I don't think he understands you," I told her. I was trying to help hold him still but we hadn't had much success. We, with Oscar, Tabitha and Zagros had tried several positions and had taken many breaks but it had turned into a tedious affair. We had been at it for over an hour but, thankfully, there were only about a dozen sutures left to remove.

It hadn't helped that Cassiel was poking her head into things, under our arms, around our bodies, to see her brother. Whenever she did that Helios would look at her and try to get away from us. As young as he was he had some pretty good strength. I had already felt that when he'd slammed me to the ground, of course, but Jackie and Oscar got a first-hand feel of how strong he was.

"I will say, I'm actually happy he has the strength to resist us this much after all that he went through," Jackie told us. "I love when my patients can make suture removal a real test of my skills."

In the two weeks since I saw Callum and Lindsey together I had been fortunate enough to not have run into Gwen. Jackie and I brought leftovers for lunch a couple of times and another time we ate at the café Gwen wasn't working.

Lindsey was, though, but she let the older lady who worked there serve us and hadn't come by our table the whole time we were there. Jackie never asked and I didn't volunteer anything. I tried not to think too much about the whole situation but I knew that Bethany and Mollie had an appointment at the clinic later that afternoon. I hoped her parents would be there and that we wouldn't talk about Gwen but I also knew that Bethany lived for gossip. Even if it was about her best friend.

"Luke, hold on," I suddenly heard Zagros tell me.

The little dragon tugged his chubby arm from my grasp and his hand came up beneath my chin with a slap when he got away. I looked into his eyes and sensed a smile that was almost a smirk and quickly grabbed his arm again.

I thought the words, "Clever little fart" in my head and hoped he could sense it.

I wasn't so sure about the relationship that was developing between Helios and me. I also wasn't sure what my role was with the young dragons. Helios seemed to treat me like a brother but also as a threat sometimes. I didn't know if we had got off on the wrong foot that summer when I had startled his sister or if it was just our personalities clashing.

"You will be fine, Luke," I heard Tabitha say. "You will have a wonderful relationship with both Helios and Cassiel. I can tell."

I looked over at her and smiled, while making sure to not loosen my hold on her son's arm.

As much as I had my doubts I also felt relieved. If there was one thing I had learned, it was to trust Tabitha's instincts. I never sensed that she could actually predict the future but she definitely seemed to know what was going on. She had an incredible way of understanding us humans as well as her own species. I figured some of that probably came from being around us for a couple of hundred years but in Tabitha's case I believed there was something intuitive as well.

"Your role with Helios and Cassiel will develop over time, Luke," Tabitha said. Her voice was so calm and confident. It was one of the many things I loved about her. If she told me the dragon babies, or wyrns and I were going to be alright then I would just have to choose to believe it.

"Are you guys talking in your heads right now?" Jackie asked. She had two more sutures to remove.

I laughed, making sure to maintain my firm hold on Helios and said, out loud, "Yes, Tabitha and I were. Could you tell?"

"No. Well, maybe," Jackie replied without taking her eyes off of Helios' abdomen. "There is just this unusual sense of calm or peace when you and she communicate. It's a nice feeling but I can't really explain it."

I smiled again. Tabitha's and my relationship extended beyond my own feelings, it seemed like. I looked at Tabitha and saw her eyes twinkle and the sides of her mouth tip upwards. I had a sense that she would pass some of her abilities onto the young dragons as they grew up and that made me feel a bit more confident moving forward with such enormous responsibilities.

I knew it would continue to be a challenge with all of my real-life obligations but I was buoyed by the knowledge that our strange group of Dragoneers and our charges had begun to feel like a cohesive team that was really starting to mesh. Each of us had particular roles on the team, just like in hockey and just like with the dog team. I wasn't sure where each of us fit on the dragon team but I was happy to spend time figuring it all out.

Just as those thoughts went through my head I felt a gentle touch on my shoulder. It hadn't startled me although it came out of nowhere. I glanced down to see a green, almost black hand with claws at the tips of the digits resting on me. Turning my head back a bit more my eyes locked with those of young Cassiel's. I couldn't hold back my smile and hoped she could sense the feelings of love and hope that washed over me.

"We're done!" Jackie exclaimed with more exuberance than I thought she would have after working that long to remove sutures.

"Good job, Dr.Yale-Houser," Oscar said. "I cannot thank you enough for all you have done, on behalf of dragons and Dragoneers everywhere. Every dragon is a gift to the world and to their species. Without you we would have lost this precious one."

Jackie lowered her head and looked almost embarrassed by the compliment. Or maybe it was the weight of Oscar's words that caused her to do that.

"Thank-you, Oscar. I'm humbled to have been able to use my training to help. In honesty," she said, as she raised her head and looked around at everyone, "doing veterinary work on these magnificent creatures has brought my old love of medicine back to the forefront of my mind and it truly is an honor."

"You are an important member of our family, and we all thank-you," Zagros said. I saw Jackie and Oscar smile so he must have shared that thought with everyone.

"As much as we would love to stick around, Luke and I have appointments this afternoon at the clinic so we'd better get back there," Jackie said. She and I shook Oscar's hand and hugged Tabitha and Zagros. I remembered to remove a shiny silver clip board I had taken from the clinic from my knapsack to give to Tabitha before we left. I had hoped Jackie wouldn't notice but she busted me.

"Luke, did you steal that from the clinic?" she asked as we got ready to get into Oscar's golf cart.

"Yup," I answered. "Are you going to take it away from her?"

We both looked back to see Tabitha clutching the clip board to her chest with both arms. I swear I saw her wink at us.

Jackie turned back and climbed into the bench seat of the cart and said, "Nope, I guess not."

On the ride back down to Missing Lake I figured I should tell Jackie about Gwen and Callum before Bethany arrived. Bethany's mom had made their appointment specifically for a day that I was working so obviously we were going to talk. I didn't want her to blurt something out and have Jackie be shocked, even if it meant talking about relationship stuff with my step-mom.

I hadn't been sure how to bring it up so I just threw it all out there after I hit the power button on the CD player to turn off Tom Petty. While I hadn't wanted to end the time I got to enjoy cooler music than disco I had, at least, felt bolstered by hearing him sing the words, *Well, I won't. Back. Down.*

"So, um, Bethany might say something about Gwen today when we see her or she might want to talk privately if that's alright," was how I brought it up.

Jackie, with her hands reliably at ten and two merely said, "Oh?" in a questioning tone.

"I don't know if you knew, or why you'd know but Gwen has been seeing a guy who is a grade higher than us. It started at the last dance we had."

Jackie didn't comment so I kept going.

"It really isn't any of my business and its kind of awkward but one of the times I took my bike to get our lunches I saw her boyfriend kissing the newer server at the café, who is in our grade."

That got Jackie's attention. Her eyebrows just about lifted off of her forehead and she sucked in a big breath of air.

"Did they see you?" she asked.

"You could say that," I answered with a wry chuckle. I told her how I almost ran into them with my bike and how Callum had told me he hadn't broken up with Gwen and that I pretty much wanted nothing to do with either of them. I explained that I hadn't seen Gwen since then and had no idea if they were still together or not.

"Is that why Lindsey was avoiding us the other day at lunch?"

"Yeah, I'm pretty sure. I mean, I don't really know her that much and I know its not just her fault, that Callum was just as much to blame but it definitely is weird between Lindsey and I," I said.

We rode in silence for at least a mile before Jackie said, "It must have been difficult to not get angry with this Callum fellow, Luke. And I'm sorry you've had to keep this to yourself. What an awkward situation."

"Zagros let me kind of vent to him by the bonfire the other night," I admitted. "He's a good listener."

"I can imagine," Jackie said. "Feel free to go outside with Bethany and visit if you'd like. Her dog, Mollie is pretty hyper but her parents are usually there when she comes to visit. I'm sure one of them can help hold her. If not, we'll keep you for a few minutes. I have to check her ears so the more I think about it the more I know I'll need you."

I laughed as I pictured the rambunctious liver and white spaniel. She was already famous amongst our group of friends. I almost felt like we were all part-owners of Mollie.

Before long we were back at the clinic where we devoured leftover lasagna that we'd brought for lunch. Dad had outdone himself with that batch the night before.

After a few routine vaccine appointments and phone calls, Mollie came bounding into the waiting room, almost dragging a breathless Bethany behind her.

"Whoa, Horsie," Bethany said as Mollie skidded to a stop on the tiled floors in front of Jackie. Bethany's parents came in behind her with a lot less commotion and we all made our way to the examination room. After we weighed her, Bethany's dad offered to lift her up onto the table.

"At forty pounds is she doing alright, Dr.Yale-Houser?" he asked. I heard him grunt a little as he hoisted the wiggling patient onto the table. I stepped in to try to help hold her still. Her head was swinging left and right with her tongue hanging out. It felt like she was going to burst with excitement. Bethany laughed and I caught her eye as her parents started telling Jackie about Mollie scratching her ear and tilting her head to one side.

Bethany's eyes told me all I needed to know. She nodded her head and raised her eyebrows at me before she joined in on the discussion about ears. I wasn't sure if that meant Gwen was heartbroken or if it meant she knew that I knew about Callum and Lindsey. I tried to focus on holding the squirming Mollie in one place.

Jackie got her scope thing with a light that looks down into ear canals off the counter and went to work in Mollie's left ear. The room grew silent as she squinted and Mollie made an almost moaning sound. Her back leg flipped a couple of times on the same side as her bad ear that Jackie had been looking into.

I thought she should put exam gloves on but she was too fast in getting her ear cleaning fluid out and into Mollie's ears. I heard Jackie tell the usual stories about how yeast likes moist, dark environments and that spaniel ears definitely provided that. Bethany and her parents got to learn all about ear cleaning and cotton balls and medicated ointments and Mollie seemed to actually enjoy the process as well. She leaned towards Jackie and made happy-sounding grunts as Jackie continued.

"Oops, now my hands are all waxy," she said after she stood back and Mollie let the head shaking fly. I knew to close my eyes and mouth when they did that having learned a gross lesson about how ear gunk tasted the year prior.

Bethany and I went outside and sat on the lawn behind the clinic when Mollie's ear cleaning was done. Her parents had an errand to do so they left Mollie in the kennel room and Jackie went to do notes on her computer.

"They broke up, you know," Bethany said as she crossed her legs on the lawn. The sun was shining and the sky was an incredible blue without any clouds to be seen. I had spent my morning with my dragon friends and it had been a great day so far.

"Yeah, I figured," was all I could say. I looked down at my lap where my hands were fidgeting away.

"Callum told her that you saw him and Lindsey." I looked up at Bethany and raised my own eyebrows.

"And she's cool with it, Luke, really."

"Is she mad that I found out before her that he was cheating on her?" I asked. That stupid squeak that still threatened any ounce of coolness I could have had crept into my voice again.

"No, I don't think so. I think she's really embarrassed and she was super upset and kind of heart broken about Callum and Lindsey," Bethany told me. "But she was mostly pissed at Callum." She paused before adding, "Ass," under her breath.

I nodded my head but didn't know what to say. Bethany stayed quiet, as well, which was remarkable given the fact she was Bethany.

"She's doing great though," she finally said, "I mean, its been two weeks, right? And it isn't like they were together forever or anything." I figured she was trying to make me feel better about the situation. I wasn't happy that Gwen had to have her heart broken or anything but there was a tiny little part of me that was glad she was single again.

I was startled then to hear Gwen's voice from behind me.

"Hi, guys," she said as she walked towards us. Both Bethany and I leapt to our feet and Bethany met her with a big hug. They hugged long enough that I started to feel stupid before Gwen took a few steps in my direction.

"Hey," I said, feeling immediately stupid for not having something more grown-up or mature to say.

"Hey, back," she said. "I knew Mollie had an appointment today and I just got off work and thought I'd come by, too." I watched Gwen look down at her own hands that were clasped in front of her.

"Say, my folks have just come back so I'm out of here, okay?" Bethany said, her dark hair spinning around as she turned back and forth between the clinic and us. She gave Gwen a shorter hug and then surprised me by giving me a quick squeeze as well. Gwen and I watched silently as our friend ran to the parking lot and Mollie and her family drove off.

At that point, it was just Gwen and I.

"So, yeah, that whole thing with Callum kind of sucked," she began. She looked up and made a funny, scrunched-up sort of face that made her dimples show. Her hair shone a brighter golden color in the sunlight and she had a light blue ribbon tying up her ponytail. It matched her eye makeup and her shirt that had little flowers around its curvy neckline.

"Um, yeah, you could say that," I said. "I honestly felt really uncomfortable but it wasn't my place to tell you."

She smiled at me and said, "No, Luke, I'm glad you didn't tell me. I would have been really mad at you and I probably wouldn't have believed you anyways." I chuckled and nodded my head.

"I actually thought about punching him, to be honest but then the image of me trying to do that was horrifying and even more embarrassing so I didn't try anything," I confessed. That, at least, got her giggling. I had forgotten how much I liked the sound of her laughter. It reminded me of pretty bells at Christmas.

Before I knew what happened, Gwen stepped forward and reached her hands up on either side of my face and kissed me.

Just like that.

Standing in the sunshine on the lawn behind my step-mom's veterinary clinic Gwen kissed me. And I liked it. I realized I was thinking about it too much so I decided to try to kiss back.

Thankfully, Gwen didn't freak out and I learned right then that you could smile when you kissed someone. I also learned that even though the sudden feel of her wet tongue touching mine didn't gross me out, it did startle me. Then I felt her smile as well. My hands reached up to her waist as if they were moving by someone else's control and the kiss seemed to last forever.

Eventually she lowered her hands and took a step back. She told me she had to get home and I stammered something about going back to the clinic even though I was already there which brought her sweet laughter to the air once again.

"I don't want to have a boyfriend for awhile, Luke," she told me, "but when I do if you're available maybe you'd consider it?" I watched her face turn more pink than usual and her freckles stood out even more. I smiled and nodded my head.

I watched her walk off with her pony-tail and its pretty blue ribbon swinging in circles above her head.

That night, with Baxter snoring away cuddled tight into my side and two purring cats nestled into my quilt at the foot of the bed, my mind kept drifting to the adventures and emotions of the day. I hadn't said anything to Jackie or Dad about Gwen and I was grateful for that. I was pretty sure Jackie would tell Dad what I had told her about finding Callum and Lindsey together but I hoped they would just let it go and let me figure out my own path with my friends.

With my dragon friends, or team, or family, or whatever we were.

And with my high school friends, or best friends, or maybe even girlfriends.

As I tried to close my eyes a vivid picture came to my mind. It was as if I was looking through a window and I sat bolt upright in bed. My forehead was suddenly sweaty and my back felt clammy as I realized Zagros was giving me a look at what he was seeing. I didn't want to open my eyes as I watched the impossible happen as though it was right in front of me.

Josh was reading to his little sisters in their bed. The bedroom was pink and one of his sisters already looked asleep. I could see my good friend clearly. He looked like he had joined the club of guys who were starting to need to shave and I smiled. My eyes were closed but I could actually see him close the book and place it on a nightstand next to the bed the girls were sharing. He bent down and kissed them both, tucking them in beneath their covers.

He looked as serious as I had ever seen him and maybe even a little bit older. My heart tugged at how fast he had to grow up and at the responsibilities he, too, had to shoulder in his young life.

Just before he turned off their bedroom light I watched him abruptly stand in place, as if he had heard something and was startled. He looked even more concerned until he turned his head and seemingly looked right at me. A confused look appeared on his face and he shook his head as if to shake whatever he had felt from his mind. Then I saw him smile and he turned out the light.

All characters and places in this book are fictitious and are not meant to represent any specific person or place.

ACKNOWLEDGEMENTS

This book, like my others, is the work of combined talents and inspirations and I appreciate everyone's efforts immensely.

Thank-you, Dona and Gary, as ever, for helping with the edits, particularly with the sled dogs. Thanks, Bethany, for being the first set of teen eyes and for encouraging me to hurry up and get it finished so you could enjoy the characters once again. My dear friend, Lynn is always up for a phone call and a good laugh and her support is boundless and much appreciated. (You just have to believe, right, Lynn?) Jessi and her family have been amazing friends who have taken care of our Montana farm at a moment's notice so I could attend conferences, book events, or other activities out of state while knowing in my heart that our animals were loved and cared for as much as they are when we're home with them. Thank-you, Deb Kolegraf, Tim Bakker, Tessa Stevens and Theresa Magelky- whether we were sipping coffee or discussing the book, the state of the golf course, animal crises, the fabulous bling or the lunch menu in front of us, I appreciated every visit and every question about the book's characters and my own sanity.

Thank-you, Ben Brick, for once again leaping at the chance to create the wonderful illustrations for *Secrets Abound*. Your talent and humor shine through in your work and I am so excited about this cover and inside artwork.

I thank my brother, Dan for his encouragement and support of this book series. His insights and questions offer different directions for me to take the story and I appreciate every late-night phone conversation about Canadian songs for Sharing sessions and what happened to Josh. Thanks for proudly serving Canada in our Armed Forces for all those years, too, eh?

Thanks to every single one of you who has commented on social media pages and my blog and to all of you for buying and reading my stories. I love seeing old friends and making new ones at my book events and can't wait to get out there to market *Secrets Abound*.

My number of animal companions and muses has dramatically been reduced over the past two years and we are almost a normal family now with two dogs and three cats. Most of this book was written, however, with Loki and UB at my feet, Sport behind my head, ferrets tunneling through the couches behind me, Jockey the barn cat staring at me through the window by my side, and Cleo lounging on the couch. There is nothing like the unconditional love of a good fur ball and they all have certainly provided me with much inspiration.

Finally, Alistair, I thank you from the bottom of my heart. You have put up and gone along with almost every zany idea I've had for over twenty years and you make me smile every single day. I appreciate the time you take to help edit these books and the fact you work so hard, so far apart from me and our beautiful mountain home to provide us this incredible life. Here's to another season of laughing together on our golf courses, Aloha hot tubs with the tiki torches and getting these books out there. I love you. Always.

ABOUT THE AUTHOR

Tanya Fyfe dreamed of writing books her entire life. The hours spent in frigid ice rinks in British Columbia, Canada, training to become a professional figure skater gave her plenty of time to think of stories to tell while tracing minute lines on precise figure-eights during "patch."

Tanya toured in two professional ice shows in Japan and then returned to Tokyo to teach English. Her story-telling skills increased exponentially at that time as she pretended to be a twenty-five year old with a degree from the "University of Vancouver." (At the time, she was nineteen and there is no such institution.)

While her figure skating career has been good to her (she met her husband, Dr.Alistair Fyfe while she was guest-skating in Creston, BC and the veterinarians interviewing her for veterinary school were more fascinated with her ice show experiences than the fact they raised American Paint Horses and had ferrets), she became a veterinarian in 2005 and has worked in small and large animal practices in North Dakota and Montana.

Taking a break from full time practice has given Tanya the time to create the fictional Missing Lake series featuring teen-aged Luke, his step-mom veterinarian, Jackie and the fabulous dragons and their family. She blogs regularly at *tanyafyfe.com*, still guest coaches figure skating on occasion and collects and sells jewelry from the Bling Emporium in their Montana home.

The doctors Fyfe split their time between their ranches and golf courses in North Dakota and Montana. They enjoy cuddling with their remaining pets, riding horses, canoeing, hiking, snowshoeing, skiing, and planning trips to the Hawaiian Islands. Their latest dream is to load their golf cart, Norman into the four-horse trailer and golf their way back and forth across North America. Tanya is certain there is a good book in that!

On the last day of fifth grade, Ben Brick's teacher put stacks of math homework sheets around the classroom. She encouraged the children to take as many as they would like so they could stay sharp over the summer. Surprisingly, Ben was the first to the piles of paper. He inspected the sheets and began stuffing his backpack to capacity.

Impressed with Ben's eagerness to excel, his teacher stopped him to express her excitement. Ben quickly threw the heavy bag over his shoulder. He looked at her and, with a smile, told her, "So glad they are one-sided. I can draw on the back!"

To this day Ben doodles all summer long and has become fortunate enough to do it for a living.

Tanya Fyfe met Ben through his lovely wife, Rebecca, who was one of her figure skating students many years ago in Creston, BC. Her father also happens to be Alistair's partner and one of his best friends, and one of the team of people who set the Fyfes up when Tanya guest-skated there. Tanya and Ben share their creativity and laughter over random lunch meetings in North Dakota.

Made in the USA
Coppell, TX
26 January 2021